INCOGNITO

INCOGNITO

Susan Trott

Harper & Row, Publishers, New York
Cambridge, Philadelphia, San Francisco, Washington
London, Mexico City, São Paulo, Singapore, Sydney

This story is dedicated to Roger Gordon

A hardcover edition of this book was originally published in Great Britain in 1983 by Severn House Publishers, Ltd. It is here reprinted by arrangement with Jonathan Dolger Agency.

First PERENNIAL LIBRARY edition published 1987.

Library of Congress Cataloging-in-Publication Data

Trott, Susan.
  Incognito.

  I. Title.
PS3570.R59415   1987   813'.54   86-46234
ISBN 0-06-097106-1 (pbk.)

87 88 89 90 91 92   MPC   10 9 8 7 6 5 4 3 2 1

PART I

1

Jenny Hunt was so surprised to see her adviser labouring up the forty-two steps to her house which was high on Hillcrest Avenue in the town of Mill Valley, California. He never came on Tuesdays. This was unprecedented. She wondered if she should feel alarm. She never had before. Anxiety, yes, she had felt plenty of that and it always got her into trouble. She was learning not to betray it, but it was hard – the rocks were always a giveaway.

She opened the door, greeted him graciously, offered him a cup of coffee, which he refused. He looked quite grave about the eyes, she thought, and positively grim about the nose. He had a way, when perturbed, of indenting his nostrils, almost closing them, the way camels did in a sandstorm.

Damon Carner was a small, spindly, kindly man. Jenny was not fond of him. He was simply her adviser, who told her what to do and what not to do and handled for her the super-abundance of her wealth.

She tossed back her glossy brown braid. Her hair had never been cut and it came to her thighs. Her eyes were brown, too, and shiny like her hair. Her teeth were regular and her smile was sweet. At a glance she looked seventeen but was twenty-nine.

It appeared that her adviser was saying goodbye. He was giving her a present, a painting, which was wrapped in brown paper. How nice. She was a painter herself, but he'd never shown the slightest interest in her work. She didn't know he liked art or was even aware of it.

'This painting,' he said, 'is by a very great contemporary artist. There are only ten existing canvases by him because

7

he's so choosy he destroys most of what he creates. His family owns one, two other private persons do, you do, and the rest are in museums. I'm sorry to say that the man is now at death's door . . .'

Jenny envisioned 'death's door'. It would have a shiny brass knocker in the form of a skull. Or perhaps the knocker should be of bone, whalebone, scrimshaw, and the door white as well. Maybe the entire door should be bone.

'What this means to you is that, when he dies, this painting will at least triple in worth. It cost me, you, a hundred thousand dollars. When he dies, it could very well be worth half a million dollars.'

Damon Carner looked sorry, not because the man was dying but because he knew it was so tasteless to profit from it.

Jenny listened attentively as she always did when Damon Carner was instructing her. 'It's sort of my own legacy to you,' he said, mysteriously she thought. Could Damon be at death's door too? 'Take very good care of it. Also, do you remember Arthur Huntington – another close friend of your father's?'

'Why yes, I do! ' Jenny had a far-off memory of a joyful man.

'I have written him and you will be hearing from him soon. He will invite you to stay at his estate in Sonoma and you must go.'

'That will be nice.' Jenny waited for him to tell her to be sure to go incognito to Arthur Huntington's, but surprisingly he didn't. There was an awkward moment while this was glaringly left unsaid. But I know by now to go incognito without Damon telling me to, she assured herself. There's no *need* for him to say it again. I don't need to be told every time. It's understood.

'Are you really going away? Shall I not be hearing from you ever again?'

'No, my dear, you won't.' He looked concerned. 'I hope you will be all right. There's your grandmother, and Arthur, and your friends.'

She smiled. 'Oh, I'll be fine.'

8

They shook hands and he departed. She watched him out of sight but he never turned round. She raised her eyes from his downwardly departing figure to look over the trees to San Francisco, fifteen miles away, then back to the dirt road, where she could now see his green BMW move hesitantly round the curves.

There went her adviser, who'd been an integral part of her life since her father's death when she was eleven. He'd made absolutely every decision for her. Now he was gone.

She stepped back into her house and warmed up a cup of coffee. Her house straddled a ridge, perched like a hang-glider about to take flight. From the kitchen side, she could see Mount Tamalpais.

She supposed she would feel Damon's absence in time. Right now was too soon to feel anything. Except afraid. But I always feel that, she reminded herself, except when I am painting or reading.

My life is bound to be different now, I imagine, she thought vaguely, unable to envision the future anywhere near as well as she had conjured up death's door. She was a woman who lived very much in the present. One day at a time. One hour at a time.

Meanwhile, I guess I'll just go on as if it were the same.

She carried her coffee back to the living-room couch, where her book lay open and waiting. I'll just wait to hear from Arthur Huntington.

She began to settle in with her book, then exclaimed aloud, 'Oh, the painting! I must have a look at this very great contemporary painting.'

She carefully unwrapped it and looked at a small oil-painting about the size of a Persian miniature but with none of the content. While the colours were pretty, the overall effect was sort of blurry. 'Oh,' she said, but it was an interested oh, not a disappointed one.

She set it on the mantel for now. Then she lay down and picked up her book, about the first emperor of China. She became lost in the book, even to forgetting her coffee, let alone her life that had just suffered a cataclysmic reversal.

2

Arthur Huntington took his breakfast in the living-room of his new estate in Sonoma County, with his cohort, Laveen. His wife, Jess always ate earlier and more slightly. Laveen read the morning paper; Arthur his mail.

He was a large, powerful man in his sixties whose face wore the graceful ruins of what once must have been devastating good looks. He looked like an ageing scoundrel playing the role of a Boston Brahmin to pull off a scam. But he actually was a high-class Massachusettsonian who had elected to live abroad and in California because he was also truly a scoundrel, of the unmitigated variety, and his outrageous behaviour, by his fellow Bostonians, would not be brooked.

They sat at a round table in a bay window that overlooked a jewel-like pond. A tennis court reposed on a rise above the pond and Arthur allowed himself to look longingly at it. He'd made a recent rule for himself: no tennis until he'd accomplished any business of the day.

Happily, aside from the mail, there wasn't much business. He liked to say, 'Jess runs the place, gives all the orders, makes all the minor decisions. I make all the major decisions and there are no major decisions.'

He looked at Laveen, who was all suited up for his return to the Fair Haven Sanatarium, which he owned and sometimes administrated and which was located some twenty miles away. While Arthur was garbed in baggy shorts and a Brooks shirt unbuttoned with the tails hanging out, Laveen was sartorial in beige linen, white shirt, pale yellow tie.

Arthur perused a fat letter from Damon Carner. After several minutes, he said aloud, 'Here's a tragic business.'

10

Laveen lowered the paper.

'Damon Carner is about to put a bullet through his head because he's lost the fortune of the little Hunt girl.'

Laveen apparently failed to see what was tragic or even interesting about it and raised his paper again.

'I'm not surprised,' Arthur went on, knowing Laveen could easily read and listen at the same time, missing nothing, probably using another part of his mind to plot a murder. Laveen's mind never stopped for a minute for fear he'd die of boredom if it did. As it was, he was always gravely ill from boredom. 'Alan Hunt was a fool to name Carner her adviser instead of me. Granted, he was much more trustworthy. I would have dipped into the fortune with an enormous ladle. I would have squandered it but I *never* would have mishandled it. It took him eighteen years to lose the whole thing. Kept throwing good money after bad, apparently. He feels awful about it. I must say he took his responsibility seriously. Too seriously. He over-protected her fearfully. He was so afraid someone would try and take her fortune from her and, in the end, he did. It would have taught her to live. At the very least I'd have made a first-rate tennis player of her. Under my tutelage she would have become a gourmande, an athelete, an incredible lover, an astute spender of money. What a shame. It's too late now. And now he wants to hand her over to me with none of the money to go along with her, and when I can no longer play Pygmalion to her Galatea. What a fool he was. How I deplore stupid, honest, little men. What a waste. It's enough to make a man weep.'

'How much money was there?' Laveen asked from behind the paper.

'Millions. Twenty, fifty, possibly hundreds of millions! And she never got to enjoy it. He hid her away. Kept her in moth-balls. She's in some dopey little house in Mill Valley, and that's her *only* house! He says she has her house, mortgage free, and her car and her bills are paid for the next year.'

'How's her state of mind? I expect she'll be showing up soon at her old Alma Mater, Fair Haven.' Laveen turned a

11

page revealing, Arthur thought but wasn't sure, a smile. Currently Laveen was so very bearded it was hard to tell. Also he wore dark glasses and a hat. He was in disguise. This was his persona for Fair Haven. Laveen was always in some disguise or other. Arthur couldn't remember what he really looked like, although they were cousins.

'He hasn't told her that her fortune is gone. That's up to me. He couldn't bring himself to tell her. In any case, she can no longer *afford* Fair Haven. What's her mental problem? Were you ever actually there the times she was?'

Laveen used Fair Haven for a cover for his other nefarious dealings – and also to meet rich people.

'Yes, I was. She experiences anxiety, paranoia, when life gets too much for her, which it easily does. It's interesting because when she gets anxious, she collects rocks, keeps them close to hand.'

'In order to throw them at people?'

'That's what Damon Carner was morbidly afraid she would do, but she never actually hurt anyone. He liked to put her away before she did.'

'Poor thing,' said Arthur. 'The rocks probably comforted her. She must have very little strength or confidence in herself due to his unconscionable cosseting.'

'I remember this adviser of hers always treated her as if she were retarded,' said Laveen. 'People often do with people who are crazy or terribly sweet – although he may have believed she was retarded, which is why he over-protected her.'

'Is she?'

'In some ways. But that would be due to a lack of experience not a lack of brain.'

'Is she sweet?'

'Disgustingly.' Laveen folded up the paper in its original form and gave Arthur his full attention. 'What about the painting?' Like Carner, Laveen had kept a keen eye on the whereabouts of the ten existing paintings of the Great Contemporary Artist as well as on the good investment opportunities inherent in the artist's poor health. He and Arthur had decided to 'collect' the three paintings owned by private parties.

'Ah,' Arthur smiled, 'that's the good news. He gave it to Jenny. His legacy, he calls it, since in time it could restore her to a comfortable life, which is all she's accustomed to, anyhow, a modicum of comfort.'

'Excellent,' said Laveen. 'Then you'll be inviting her down?'

'Yes,' Arthur replied, 'I'll be inviting her down.'

3

Horacio Huntington stood on the cornice of a building on Pacific Heights in San Francisco, four floors up, and knew a moment of black despair. It dropped upon him like a shroud, falling softly, slowly, so that he didn't know it was upon him until he was actually covered by it, felt its weight. His heart felt like a stone. His chin dropped slowly to his chest. He almost lost his balance. He sighed deeply, as if to ease the stone from his heart, and it came out like a groan, loud enough to alert the sleeping victims within. Maybe that's what he wanted, to awaken these people whose hospitality he had abused, to be discovered, set upon by them, chased, caught, strung up, dismembered.

Not that he felt any desire for justice, only for some excitement. It was all so boringly simple. That fool, his host, had gone to his safe before the very eyes of his guests, after dinner, to get out cigars and cocaine. Although he hid the dial with his body, Horacio easily caught the combination with his ears. No challenge. Like taking candy from a kid. Not

13

that the idiot even needed to keep the stuff in a safe – although they were damn good cigars. He was only showing off that he had a safe.

So Horacio had returned to the mansion a few hours after the party ended, entered through the front door, cracked the safe, pocketed the diamonds and gold brick, blown the cocaine over the brown velvet sofa, purely out of meanness, then decided to make his way out by the exterior of the building to add a little zest to the escapade.

It was there that, instead of the hoped-for adrenalin rush, he was assailed instead by this terrible despair to the point where he lost his balance, his perfect balance from the Iroquois blood on his mother's side, and teetered on the cornice's edge thinking, what the hell, why not go over and bloody the pavement? Who cares? God knows, I don't.

Then a voice from the street called up, 'Are you all right? Can I help you in any way?'

Horacio snapped out of it, regained his alertness. He waved a reassuring hand to the blurry figure below and ran along the narrow cornice to the corner of the building, where he disappeared into the branches of a black walnut tree.

He slipped through the tree with ease, from branch to branch descending. An old friend of trees was Horacio, their rough bark more dear to him than any woman's skin, har-bourers and ladders as they'd always been for him. But then – a branch broke! This black walnut, one of the most depen-dable of trees, had let him down, hard, an eight-foot fall to the sidewalk. His body twisted just in time to take the impact on his side so he could roll with it. 'Oomph!' He didn't roll. The breath was knocked out of him and, for a moment, his consciousness.

4

Jenny Hunt was also in a mansion on Pacific Heights that night. She was spending the night with her paternal grandmother. Going to the city was a trial journey for her in preparation for her monumental trip to Arthur's. Having covered the fifteen miles from house to house, she felt no less accomplished than Vasco da Gama after he went around the entire continent of Africa to India from Portugal, discovering the sea route thereby. Jenny had discovered Route 101 South. When she went to Arthur's she would penetrate the deep recesses of Route 101 North.

She had dined with her Gram and told her the Damon Carner abandonment story. Mrs Hunt, as usual, was exasperated with Jenny. Why had she not questioned him closely? Why had she so little information regarding his mysterious and sudden exit from her life?

After dinner they both settled comfortably with their books, which was their custom before bed, but Mrs Hunt felt unnerved by Jenny's new situation. 'What are you reading?' she asked.

Jenny quoted aloud,

> ' "Come, my friend, and remember
> That the rich have butlers and no friends
> And we have friends and no butlers?
> Come, let us pity the married and the unmarried." '

'That's ridiculous. They needn't cancel one another out at all. Having friends or butlers, that is. Who wrote it?'

'Ezra Pound.'

'Oh yes, he's that crazy redhead I played tennis with one time in Lugano. In the Twenties, I guess it was.'

'There's nothing wrong with being crazy.'

'Yes, there is, Jenny, as you will be the first to admit. Jenny, what are you going to do? Who will advise you? I can't. I'm much too busy. I'm always on the move.'

'Perhaps Arthur Huntington will. Do you remember him? What's he like?'

'He was easily the handsomest man I ever met in my life. I had an affair with him. He was a decade or so younger than me, but that didn't matter.'

Jenny looked at her admiringly. Even in her seventies she had a certain sexual force.

'Perhaps I'll have an affair with him too,' Jenny said musingly. 'Imagine having the same lover your grandmother had.'

Mrs Hunt smiled. The child's mind continued to astonish and delight as well as exasperate her.

'That would be one for the books,' she said dryly.

Jenny had not had many lovers. She was like a night-blooming cactus that flowered once a year for twenty-four hours. She would swell and burst into bloom and scent and moisture for a brief period and then become dry and prickly and sexless for another extended period. These blooming cycles always happened when she was incognito, when she wasn't Jenny Hunt but some assumed person. Maybe that freed her.

'The poem finishes in quite a different mood,' she said.

> ' "The dawn enters on little feet
> Like a gilded Pavlova
> And I am near my desire
> Nor has life in it aught better
> Than this hour of clear coolness
> This hour of waking together." '

'That's quite beautiful.'

'I don't know what that's like, being together with someone, being in love.'

16

'You will, dear.'

'I doubt it. Nor do I necessarily want it. I love being left alone.'

'You're too much alone. Much too much alone. You should –'

Jenny held up a hand, fending her off. 'Don't,' she said gently. 'Just this once, don't rail at me. Why can't you, finally, accept me for what I am?'

'I will when I see you happy. What are you?'

'An artist. A crazy, non-redheaded artist.'

'I think you should cut your hair.'

Jenny lit up. 'Good idea. I will. What good advice! I'm so glad you thought of it. Do you really think I should?'

'Yes, I do. I think it saps your strength.'

Jenny lay languidly on the couch, the book drooping from her hands, the picture of sapped strength. 'I think so too,' she agreed. 'It's a drag. It drags me down. I'll cut it off, and who knows, there may be new spring to my legs, a new rich timbre to my voice. I will paint powerful pictures. What vigour, they'll say, to her brush strokes, now that she's shorn her hair. I will electrify people whenever I walk into a room. Like you do, Gram.'

'You must go to a beauty parlour and have it done properly, have it styled.'

Jenny said nothing to that, knowing she wouldn't. 'It will be good for my incognito at Arthur Huntington s to look different too. I'm going to look different and be different.'

'Poor child, why don't you just go as yourself?'

'I can't. They'll get me if I do. Damon said so. He said people would always be after my money. They will make it their business to find me. They'll never love me for myself. Maybe going incognito gives me a chance to be loved. Anyhow, I *like* going incognito.'

'Maybe,' said Gram, 'because instead of being in disguise, you are really being yourself, in a way that you can't be whilst living your morbidly reclusive life as Jenny Hunt. It gives you a chance to spread your wings.'

'I'm not so reclusive. Look! I've come all the way to the

17

city to see you.'

'First time in ages.'

'Still!'

'Still, it was good of you.' Gram knew she must encourage her. 'It was a great accomplishment to come all this way yourself.'

'Across the bridge!' Jenny said proudly.

'An absolute act of derring-do, my dear.'

Jenny smiled at the praise.

Presently they went to bed. At four in the morning, Jenny woke up and couldn't get back to sleep. She decided to go back to Mill Valley and left a note for her grandmother to that effect. It was while walking to her car, taking a gander at the stars, that she saw the man on the building looking very much as if he was about to take his life. His body language emanated suicide. She's been around enough suicides at Fair Haven to know. Her concern took her out of herself. She overcame her habitual paralyzing reserve, and called up to him, 'Are you all right?' and was relieved to see him respond with a total lifting of his mood. He disappeared until a minute or so later, when he dropped right at her feet, not from the building, thank goodness, but from the tree she was passing beneath.

For the second time that week, she felt alarm. This event, too, was unprecedented.

5

'Are you all right?' she asked again, bending over him. 'You made a terrible sound when you hit the concrete.'

Damn! The girl. Getting a good look too. Luckily he had

18

the most forgettable of faces, even when it was grimacing in pain. And the light was bad here under the tree.

'Shall I call an ambulance? You probably shouldn't move.'

Horacio sprang to his feet to show how fine he was, reeled, then settled square on his legs.

She stood up slowly, looking both relieved and embarrassed.

Horacio did not speak because his voice *was* memorable – for its monotony. It was the most tiresome, flat, lifeless voice in the whole world. Over the years he had tried to put some life and expression in it, nothing so grand as an actual lilt but just some subtle variation to the droning tone – to no avail. If anything, it got worse. The most he could do was try to put some amusing content into his talk, but that was wearying. He gave up that idea pretty quick.

Horacio was a quiet man. Now he bowed gravely to the girl, turned on his heel and walked briskly up the hill, although his car was downhill, because he figured it was easier to shake her going up, in case she had a mind to follow and be sure, once and for all, that he was all right. However, it was not easy to walk briskly. *Ow!*

At the top of the block, Horacio glanced down to see that she was not looking after him. She had gone on her way. Well, he thought, the caper had turned out to be mildly exciting after all.

He walked over one block and down two to his 1958 Porsche speedster convertible, which he called his white lady, since most of his lovers, being Third World, weren't.

Going north, he passed Jenny on the Golden Gate bridge, but as her hair was under a hat by then, he·didn't recognize her as being 'the girl'.

It was five a.m. when he garaged his car and entered the house he was building for himself high on a hill in Mill Valley. His old dog, Abraham, a German short-haired pointer, struggled up from his slumbers by the door to greet his master – he not barking and Horacio not speaking. Their greeting was more a mutual acknowledgement, having little in it of love, respect, or even dependence.

19

Abraham had wandered into Horacio's life some years ago and stayed. The agreement was: I'll guard your house and keep off the furniture if you'll feed me and not expect me to wag my tail.

Both Abraham and Horacio were singularly laconic, fearless, lawless, physically strong, rich in experience and sexually active. This last attribute got them both into lots of trouble, but their fearlessness, lawlessness, and quietude got them out of it.

There were three letters that had been pushed under the door and Horacio wiped his feet on them. They'd be from women. He didn't have a phone, so his women left notes. It was a wonder, he thought grumblingly, that they didn't bump heads with each other as they pushed them under the door.

There would be more notes in the mail box: clever, cute, poetic, endearing. He could predict each one. There was no new note under the sun.

He put the gold and diamonds in the body of a six-foot-high wooden soldier which was standing in his bedroom, and stripped out of his clothes to go straight to his shower, the place he loved next-best to his bed. He had built himself a double-sized shower of crimson tiles with three shower-heads.

Afterwards, feeling clean, massaged, rested, and healed, wrapped in a terry kimono, he traversed the fifty feet of plywood floor of the living/dining-room to the kitchen, where he made himself a batch of pancakes.

From the dining-table beneath the huge chandelier, he surveyed the room. Fabulous oriental carpets were laid over the unfinished floor all the way from where he sat to the twelve-foot-high fieldstone fireplace at the far end, but no chairs or couches interfered with his gaze.

Magnificent but bleak, he thought. Not exactly cosy.

The actual construction was almost done, or it could be almost done (mostly just finishing work remained) if he would only stop adding more rooms. Friends compared it to the Winchester Mystery House, to which an old lady had kept adding rooms as a way of battling off death – rooms and stairways and passageways that went nowhere.

I'm just battling off finishing the damn thing, he thought.

But even if he did finish it, then what? Who was it all for? Did he still fool himself that he would marry and have a family? Already he had four children by three different women – three separate families that were an emotional and financial drain on him. He loved the kids but could not have borne to live with any of the mothers.

So many women threw themselves at him that he never had a chance to choose one, was never free to, was always involved with new women and could never shake off the old. The dick has no brain, no memory, cannot see two minutes ahead. It's only a rush of blood. You cut yourself and you bleed. Likewise, you see a woman and you bleed, but the blood, alas, fills the penis instead of leaving the body, leaves instead in the form of an abundance of seeds, any one of which can combine with a woman's to heedlessly create a poor little innocent human.

Horacio remembered the black despair on the cornice, felt its shadow. He should get away for a bit. Where? Mexico? Hawaii? No, at any resort there'd only be more women. Where, then? Some haven. Some treehouse where the branch won't break.

His heart lightened, lifted, beat almost with joy. Uncle's! He'd asked him to come and see his new house some months ago, but it hadn't been a good time. Now it was. He'd go and see Uncle – that old rogue. Just the person to give him a new lease on life. He'd take a few days to organize his affairs, arrange for the house and Abraham, answer his letters and notes, then he'd throw a few things in the white lady and be off! Off to the Valley of the Moon and the new abode of old Uncle Arthur Huntington the Great!

6

Dear Jenny,
I've returned to the Coast after many years abroad and
have built a little place in Helena Hot Springs to dodder
about in in my dotage. Jess continues to look after me
with heroic love and tolerance. Won't you come and
spend some time with us? I'm expecting a few friends
for the month of September in honour of the Harvest
Festival. Come and join us. Love, Arthur.

Jenny replied that she would come. Then she prepared for
the major undertaking of the trip, her first one alone. It
would be her longest lone drive ever – about seventy minutes.

When her adviser felt the time had come for her to have her
own car and no longer be chauffeured, she had made her
choice carefully. She wanted one that was aesthetically pleasing but not ostentatious. She chose the Alfa Romeo Spider, a
cabriolet sports car, and had it painted a shiny aubergine
purple, almost black. The interior and top were buff-
coloured.

She was taught to drive it – private instructions from an
ex-racing-driver who, after many crashes, could no longer
walk very well but could still drive like the devil. 'This was a
good choice,' he said. 'When you get behind the wheel of a
Porsche, it says to you, Now ve vill have fun. When you get
behind the wheel of an Alfa, the car says, Where do you want
to go, big boy?'

He taught her more than she'd ever need to know: how to
corner at eighty, how to brake and reverse at sixty, how to
drive on two wheels, or one, how to take it up to a hundred

and twenty, or take a rocky mountain road in first gear for ten miles. She was terrified the whole time. She drew the line at learning how to roll over in it. She did not want a roll bar put on the car: it was not aesthetic.

She was a good driver, he said, when she concentrated, but she tended to let her mind wander and not keep her eye on the r.p.m.'s, or the road.

After four years, the car had done only ten thousand miles. Mostly she used it to drive down the hill to the market and back up again. It had never yet said to her, 'Where do you want to go, big boy?' In any case, she only wanted to go home. But now she wanted to go to Arthur Huntington's. She really looked forward to her visit. She was going to spread her wings. Also, on Gram's advice and her own deep desire, she was going to cut her hair.

Her immensely long hair drew attention to herself and she was sick of having to hide it under hats or put it up where it weighed heavy on her head. She knew it would be terribly traumatic to have it shorn, and decided to do it herself rather than possibly, probably, suffer a crisis of nerves at a beauty parlour. She hated to swoon in public or, worse, weep.

She did as people have done since time immemorial: put a bowl on her head. She held it steady with one hand and cut round it with the other. She took the bowl off, shook her head back and forth, smiled. It was not traumatic at all. It looked good and felt great. What a relief. What a big girl she was getting to be. Now, if she could only grow bosoms . . .

She cupped her breasts in each hand. They were not entirely insubstantial.

She packed some summer clothes; it would be warmer in the valley. She put her paints neatly in a paintbox and collapsed her easel. Maybe she would even try to paint outdoors, she thought. That would be a change. She would not take her little collection of found objects that she liked to paint over and over again. The only departure she ever had made from these objects was when she had once painted her rocks in an attempt to disguise her mounting anxiety and confound her adviser. She pretended to herself, and to him, that she had gathered the rocks in order to paint them, not because she was scared. It transpired that she became fascinated while painting the rock assortment. On canvas it assumed the aspect of a gigantic desert landscape rather than a still life of rocks on a tabletop. But when her anxiety retreated, she relinquished the rocks so they wouldn't be around to remind her of her fear. She hadn't painted rocks since that one time she snookered her adviser – her deception had worked and deprived Fair Haven of her presence for the nonce.

In her circle of five friends, all of whom assumed she had money but never dreamed how much, was one who was also an artist – a professional, successful artist. She always spoke of Jenny's paintings as 'amusing', which hurt her deeply. Sometimes her friend said, 'They're so like you. They *look* like you,' a comment that might have pleased Jenny, except that it was said with a laugh which meant that that was part of what made them so 'amusing'.

She knew she was an artist and that she would live and die an artist. Her painting was the most important thing in her life. It *was* her life.

Gram believed her life was stifling and had been thrust upon her by Damon Carner's fears, all of which he had imbued her with. That was true as far as it went, but it was also true that she had chosen this life, that she saw it as one of absolute freedom where nothing was required of her, not even the smallest decision. She had the freedom to be herself and do exactly what she wished – which was to paint pictures.

The only problem was that the nature of her existence did not allow for much self to be, did not allow for growth. She was beginning to suspect that this was so, and if it was so, then it followed that there was truth in her friend's estimation of her work – that it was nothing more than amusing.

It was curious about the painting Carner had given her: the more she lived with it and looked at it, the more extraordinary it became. It completely changed in her eyes. What her eyes had first received as pretty-coloured-blurriness, paint laid on by a superb colourist, emerged in time as shapes and forms. The picture actually changed shape and form.

24

That image there was a boulder and, another day, a person appeared from behind the boulder to go, another day, and sit by a tree that previously had appeared to be a cloud.

The painting's mood changed with the light and the weather. It seemed to absorb its own light and weather accordingly so that Jenny actually expected the ethereal, perambulating person to hoist an umbrella on certain days or bring out the old *bain de soleil* on others.

She had grown attached to it and decided to take it with her to Arthur's. In fact she *had* to take it with her because she had been advised to take very good care of it, and that certainly meant keeping it close by.

Furthermore, she had had one final call from her adviser (the poor man was so accustomed to advising her she doubted he'd be able to stop until he was dead and buried) in which he urged her to put the painting in a safe. 'It is too valuable now to be out and around; the artist has died.'(Death's bone door had opened and closed.) 'You ought not to have it on your wall. He isn't that well known but people-who-care make it their business to discover who owns certain paintings. Because he is not yet famous, you can't pass it off as a reproduction.' (While most people pass their reproductions off as originals, Jenny had been taught to do the reverse.)

However, by the time of this last plaintive call, Jenny had already begun to learn to live without Damon. She had cut her hair, bought tapes to play in the car on the way to Arthur's, made her trial run to the city, and assumed her new identity. Although her responses to her adviser had always been Pavlovian in their dependable obedience, this time she said, to their mutual amazement and dismay, 'I'm afraid I can't do that. This painting would be wretched in a safe. It would be stifled without colour and light. It needs to be with someone.' (Was she talking about herself?) 'I mean, it needs to be out and about and looked at. It should be in a museum, looked at by multitudes of art lovers but, for now, I want it with me. I assure you I will protect it. And, if you don't think I should, I won't show it to anybody from now on.'

'Very well. Goodbye again, dear child.'

Damon Carner was anguished that he had been so indiscreet as to mention the painting to Arthur in his letter. He had done so to assuage his ego, to show Arthur that in one astute move he had left the girl partly provided for, that she wasn't a complete pauper at the end of his advisorial tenure. Also, since it was necessary to apprise Arthur of her exact financial situation, he simply had to include her possession of the painting. For those two reasons, he decided to tell Arthur about it. It was in keeping that his hundredth and final decision about Jenny's fortune was another wrong one.

Jenny also was feeling some anguish. She felt bad that she had not told Damon that she'd already heard from an art dealer with an offer for the painting – ergo someone had already made it their business to discover its current owner.

Naïvely, she'd responded:

'Dear Mr Smith, Thank you for your offer of $350,000.00 for my painting. I do not wish to sell at this time but I'll let you know if and when I do.
Sincerely, Jenny Hunt.'

(Upon receipt of her letter, Smith told his client, 'She doesn't want to sell.'

'Hmmnn,' said the client, whose name was Laveen.

'But keep in touch. She may change her mind.'

'She definitely is in possession of the painting?'

'Yes.'

'Thank you.' Laveen rose from his chair, which faced Smith across a desk.

'You might try offering her more. It really wasn't a particularly fair price,' said Smith.

'I'll be the judge of that,' Laveen said as he turned on his heel and exited.

Of course, he hadn't wanted to buy the picture and he knew very well that Jenny had it in her possession. What Laveen wanted was: one, to get a good look at Smith and, two, to forge a connection between Smith and Jenny.)

Dear Arthur,
Thank you so much for your kind invitation, which I
accept with pleasure. Once reminded of you by Damon
Carner, I found I had such extremely happy memories
of the times as a child when my father and I would visit
with you. Please don't think it odd if I ask to remain
incognito during my stay. Would you please introduce
me to your friends as Beulah Ludwig? See you on
September first. Looking forward with all my heart.
Love, Jenny.

Arthur confessed himself moved. What an open,
vulnerable, susceptible, wanting-to-please, darling child-
woman this letter portended Jenny to be.

He too remembered her visits as a child. How her father
had loved her. Although many women don't know the father
of their child, Alan Hunt was unique in not being sure of the
mother. Jenny had been left on his doorstep, looking like a
Hunt from day one, with the blood type to prove it.

Arthur cleared his throat. 'She's coming,' he said to
Laveen.

'Who's coming,' asked Arthur's wife, Jess, from her
corner of the living-room.

'Jenny Hunt.'

'Who is she and what brings her here?' Jess got up from the
long couch which undulated with pillows, where she'd been
languishing in a fit of ennui. She walked back and forth in
front of Arthur in the way that she did when she wished to
receive his full attention. At forty-three, her figure was still

attention-getting. She even drew Laveen's gaze. Laveen raped her briefly in his mind and found her wanting. Too used.

'She comes because I invited her,' Arthur replied simply. 'She is the daughter of a dear friend of mine, Alan Hunt, who took his life when she was eleven.'

'Is she pretty?'

'I imagine so. She was as a child.' Arthur anticipated Jess's next question, 'She's now twenty-nine,' and then her next, 'Not married. She wishes to remain incognito. The poor thing doesn't realize it's no longer necessary being a lowly ex-millionairess, which has none of the cachet of being an ex-president, ex-hero, ex-almost-anything-else. For Nixon is still Mr. President and generals and colonels retain their titles till death. A hero is always a hero, and even a crook can become a legend, but a poor ex –'

'They all earned their titles,' Jess pointed out, 'by doing something. Chances are a thousand to one that this girl inherited.'

Jess wished to diminish the girl with or without her money – Jess who had never earned a nickel in her life.

'She wishes to be called Beulah Ludwig,' Arthur went on.

'What an ugly name.'

'Why did you tell us her real name, then?' Jess asked. 'You've already blown the cover she desires. Not very nice.'

Arthur spread his arms to them both, smiling with all his formidable charm. 'But you are both my close friends, my confidantes. I trust you not to tell a soul. She only needs this incognito for her own peace of mind. You will not let on that you know who she is. We will give her the safe haven that she requires. I will ease her into the wonderful knowledge that from now on, being quite out at pocket, she can go everywhere being exactly who she is.'

'Which isn't much of anybody,' said Laveen, a crook who had become a legend. Laveen not only was Somebody (master criminal wanted on three continents) but Everybody (master of disguise). From this pinnacle of being he could pretty much scorn everyone else as nonentities, except Arthur, who was uniquely himself.

'Jess, darling, will you go and tell Rowley to drop his chores and get ready for a set or two of tennis?'

Jess departed and could be seen from the window accosting the hired man, a tall, scruffy-looking young person, who was setting water-lilies into the pond edge.

Laveen showed some teeth.

'Are you smiling, Laveen?'

'Yes. I like her being incognito. I can use that nicely. It definitely manifests the mindset we want. I'm excited.'

Never did a man look less excited, Arthur thought. His heartbeat remains ever constant – which is remarkable in itself since he is so completely heartless that there is nothing there to beat. I bet his heart stays the same during orgasm. I bet he doesn't have orgasms.

'Yes,' said Arthur musingly, 'it begins. Now with this letter, it begins. There is no moment quite so pleasing as the beginning one. Tell me, Laveen, what is your resting pulse?'

'Sixty.'

'God, that's wonderful! I won't tell you what mine is. Or what my blood pressure is. My pulse doesn't even know the meaning of the word rest, and my heart is so unstable it thinks it is my balls. It thinks it actually hangs outside my body like my balls do, bouncing all about, expanding and contracting, subject to weather, women, alcohol, and ire.'

Arthur stood up. 'I must hie me to the court. Have a day, Laveen: good, bad, or indifferent. You choose.'

'Have an indifferent day yourself. It will be good for your heart to cultivate indifference.'

'How touching of you to care.'

As Arthur got into his tennis whites, he reflected that it wasn't just Jenny's coming that pleased him, it was Jess. She had exhibited her first jealousy symptoms for a long time.

29

Their love throve on her jealousy. In his prime, there had been no problem. He had had to beat off the women and Jess had been ruled by, in thrall to, the green-eyed monster. But of late they'd been living quietly and all the women in their party circuit, such as it was, were damned dowdy. Jess became bored and dispassionate when she went too long without feeling threatened. She did not know what to do with herself, had no *raison d'être*, so that he actually worried for her health. An attractive woman around would put her on her mettle, revive her spirits. Arthur smiled. The truth was, it had been many years since he had entertained the smallest desire to be unfaithful to Jess. He loved her. She was the only woman he wanted. But, every so often, he made an effort towards another woman if only to displease Jess – and keep her happy.

Instead of watching Arthur and Rowley play tennis, as she usually did, Jess got into her yellow MG, let herself through the gates and sped to the town of Sonoma – a woman on a mission.

The people in the park of the historic old town square, which was flanked by the historic old Mission, were in the throes of a barbecue. Hundreds of pieces of chicken, encouraged by hands full of spatulas, turned russet above smouldering coals.

It seemed that every time she came to town, the park was in some stage of a barbecue. Every time, bar none. It was amazing! What a town this was for barbecues. It was like Spain and its saint's days. This one was probably to celebrate the harvest festival. The grapes were in. The wine-making would begin. Meanwhile, let's eat.

A stage-coach, pulled by four horses, was careering wildly around the square, selling rides to kids. It was all hokey as could be but Jess ambled through the park, enjoying the sights and scents, the Americanness. Sometimes she felt jealous of unexotic lives. It was her cross always to be jealous of something.

In the phone booth, she dialled the private number of a nationally syndicated columnist. Arthur had a penchant for listening in on extensions and there was one at the tennis court. Often, if absorbed in a game, he would make tapes of any incoming or outgoing calls. It wasn't that he was suspicious, he just couldn't bear to miss out on anything or not to be included in anything that might pertain to him in the slightest degree. Therefore Jess sometimes had to repair to public booths.

She was put through immediately to the big cheese.

'Tell me all you know about Jenny Hunt,' she asked, and was answered, 'Very little to tell. She was the only inheritor of Alan Hunt, who invented and produced some essential component for the space shuttle. He died at forty-five when Jenny was eleven. She has never made the national or international scene. She went to art school and now lives as a recluse, painting pretty much the same picture over and over. She has periodic nervous breakdowns and is, all in all, a nice kid. I've no pictures of her. Her father was a knock-out. She hasn't married. Most of her friends are women. She could be gay.'

Jess thanked her, gave her some excellent gossip in return, made her farewell, and after a swift passage through the park, resumed her seat in the car, feeling apprehensive.

One never knew. Sometimes weird women, as it appeared Jenny Hunt was, had their ways. A man could be drawn to them for no apparent reason. True sexiness hadn't that much to do with beauty, money, or youth. Often it had to do with weirdness. Such people could be compelling. Young, neurasthenic artists, with or without millions of dollars, could captivate.

Hmmpf. She sat thoughtfully for a few minutes. She did not need to look at herself in the rear-view mirror to reassure herself. She knew exactly how she looked: fantastic. She had only to look at her hands, which were poised on the leather-wrapped steering wheel. They were small, finely boned, beautifully formed, exquisitely kept, white, soft, perfect. They spoke for her entire self. Only the keenest inspection

31

would betray that they, and she, were old.

Her hair was still lustrously brown. She had had only one face-lift and two eye-jobs. Her body remained naturally firm, smooth, and light. Two hours a day she gave to floor exercise, lotions, and make-up. She looked to be in her mid-thirties. She still had her menstrual periods. She was fifty-two. Ten years ago she had lied to Arthur about her age by nine years, and she had had to live that lie ever since. She lived it well.

Her eyes turned inwards as she experienced, not for the first time, a fleeting vision. This vision was of two people walking slowly along a street together, arm in arm. Grey-haired they were, comfortably stout, wrinkled of mien – a vision of her and Arthur just walking along being old together, just being themselves as old people. And the picture gave Jess such a curious, momentary happiness that she lit up with a smile that would put the weirdest of young millionairesses in the shade, but this was followed by a pang of intense sorrow because it was simply not in the cards for them. Unimaginable. Too hokey and comfy and barbecue-ish. She and Arthur, instead, would have a calamitous old age, holding on to their youth with all their combined might, until finally being extinguished by a bizarre and hideous end in some unnatural corner of the earth. Well, the earth being round, any corner would be unnatural.

Although, she thought, what we have now is the closest we have ever come to a peaceful time together, a retirement. Or we did have peace until that awful Laveen started coming round.

She drove back to the house to watch the hired man, Rowley, let Arthur beat him at tennis.

8

Jenny was set to go. She stood a last moment in her little house that gave the illusion of teetering on the ridge, a seemingly friable structure spun of bits of glass and wood and stone, and said goodbye to it. She had chosen this house as she had chosen her car, for its lines, but she sometimes thought that only she and the architect saw how wonderful it was. It seemed to give a lot of people the jim-jams. People were funny. Last night her friends had come to say goodbye and she had looked at them and realized how little they knew her. They didn't know that she was one of the richest women in America. They didn't know about her rocks and break-downs, that she was afraid of almost everything, that despite the foregoing, she was happy most of the time.

No, they did know she was happy, and that's why they liked her and liked to be with her. Would knowing the rest allow them to know her better, or did they perhaps know her best? Why did she not divulge more of herself? Doctors would say she was afraid to be known, therefore loved, therefore abandoned. Both her mother and father had aban-doned her even though they'd loved her. Her father said she was a loved and happy baby when she was left with him at the age of about four months. Why, then, did her mother give her up? Why did her father, eleven years later?

Jenny would not let that happen again. Maybe the rocks were to fend off lovers not enemies. Whenever anyone got too close she went crazy. She left. Walked out of her mind. So they couldn't know her and love her and leave her. These were doctor's ideas – grasping at flies before giving the helpless shrug preparatory to condemning her to Electro-

33

convulsive therapy, the great cure-all. It works! We don't know how it works but it does! It'll bring her out of it!

It did. For the time being.

'Goodbye, house,' she said. She picked up her duffel bag, her easel, and her paintbox, into which, making a false bottom, she had put the valuable painting. She wore a blue cotton skirt and a coral-coloured blouse imprinted with small blue roses. Although she was five feet six inches tall, she wore a size five, being very slender. What with this thinness and her pallor from always being indoors, and a perpetual blueness under her large dark eyes, she looked rather frail, if not positively ill, but she was in fact amazingly strong and healthy. She never caught cold or flu, although that might have been because she never went anywhere to catch them and because, since she looked so ill, her friends were careful never to bring them to her.

'Hello, car. We're off on a great adventure.' She put the top down and threw her things on the seat beside her. On top of the dashboard she put a California map, folded to the pertinent territory, and a hand-drawn map Arthur had sent her, showing the way to his house. She put Stevie Wonder's Master Blaster album into the tape deck and, buoyed up by his energy, she started the sensational engine and set off.

'Goodbye, town.'

Feeling every bit as brave, every bit as much of the right stuff as the men who flew to the moon (thanks to another indispensable part provided by her father), Jenny turned north on Highway 101 and roared off, her heart beating like a humming-bird's wings, into the uncharted lands of her sudden future, where she would create herself anew under the aegis of Beulah Ludwig.

An hour or so later, Jenny was flying high. She had successfully completed her journey to the Valley of the Moon, navigating freeways and highways and byways with nothing untoward happening. No accidents befell her, nor was she waylaid by brigands.

She rang the bell at Arthur's estate gate, and presently an

34

incredibly dirty person (Rowley had been doing some plumbing) came down to the gate to let her in.

He took her bag, tried to take her paintbox, and led the way up the driveway to the house. It was a large, rambling, one-storey adobe and fieldstone house with two wings, set by a natural pond which had had some work done on it to make it less natural and more swimmable. Only indigenous trees and shrubs grew in the grounds, except for a garden of yellow and lavender roses by the front door. An emerald lawn surrounded the house and sprinklers swirled over it, rainbows dancing in the spray of them. Beyond the walls, in the valley's vineyards, the impeccable rows of grapes seemed to stretch off to infinity, but eventually reached the blue-green steeply-rising hills.

Rowley, carrying her things with his fingertips as if they were weightless, led Jenny round to the patio at the side of the house and left her there. Arthur was going over some papers at a glass-topped table. He rose to greet her and she smiled to see her old friend. Dressed only in baggy white shorts, he still looked every inch the aristocrat as he walked towards her in a slow, light-footed, majestic stride.

He hugged her hugely and warmly. It felt so good. It was the first physical affection she'd had for months. It brought tears to her eyes. She hastily blinked them away.

'Welcome, my dear, welcome.'

She was loath to let him go. I would like to be incorporated into him, she thought. I would like to fall asleep standing there in his arms. He let her rest there. She did seem to doze blissfully for a second. Then they separated.

She smiled. 'What a heavenly place.'

'You like it?' he exclaimed, terribly pleased. 'It's not half bad. It's coming along, I think. A few things still to be done.'

'Oh yes, I do like it. My house, although high on a hill, is in the woods, and this looks so bright and big and open. I feel like I've come out of a cave, a hibernacle. The space and light almost hurt my eyes. And you – you hurt my heart! You just seem to emanate memories of Daddy – in a way that Damon never did.'

'I loved him, that's why. What a prince he was! A prince of good fellows. But you must meet Jess. Jess!' he called into the house. 'Come and meet Beulah Ludwig, who's just arrived.' Arthur winked at her.

Jenny had forgotten for a moment about her incognito. What an ugly name, she thought, as she heard it called aloud. Couldn't I have done better than that?

A beautiful dark-haired woman stepped out on to the patio. 'How do you do?' Jess said correctly if not very warmly. 'How nice of you to come to stay,' she said, like Eliza Doolittle reciting to Higgins. 'I hope it won't be too boring for you here.'

'Oh no, I love the quiet. I want to do some painting while I'm here. You're very kind to have me to stay,' Jenny found herself reciting back. 'What a gorgeous place,' she said lamely, her enthusiasm deflated by Jess's coolness.

'Why, thank you.'

'You're welcome,' Jenny said helplessly.

'Follow me and I'll show you to your room. Perhaps you'd like to lie down. You look hot and tired, as if you'd come by foot instead of car.'

Jess managed to make her feel ghastly-looking. 'I'm not really tired. This is my normal look,' Jenny mumbled, but her hostess, uninterested, had turned towards the house. Jenny followed submissively with a parting wave and smile towards Arthur, remembering to pick up her paintbox, which she'd dropped for the hug.

She trailed behind Jess into the house, through a gracefully proportioned living-room made out of adobe with big brown beams across the ceiling and a fireplace at each end.

They went down a slender hallway with several doors off it, to the end. 'Here's your room. Relax for a while and I'll call you when it's time for lunch.'

Jess smiled as she opened the door for her, but after she had let Jenny in she shut it, rather sharply Jenny thought, leaving her alone. Dismayed, she said to herself, I've been sent to my room. But what a lovely room it is!

It was pleasant and cool. A fine old Bukhara carpet lay on

the shiny oak floor. There was a big green velvet armchair in front of a small stone fireplace. Jenny loved fires, fuel for her senses. The double bed was covered with a pale orange spread, and on the table was a vase of the yellow roses that grew by the entrance. There was a book-shelf crammed with books. A pair of french windows led to the lawn and the pond.

She stepped out of her sandals, lay on the bed just to try it out before unpacking, and fell into a deep, sweet sleep – Jess having been quite right, in fact, about her fatigue.

Jenny slept a long sleep. She slept off the strain of the trip which, despite her pretence to the contrary, had been immense, and she also slept off the strain of the previous week: the hair-cut which, although she'd shrugged it off, had been a trauma comparable to cutting off her fingers; Damon's abandonment, which wasn't too serious since they hadn't loved each other, but still; and the man falling from the building to her feet – that had terrified her! For some reason her mind had eclipsed the tree and she thought of him as the man who fell from the building then sprang to his feet and walked away. The sound! The sound of him hitting the concrete still reverberated in her mind. Why wasn't he broken to bits? She felt she was wrong to let him disappear, that even now he might be lying a few blocks away from where he fell, bleeding internally. At the very least she should have followed him to make sure he was all right.

All these events flashed kaleidoscopically on to her mind before she plummeted into sleep.

When she finally surfaced from her sleep, she thought about Beulah Ludwig.

Beulah, she decided, would be another personality entirely, a more successful one, one who never in a million years would have a nervous breakdown or paint amusing pictures.

Beulah would be intelligent, suavely aggressive, confident as all hell. She had two feet on the ground, was down-to-earth, sexy, greedy and tough. Well, maybe not greedy. No need for that. As for sexy, how did one even *begin* to be sexy?

37

Mainly, she had to get tough. Until now she had striven for two things in life: to be honest and to be kind. She now believed, Beulah believed, that truth was illusion and kindness and gentleness really ended by being madness.

Beulah would be tough and sane. She would paint pictures that had impact, that walloped you one. Beulah would . . .

By God, thought Jenny, already I'm beginning to hate this Beulah!

But the thing is, if I convince myself of being Beulah, I won't even look like Jenny. One's expression, attitude, and affect, does more for an incognito than hair-dye and false moustaches. Although that's an idea! I could put fake hair under my arms. Beulah, for sure, would have thick, curly underarm hair. What else would Beulah do? Drink! Oh good! Jenny was such a teetotaler. But I'd better start off easy. Beulah would never get drunk. Anyone that suave, that forceful, that hairy . . .

'Beulah?' Jess peeked in the door, after a soft knock. 'Are you awake now? You slept through lunch. I didn't want to disturb you. Now it's time for cocktails.'

'Oh my goodness! I'll just freshen up and be right with you. Thanks, Jess.'

Probably, Jenny thought, she'd just as soon I slept through cocktails too. And dinner. If she had her way she wouldn't wake me up until it was time for me to go back to Mill Valley. Well, I'll just have to try to make friends with her. Or Beulah will.

Jenny washed her face and brushed her hair. She took the painting out of her box. The images looked more spectral than ever. The painting looked positively wan. She decided it wasn't good for it to be in the box and almost put it on her bureau, but was overcome by an attack of uneasiness. She would keep it in the box except when she was in the room, then she would take it out.

38

9

Arthur was drinking Anejo rum on ice with fresh lime. Jess opened a bottle of Chardonnay from a neighbouring vineyard for Jenny and herself. Arthur switched on the evening news.

'Locally,' said the newsman, after a few minutes, 'Maria Lopez has disappeared from the Sonoma sanitarium where she has been recovering from a nervous breakdown these last two months . . .'

Jenny's heart stopped. Maria Lopez was her incognito for Fair Haven! Now they were showing a picture of her she didn't know existed. It was black and white, a distance shot, and of course her hair was long. She accepted the glass of wine from Jess with trembling hands and fearfully sneaked a look at her to see if she seemed to make a connection between Maria Lopez and Beulah Ludwig, but she looked marvellously indifferent.

Arthur shot her a quizzical glance, to which she responded with rolling eyes and a shrug, then he resumed a deadpan.

'Authorities say she is not dangerous but they are anxious for any information concerning her whereabouts. Foul play is not suspected. They believe her departure from the Fair Haven Hospital was voluntary but stress it was unauthorized and inadvisable.'

Arthur punched off the Trinitron and laughed. 'It certainly is a great relief to us all that this patient isn't dangerous, since she's running loose right here in the valley. Although maybe we should man the battlements just in case. What do you think, Jess? Should we have Rowley at the gate with a submachine-gun lest the poor child comes our way.'

'I don't believe,' said Jess laconically, 'that any woman

39

with that much hair could escape from anywhere. It would drain her of her natural strength.'

Jenny remembered her Gram entertaining the same absurd idea.

'I don't believe,' said Arthur, 'that one's own hair is a parasite feeding on its owner, any more than one's teeth are.'

'Obviously it weakened her brain,' Jess insisted.

'Freud would certainly be intrigued by your diagnosis.'

'Why drag in Freud? Can't we talk amongst ourselves?'

Jenny had a wonderful vision of Freud being dragged in by the scruff of the neck – probably by Rowley.

'Let's talk about dinner instead,' said Arthur.

'Rowley has made us a little cold supper, but we could go out if you'd rather.'

'Hell, no! I love Rowley's little cold suppers. What a wonder that boy is. Let's have it out in the rose garden.'

'But there are no tables and chairs there, Arthur.'

'There aren't? Why not? This is an outrage.'

'We can eat on the patio if you like,' Jess said mollifyingly.

'No, we'll bring tables and chairs from the patio to the rose garden. A rose garden isn't just to look at, it's to be in the middle of. Grab a chair, Beulah.'

As they carried the furniture around, Arthur seized a lone moment to whisper. 'Why didn't you tell me you'd come from Fair Haven today?'

'But I didn't. It's some horrible mistake. They must have got my files confused with some one else's or given the news the wrong picture.'

Arthur said nothing.

'You believe me, don't you?' she asked, worriedly.

'Of course,' he assured her. 'Now, let's see,' he said to them both when the furniture was ideally placed, 'how shall we dress? Kimonos. Let's all wear silk kimonos. If you didn't bring yours, Beulah, we'll lend you one.'

Arthur, Jess, and Jenny, all in silk kimonos, ate Rowley's little cold supper among yellow and lavender roses. The sun went down, the moon sailed up, attended by Venus, which shone greenly down on them. They ate, drank wine, told stories, laughed. Jenny's stomach muscles, almost ossified, came back into play with all the laughter. She rediscovered what it was like to be happy, to have fun. She realized that, sexiness and toughness aside, Beulah's aim must simply be to stop being fearful and have fun.

Jess and Arthur, she saw, were blessed with the gift of fun. Despite being sophisticated people of the world, they had an ingenuousness that was enchanting.

For the first time, Jenny thought, I am with people to whom I belong. I have found my family, my tribe.

10

The next morning, which was sunny and mild, Jenny was alone with Arthur when the news came on and the escape story was repeated, this time with frills. Maria Lopez, in fact, 'could be dangerous when stressed.'

'This is all maddeningly ridiculous,' said Jenny. They were outside on lounge chairs by the pond and, in the bright sun, as opposed to a dim room, the television lost its power as a conveyer of news of any real importance – else she might have felt more upset. 'I should just call Fair Haven and straighten it all out. Don't you think I should, Arthur?'

'No. I shouldn't worry about it. The story will die down. Since it isn't your real name or the name you are using now, it really hasn't to do with you at all.'

'But it's my picture!'

'Not really your picture either, as you are now.'

'You don't think people will recognize me?'

'No. In the picture you have all that hair and you do look rather demented. If someone introduced you as Maria

41

Lopez, one might make the connection, otherwise not.'

'I wonder who took that picture and how they got it. I do not want my friends in Mill Valley to know about Fair Haven. People can't help but take a different view of you if they know you're certifiable.'

'Or if they know you're rich,' said Arthur. 'I like people knowing I'm rich. I like people to truckle to me. I wish more people did.'

Jenny laughed, then said with surprising assurance. 'The thing is, I'm an artist. I'm not a rich girl or a crazy girl, I'm an artist and that's what I will still be when I'm no longer rich or crazy.'

Arthur wondered if now was the time to tell her she was no longer rich. Instead he asked, 'How long were you in Fair Haven the last time?'

'Three months. And every minute out of it increases my resolve never to return. I can see why people moulder away for years in places like that. You forget what the real world is like.'

'Or else you remember,' said Arthur wryly, 'and dread the return to it. Prisons can also be a great relief and people don't always have places such as ours to return to.'

'This place certainly isn't "the real world", it's paradise.'

'I know. But it doesn't take much to live like this. Only a million or so dollars.'

Jenny smiled, then became pensive. 'You're sure Jess hasn't said anything about my possibly being Maria?'

'I'm sure.'

'And you don't think I should call Fair Haven, or the media?'

'No, I don't. They might come and get you, or come and interview you.'

'Oh Lord, what a mix-up. Arthur, if they somehow did discover me here, you wouldn't let them take me away, would you?'

'Of course not! I wouldn't even let them in. It's not for nothing I have those big iron gates. I should have a moat too, come to think of it. Or a crenellated wall from which we could pour hot oil . . .'

'And Arthur, one more thing, you do believe that I didn't escape and that I'm quite sane?'

'My dear, you are one of the sanest people I know.' Arthur stood up and stripped down naked. 'Let's go for a swim. Don't look so glum. We won't listen to the news any more. Come on.'

Jenny, not to seem nonplussed, followed suit, followed suitless.

He was delighted to see what a good swimmer she was.

'Oh, I'm very well instructed in everything. Damon neglected nothing.'

'Tennis?'

'Yes, but I don't like to play. I can't compete. I don't mind losing but I get upset if I win. I just do lone sports. Unfortunately, or fortunately, there aren't very many.'

Arthur pulled himself smoothly from the pond and stepped into his white shorts. 'Here comes Rowley for our tennis game. Come and watch if you like. He almost always lets me win – although I pretend not to know this – but on some days, and I never know when it will happen, he decides viciously to beat me.' Arthur gave Jenny a hand up from the water to the lawn. 'And then it's interesting and exciting to see how badly he can beat me. Or, from my viewpoint, how unbadly. My serve is more powerful and, come to think of it, all my strokes are better – prettier certainly – but he can run, damn his eyes, and I can't. It's the hell of growing old. I – oh well, I see this isn't of much interest to you. It's consumingly interesting to me. For me, the game is everything. The game is all. And how you play it. Strength, craft, cunning, surprise. Rowley knows. He is very surprising.'

'Have a good game, then. I'm going to go and do a little painting.'

Jenny put on a robe as Rowley came into view. He was looking at her. She hadn't noticed him much the two days she had been here. Now she did. What a strange look he had – really quite odd. Those eyes! Had he seen the photograph on the news and recognized her? She tried to look Beulahish. To

43

do this she drew herself up and stuck out her jaw. This also stuck out her bosoms, which briefly riveted Rowley's attention.

Relaxed and smiling, Rowley carried two rackets and a new can of balls. He stood waiting while Arhtur put on his tennis shoes.

Arthur did not introduce him to Beulah.

Well, she thought, he's a handyman, not a friend. Still, Arthur is so democratic. Probably he thinks Rowley and I have already met, but we've never actually said a word to each other. Should I say Hi, I'm Beulah Ludwig? It would be friendly and, that way, in case he did see the news, he'd know I'm not Maria Lopez.

'Hi, I'm Beulah.'

Too late. The two men had turned and were walking away across the lawn and up the stone steps to the tennis court. Jenny stood there feeling stupid, feeling confused, disoriented, feeling almost invisible.

She walked down to the gate and looked through the wrought iron bars to her car. 'I'm here, right, car? We came here together, from Mill Valley, yesterday, right? You've never been to Fair Haven.'

Right, said the car.

'That's good.'

Jenny went to her room, and while Arthur and Rowley played tennis and Jess probably did her exercise routine, she set up her easel, got out her paints, and also got out the valuable painting and set it on her bureau so it could look around. She had taken it out last night before bed, as well, returning it to the box when she went to breakfast. It looked delightfully serene today, seeming to reassure her that all was well. Although it was the middle of the day, in the painting the sun seemed just to have risen and all of nature was holding its breath like a newborn baby fresh from the womb filling her lungs for the first life-affirming cry.

'Pure magic,' said Jenny, ingesting it.

She decided to paint a rose. This was a mammoth undertaking. She'd never painted anything live. She was tempted to take it out of water and lay it down, so it could at least be a dying rose, but decided she'd go for broke. Should she paint a lavender rose or a yellow one, in the bud or the flower? In what light?

Underway at last, she realized she couldn't dilly-dally. Because it was alive, it would change hourly. She could not take days or weeks over this, she could only take minutes. How exciting. She would rip off a painting of this rose willy-nilly. She felt freed by the limitations of life – of aliveness. Concentrating intensely, she fell into the flower's centre, entered the rose through the heart of its convolutions of petals, like a bee.

11

Meanwhile, where was Horacio? Where was the man who fell from the building? Was he bleeding internally? Not exactly.

Despite his resolve to go to Uncle Arthur's, he had gone to bed instead. And pulled the covers over his head. And stayed there for days. He was damned depressed. He hadn't shaved or even showered and rarely had eaten. Every so often he'd get up and make himself another pancake, from the same batter, and drink a glass of water. Since there was no phone, no one could call and rouse him from his inertia. He also had no doorbell, and if any one beat on the door, he wouldn't be heard from the bedroom. Or rather, *she* wouldn't. And a she, naturally, would beat less loudly than a he. There was no way of looking in on his bedroom from outside as the ground fell away steeply on that side of the house. Once, during another depression, a woman had climbed a tree to look in, but she was unusual, and only did so because she was in a jealous fit and thought someone was in bed with him. What else could keep him there for days on end?

Horacio had never found any woman who could keep him in bed for days like a good depression could. Maybe if he had, everything would be different.

Since he had a sonic switch command and could do so without leaving bed, he sometimes switched on his television. So it was that he saw the coverage on the missing mildly-dangerous patient, and for a moment was bemused.

Horacio didn't have a very good memory for faces but he did for hair. Wasn't this woman the Nosy Parker who had persisted in trying to find out if he was all right the night he stole the gold and diamonds? If so, that being several nights ago, how could she have escaped yesterday from Fair Haven? The news report was a lie. The kid was getting a bum rap. It made him mad.

Going from bemused to mad lightened his depression. He decided to get up, stay up, go away.

'I'm all right, Maria Lopez,' he mumbled on the way to the shower. 'Are you all right?'

12

The next morning, Arthur waved Jenny off on a walk beyond the confines of the estate, something he'd encouraged her to do lest even here she fall into her reclusive ways – and lest he not be able to find the time to search her room. He entered her room through the french windows. He 'laundered' the room carefully but did not find the painting. Jess, passing the doors, discovered him there. 'What, may I ask, are you doing in Beulah's room?' She entered and confronted him.

'You may ask,' Arthur replied, sitting down in the green armchair. 'You may not get an answer. I'd be very surprised if you got an answer. But do ask.'

'You seem to be looking for something. Perhaps some article you left when you were visiting with her here.'

'Jess, I have not visited with Beulah in this room.'

'It is enough to swim naked with her.'

'I swim naked with everyone, you know that. I'll be damned if I'll put on a suit in my own swimming-hole.'

'You asked her to watch you play tennis – you didn't ask me.'

'Ask you! Since when do I issue an invitation? It is a given that you'll be there each day to cheer me and boo Rowley.'

'Exactly. Let it also be a given that I do not want Beulah sharing my duties, and that includes bed.'

'Right!' Arthur expostulated. 'It sure does include bed. I refuse to have her in bed with us. It's crowded enough as it is.'

'You just make a joke of everything. You don't care that I am suffering.'

'Jess, darling, come here.' He took her on his lap, kissed her warmly, licked away her tears. 'I care more than you will ever know.'

Rowley also waved Beulah off on her walk, emerging from the gatehouse where he lived just as Beulah was going through the gate, but she didn't see him. He noticed that she didn't go off into the vineyard but turned and headed for the hills. He watched her disappear from view and felt happy. Only six months ago he'd been down and out, on the skids, on the beach, and on the lam. Now he had a good job, a place to live, his health and strength, friends in the town. He had a daily litany: 'Don't let me blow it.' Now, on top of all the foregoing, he was in love. He was in love with Beulah Ludwig.

As soon as he'd opened the gate for her on the day she arrived, he'd fallen. There she stood, looking pale and wan,

47

unsteady, unsure, and yet wonderfully sweet. Since then she'd grown more and more beautiful to his eyes. Her slight body was all grace and strength, while appearing so fragile. She was quick to smile, so warm and responsive to all around her. She was serene and yet, somehow, so comical too that to see her made him smile. She was smart, an artist therefore a thinker. Who had he ever known who was a thinker? Most people only acted and reacted. Except Arthur. Arthur was a genius. Or a crook. He'd have to be one or the other to have the money he had. Of course there was no reason he couldn't be both.

Thank God for Arthur and his hidden estate. As long as he kept out of trouble, didn't blow it, there was no reason to ever be caught.

He had been in prison for two years with three to go when he decided to make a break for it. The two years of time had done him good. He'd recovered his health, strength, and brain. He'd got his high-school diploma, learned skills, discovered books, taken up sports and weight training. He was a model prisoner, trusted. Ask any guard there if Rowley would run and they'd say no.

But one day he looked around (it was his birthday and he was twenty-six) saw the guards and walls, the yard full of men without purpose, castrated cattle, and realized that he felt pretty good and that this was no way for a human being to live. So he escaped.

It was a few weeks and four hundred miles later, when he'd got some free man's clothes and a shave and was hitch-hiking on Route 37 going north from San Francisco, that Arthur picked him up. He was driving a beautifully preserved 1960 Pontiac Bonneville ragtop. It was baby blue with black leather seats. It looked twenty-five feet long and ten feet wide and Arthur, in white linen trousers and a blue Brooks Brothers shirt with the sleeves rolled up to show his impressive forearms, looked like a man who had the world by the tail.

He stopped for Rowley, who was carrying a sign that simply said *North* but, instead of driving on, they sat together and communicated, and the upshort of it all was that Arthur took him home to Helena Hot Springs and put him to work.

Rowley began by working on the grounds, being overseer and security man. Gradually, as things went wrong around the house and he showed he could fix them, his duties expanded, along with his pay. In the car he'd promised Arthur he'd be quick to learn tennis, and he lived up to his promise. Soon Jess discovered he could cook, and not only did the food taste good, he had an artful way of preparing and serving so that it looked good too. Rowley became what rich people call a treasure.

Arthur was generous with time off as well as money, and Rowley found a hangout in a nearby town, a bar and restaurant called the Always Inn, where he made friends and went to dance, drink, gamble, and look over the women. He'd learned to live without sex in prison, including not fooling with himself, and he found he wasn't hot to begin. He wasn't *ready* to begin, maybe not ready to get that close to a person, even in the most casual kind of sex connection. Even if he paid, he didn't want it.

Or maybe, he realized now, it was the casualness that was so undesirable. Since he'd learned not to need the physical release, he could continue to do without until it would mean more, be more. As it would be with Beulah.

Tomorrow, he vowed, I will ask her to go dancing with me.

One of Rowley's duties was chauffeuring, and that afternoon he drove Arthur to fetch Laveen at Fair Haven, then motored slowly around the valley so the two men could talk privately together in the back seat. Just as Jess sometimes had to repair to a public booth for telephone calls, Arthur had to repair to his car, since Jess not only listened in on extensions but also at windows and doors.

The car's top was down and Arthur, as usual, was in his shirtsleeves, bareheaded, basking in the hot, wine-country sun, while Laveen, as usual, was in suit, tie, gloves, and hat, as well as beard and glasses.

'How is everything going?' Laveen asked.

'Very well. She is a charming guest. She is *quite* sane, you know.'

'She's not under any stress right now.'

'Just because you're posing as a psychiatrist, Laveen . . .'

'I know ten times more about the human psyche than those poor fools. The entire science would be useless without drugs and electro-convulsive therapy. No, I shouldn't dignify it with the word science.' He waved his hand irritably. 'What's the plan? Has she got the painting with her?'

'If she does, it's extremely well hidden. We'll have to flush it out.'

'Ah, good, then we'll proceed with plan B.'

'Yes, as your orderly mind would have it, plan B.'

'I'll be glad to get away from Fair Haven. I'm going to assume another identity, but to you and Jess I'll still be called Laveen.'

'I'd like to give her a little more time to settle in and relish her freedom.'

'Fine. I'll arrive in, say, a week's time, as your guest.'

'My unexpected guest.'

'Of course. That was implied. I didn't forget.'

Even with the dark lenses, Arthur could see Laveen's eyes flick menacingly. He knew Laveen hadn't forgotten. Laveen forgot nothing. But he liked to tease him, to try to loosen him up. Of all the criminals he'd ever known, Laveen was the most fanatically serious. He supposed that was why he was so good – in a whole different league from himself – but where was the fun? Well, Arthur should be grateful. This art theft was child's play for Laveen, but Arthur needed the money and it was nice of him to take an interest and help out – a fifty per cent interest, but still . . .

'So it will just be us,' Laveen said. 'You're not expecting any others. Just Beulah, you, me, and Jess.'

'And Rowley. He who sits in front of us. This car isn't on automatic pilot, you know.'

'What about Rowley? Are you sure he can't hear us?'

'I'm positive. Rowley can't hear us talking anywhere. He's deaf.'

'Ah! He *is* a treasure.'

'And dumb.'

Laveen actually looked impressed as if, thought Arthur, I'd deafened and devoiced him myself as an ultimate discretionary measure. Laveen would do that. Probably has. He would certainly make eunuchs to guard his wife, if he had a wife. 'Rowley was that way when he came to work for me, Laveen.'

'Oh.' Arthur took a great fall in Laveen's esteem.

13

Horacio Huntington drove up to the gate about half an hour after Arthur and Rowley had driven off. He rang the bell, and his heart sank when he saw a young woman come down the drive to let him in. Oh, Christ, there's no respite. I should have known that Arthur would people his latest Shangri-La with young lovelies.

But even as he thought this sullen thought, it was instinctual with him to put on a winning smile as the woman approached.

Horacio wasn't strikingly handsome, but he had the most heartbreakingly beautiful smile ever conjured on a man's face. One flash of it was all it took to fatally attract the one he bestowed it upon. He would have Jenny in bed by nightfall.

But Jenny, so fearful was she to find a stranger at the gate, was wonderfully unaffected by Horacio's smile. She'd been at her painting when the ring had come. Realizing she was alone on the estate, which was unusual, she'd gone timidly to answer.

No sooner had she left her room than she was assailed by

more fear because she'd left the valuable painting out and unattended. Why this frightened her she didn't understand. She felt she was the painting's guardian and protector.

Should she go back and put it away? How silly. There was no one around to discover it. This person at the gate surely was not going to dash by her to her room and seize it. He had not come for that purpose, had he? Well, it was possible that he had – but not likely.

She wavered, reminded herself she was Beulah, went to the gate.

So perturbed and distracted was she when she arrived at the gate that Horacio could have flashed ten smiles and done fifty flip-flops to boot and she would not have noticed particularly, let alone have been fatally charmed and in bed with him by nightfall.

'Yes?' She looked gravely at him through the bars of the gate.

'Hello, I'm Horacio Huntington, Arthur's nephew.'

'Oh.'

'I've come for a visit.'

'You have?'

'Yes.' Horacio held up a hand. 'Please don't say Oh again.'

Jenny was silent. He wondered if she was retarded. 'Do you suppose you could let me in?'

'Well, yes, I could.'

'Please do,' he said jokingly. 'Or shall I show you some indentification first?'

'Would you, please? That would be a comfort.' Jenny thought that if he was named Huntington, all would be well – for herself, the estate, the painting.

Horacio was astonished but he obliged. He showed her a long-out-of-date driving licence.

'What a terrible picture,' she said, handing it back and unlocking the gate.

'Almost as bad as my actual face.'

Jenny, overcome by relief, actually laughed and joked, 'Nothing could be that bad – unless it was your voice.'

'You really turn yourself inside out to please a man when

52

you first meet him.'

'Sorry.' Jenny blushed. 'I was just joking.'

'Now that you know who I am, are you going to divulge your name?' Horacio took his bag from the boot of the white lady.

'Beulah Ludwig. I'm sort of like a niece of Arthur's. He was my father's best friend. They were at Harvard together.'

'Then we can be cousins.'

'I've never had a cousin. I'd like that.'

They were walking up the driveway to the house. Horacio considered her. 'You look like you mean it.'

'I do mean it.'

Horacio felt strangely, inexplicably, pleased. Never before had a woman wanted to be his cousin. Then he wondered, why does she want to be my cousin? He wondered if, after all, he shouldn't feel insulted. Why didn't she want to go to bed with him like everyone else? He looked at her. She had short, shiny, boyishly-cut hair. Her face was smooth and unlined, the profile and large eyes looking like something off an old Greek coin. Maybe she was gay.

'Tell me, are Arthur and Jess expecting you?' she asked.

'Not exactly. But they'll be thrilled, I promise you.'

Arthur was not thrilled. Any other time but this, Arthur would have been truly happy to see Horacio, who was a great favourite of his; but not now. His reaction to seeing his nephew was much like Horacio's upon first seeing Jenny – his heart sank. He thought sullen thoughts. But he, too, mastered by the family charm which only Laveen did not possess, (Laveen's real name was Harry Huntington) smiled generously, saying, 'Nephew!' and spread wide his arms. Horacio came into his embrace. They hugged, thumped each other's backs, called each other you devil and you old dog and all in all had a warm and manly greeting.

Jess kissed Horacio and was honestly pleased to see him, not only because she liked him but because he would command Beulah's attention away from Arthur. Horacio would undoubtedly have her in bed by nightfall.

53

As the day passed in eating, drinking, conversing, and showing Horacio the building tricks of the new house, Arthur observed his nephew narrowly. What had brought him here? Did he suspect who Beulah was? Did he, too, happen to know of the existence of the invaluable painting and her possession of it?

They were both professional criminals: both audacious, resourceful, intelligent, and careful. They had sometimes worked together. Arthur did not like to think they would work against each other.

Of course, Horacio could have sniffed out the painting, sniffed Jenny here – believing Arthur to be ignorant of the treasure in his midst. In that case, as his guest and blood relation, the only decent thing would be for Horacio to put his cards on the table. But, when you're talking half a million dollars in one easy scam, you don't always do the decent thing.

For his own part, Horacio was doing some narrow observing of Arthur. He saw that Arthur didn't have anything romantic going with Beulah – despite the fact that Jess was transparently jealous of her – and if he didn't invite Beulah here for that, why was she here? If it wasn't for sex, it must be business. She wasn't a rich woman. She didn't look it or act it, and if she was, she'd have let him know by now. Rich women use it.

He could read Arthur as well as anyone, and he was looking pretty protective of Beulah. She must have something he wants, but what? Something was going on; he could sense it. He smiled at himself, at his interest and mild excitement. Perhaps he wasn't so hopelessly depressed after all. There was life in the old boy yet. He was going to be all right. It was a good idea to come and see Arthur. Damned good.

He came out of his thoughts to see everyone disrobing for a swim. Horacio, strangely enough, was shy about nudity. He went to his room for a pair of trunks.

Beulah and Horacio swam together in the pond, suspended in silver water, under the barrel of blue sky.

Floating on her back, her nipples broke through the surface like two little fishes gulping at flies.

Horacio did not feel turned on by her. At the same time he was almost dizzy with delight in her company.

He felt he could say anything to her. She was right *there*. And laugh!

How long had it been since he'd laughed?

'I'm so happy,' she said. 'I feel so lucky to be here in this enchanted place. So voluptuous. What a treat for the senses. All of them.'

'Arthur is one of the great sensualists of our age.' Horacio said, treading water beside her. 'He knows how to live. How long have you been here?'

'I've lost all sense of time. The only thing I'm sure about is this minute. And the next two minutes when I beat you in a race to the raft.' She flipped over and went into a powerful crawl.

But Horacio beat her. And wouldn't let her up on the raft, pushing her back in whenever she tried to climb aboard. Until she pulled him in with her. Then he pulled her under. And so forth . . .

'How soon before he has Beulah in bed?' Jess asked Arthur as they lay on their double lounge-chair watching the horseplay.

'By nightfall,' he answered, rather wishing they'd go to it in the water, or on the raft, so he could watch.

'How is she in bed?'

'Talk to Horacio about it in the morning.'

'Or I could just listen to the two of you compare notes.'

'Jess, this is an illness of yours, you know. Every so often I think it will give you a lift to feel jealous again, but it is like an addict getting lift from a shot of smack – you are only getting energy from that which is devouring you.'

'Do you love me?'

He sighed. 'I love you,' he said, hating her at that moment. 'Really?'

'Yes, really. I love you with all my heart,' he said truly, hating her for forcing the statement, for needing to hear it so desperately that she would accept only the husk of the feeling, which was the words.

She spoke bitterly, hating him equally. 'You only say it because I ask you to.'

<h1 style="text-align:center">14</h1>

Horacio and Jenny remained inseparable all through dinner, and after dinner sat very close to each other on the couch in front of the fire. They ran out of talk and laughter at last, falling silent, feeling a happy awareness of each other, a cosiness, a trust. The last lingering light of day dissolved into the nigrescent air, which is to say that it was almost nightfall.

Horacio didn't know how to proceed, how to translate this cosy companionable feeling between them into an inferno of desire. It was his custom to sweep a woman into bed from the force of his ardour so that she hardly knew what was happening. But right now he felt too comfortable even to get started. The fire was all in the hearth, not in his loins.

Still, it never occurred to him not to go ahead with it.

He looked at Beulah and was amazed to see that she was nodding. She yawned enormously, begged his pardon, and said, 'I must get on to bed.'

'At eight-thirty!'

'I was up at six. I like to go to bed around nine. Then I read for an hour or so.'

She was leaving him for a book! That put him on his mettle. 'I'll walk you to your room,' he said.

'How gallant,' she laughed.

Yes, it was nightfall and, as everyone but Beulah had foretold, Horacio had her in bed by it.

However, nothing doing.

'I'm sorry,' Horacio said. He racked his brain for an explanation. He could say it had never happened before, but that would just make her feel bad and in any case it would be a lie. Tired, then? Was he too tired to get it up? The long drive? Sure, the hour's drive really tired him. And the swimming too – that was damned tiring. Too much to drink? One beer.

He looked at Beulah lying next to him in all her youth and loveliness and thought grimly, I'm fucked. There's really something wrong.

But also, there was something curiously sexless about her. Unawakened. Maybe she *was* gay.

'Don't feel bad,' Beulah said, sensing his look, his dismay. She got out of bed to put a flaming match to the fire she'd set earlier. She watched it catch and blaze up, felt pleased. Fire-building was tricky, she thought, metaphorically. It could take one match or endless tending. Of course, a lot depended upon the wood.

Horacio did not look at the fire, he looked at her. She was completely unselfconscious in her nudity, like a very young child. 'You're a beautiful woman,' he said sincerely. 'A fox. A stone fox.'

'Thanks, Horacio.' She walked back and got into the bed beside him, plumping the pillows behind her, sitting up so she could see the fire. 'You're beautiful too. You have the kind of body that looks strong from use, not sport. The muscles seem to be there for some serious reason. And your face is also strong-looking, but at the same time sensitive, almost feminine.'

'You're telling me I look like a girl?'

'Well, a muscular girl.' They both laughed. Laughing together, Jenny thought, is just as good as having an orgasm together, just as nourishing and pleasing and much easier, at least for us. At the same time, I bet there are more men I could have an orgasm with than I could laugh with. 'How old are you?' she asked him.

'Thirty-six.'

57

'I'm twenty-nine.'

'I thought you were younger, *much* younger.'

'You child-molester.'

'I draw the line at twenty, since a girl that age or younger could, unbeknownst to me, be my daughter. You know, I'll tell you something. When you said you wanted to be cousins, I felt glad. The idea of being friends with a woman, relations, was wonderful to me.'

'You mean, having blood relations instead of sexual ones? Then why are we in bed together? Seems like it was pretty much your idea.'

'I can't help myself. It's something I just do automatically. It's expected.'

'I didn't expect it. But then, when you kissed me goodnight so warmly I thought, how nice, what a good idea, I'm going to give it a go.'

'It's still not a bad idea. I like being here beside you. Although I know I'm keeping you from your book.'

'Yes, you are, and it's such a good book too. But this is nice, being cosy together. Isn't it a beautiful room? And the fire! But the truth is (now I'll tell my truth) I was feeling hot for you once you got me started. I haven't been with a man for –'

'How long?'

'Oh, for a year at least.'

'God, that's terrible. Why not? Were you sick?'

'One reason and another, that I really don't want to go into now.' Jenny hung her head, feeling sad about herself.

'Now I do feel bad to have let you down.'

Jenny smiled. 'So you didn't feel bad before? What a cad.'

And he doesn't now either, she realized. Why should he? The only thing that could hurt would be his ego, but his ego is too strong for that. He couldn't feel bad for *me*, because he doesn't know me. Still, it was nice of him to say.

'I'm trying to change myself, be another sort of person,' she suddenly offered.

'People can't change.'

Jenny felt shocked. 'Of course they can. Otherwise, what

58

would be the point in living? The trouble is, we get to like ourselves, even to like our flaws and weaknesses. They're familiar and therefore dear.'

'I think my main trouble,' Horacio said, 'is that I don't have any flaws. I'm not sure you do either. Don't change. I like you this way, Cousin.'

'I'm afraid I must change, to survive.' Jenny felt a moment's desperation as she said that. She calmed herself. 'Since we're being so frank, tell me, have you been with lots of women?'

Women always liked to ask that. 'Hundreds,' he said. 'Beyond count.'

'You must be very promiscuous.'

Horacio resented the adjective, found it distasteful, although it was an entirely accurate description. 'I'm not promiscuous, I'm a stud – only women are promiscuous.'

She smiled. 'I see. But I bet none of *your* women are. I bet you think they only sleep with you.'

'Of course they only sleep with me. Why would they go elsewhere? Anyone else would be such a come-down.'

'Not for me. It will be a come-up.'

They both collapsed with laughter.

'How about you?' he asked, when he'd collected himself. 'How many lovers?' Women didn't like to be asked this back. They always lied – some saying more, some saying less, according to what was their vision of themselves.

Jenny was quiet, wondering how many lovers to pretend she'd had. There'd been three real lovers, three flings that is, since there wasn't love involved, but she'd had quite a lot of fine fantasy lovers, all of whom seemed very real to her, more so than the real ones, each with a name, description and history – around seventeen of them all tolled. If she divided the three real ones into the seventeen imaginary ones and . . .

But Horacio was falling asleep.

She shook him. 'I'm sorry, Horacio, but would you please go to your own bed now? It's much the best idea since we've decided we want to be friends and cousins most of all.'

Horacio good-naturedly got up, dressed, and left quietly. Jenny released the painting from its captivity, slipped back into bed, and fell asleep, lulled by the crackling fire and, out by the pond, the frogs singing hymns to the fallen night.

★ ★ ★

Arthur, listening the next morning to the voice-activated tape he had placed under Jenny's bed, shook his head, thinking, tch tch, Nephew, shame on you. This is a blot on the Huntington escutcheon.

15

Jenny was intercepted by Rowley as she passed his gatehouse on the way back from her morning walk. She had a key to the gate now so she didn't have to disturb him, but he was waiting there for her and swung it wide when she appeared.

She smiled. 'Thank you, Rowley.' (She had given up the whole Hi,-I'm-Beulah Ludwig-idea, since this was now the fourth day.)

Rowley smiled too and passed her a note. Surprised, she looked at him as she took it from his hands and was struck again by his eyes. They were so full, so soul-ful. And, without looking particularly sharp or quick or bright, they seemed, gently and fluidly, to scan and absorb an immense amount of visual information. She felt he could see over the hills to the other side, as well as into her heart.

But he's only a hired-man, she reminded herself.

Although his hair was blonde, his eyes were brown and his brows were a dark joined line above them. His face was long and bony and looked older than he probably was because it was so lined, this face, so scarred, tanned, weathered, and

60

pocked. When he smiled she expected his teeth to be stained, broken, crooked, and lost, but they were astonishingly white, straight, and pearly.

The note said? *'Will you come dancing with me tonight?'*

Jenny was thrown off-centre. She had throught he was giving her a note someone had left for her, but apparently it was from himself. She looked into those eyes, feeling surprised and baffled. 'Rowley, I – uh . . . '

He handed her another note that said, *'Please?'*

'But, Rowley, I don't get it about these notes.' She looked to see if there were more, if he had a whole sheaf of them he was going to dole out to her one by one. She wondered if he were crazy. She felt like she was back at Fair Haven, where one could expect any kind of behaviour (except from oneself).

Now it was Rowley's turn to look surprised. He reached into his shirt pocket for a card, which he handed to her. It said: 'I am a deaf mute but I can read lips.'

'Oh, I didn't realize. I'm sorry. Well, about this dancing . . .'

Jenny did not at all want to go dancing with Rowley. She didn't want to go dancing with anyone, but with Rowley least of all. She didn't want to leave the estate except for her lone morning walk. She didn't want to appear in public anywhere.

But this was wrong of her. Was she to imprison herself yet again? When was she going to take on the world like a normal person? Wasn't she tough old Beulah Ludwig now, and wasn't this a good opportunity to test her new self in the world? Even if Maria Lopez was being pursued, no one was going to expect her to be in Sonoma dancing with a deaf-mute handyman. Plus, how could she say no to that pathetic and irresistible *'Please?'* which she still held in her hand?

He waited, and she could see the smiling, hopeful look on his face fade and his face harden in the way it must have learned to do to handle rejection. He turned away. She grabbed his arm so that he would look back at her. 'I'd like to come, Rowley. What time?'

She was so touched to see the gladness in his eyes. He was

trying not to show it, so his face didn't know what to do with itself. The hard, concealed look it had been forming crumbled under the force of his happiness. His lips smiled crookedly, fell open. He spoke! 'Seven o'clock. We'll have dinner first. At my place. I'll cook for you.' And then he looked terribly confused and upset because he'd spoken aloud, used his voice.

'But, Rowley, you're not mute!'

'I know. But my voice is so terrible. I gobble like a turkey. Nobody can understand what I say. I gave up trying to communicate that way. My voice would scare people. They'd think I was crazy.'

'I understand you. I don't know how I do, but I do.'

She did. Every word. His voice *was* terrible. It was all up in his nose and in the roof of his mouth. Not a pretty sound. Ugly. And the words were totally incomprehensible, no consonants at all. And yet, it was uncanny, she could understand him, as if she were somehow tuned into him and could unscramble the sounds as he went along. She had some kind of unscrambling device in her ears or in her heart for this hired-man.

Tears stood out in his eyes. And in hers too. It was so moving, so uncanny.

'Can you read my lips ok?' she asked him.

'Yes, you speak clearly. Better than most people. I bet you have a beautiful voice.'

In their excitement they had clasped hands. Now, awkwardly, they let go and stepped back from each other.

'I'll see you at seven, Rowley. I'll come down.'

'No, I'll come for you.'

All of one hundred yards they were talking about.

'Bye, Rowley.'

'See ya.' See ya, babe, he said to himself. Beulah babe. My baby.

Back in her room, Jenny removed the valuable painting from the false bottom of her paintbox. Most of her paint-tubes were out on the table now, laid out in neat rows, just as her brushes now resided in jars she had got from the kitchen. It made her nervous that nothing was in the paintbox but the hidden painting, but she could not think of another good place to hide it.

As usual, she gazed a while at the painting before beginning her work. It gave her strength. It inspired her. Daily she was impressed anew with its excellence, its art, its vision, its statement, which continued to elude her but she knew was there, lurking hologrammically like its images. And, just as the painting's images came and went in ghostly guises, so, in life, no one was who they seemed at first glance – or second or third. How much, Jenny wondered, was in the looking? How much was in what the painting or person chose to reveal?

At cocktail time, Jess said, 'We're all going out to dinner tonight. There's a fabulous new French restaurant that's opened up ten miles down the road. I'm wearing my Dior in honour of the occasion.' She did a little turn in her stunning dress.

'And I'm wearing my *merde alors*,' said Arthur, displaying his usual white trousers and blue shirt.'

'You both look gorgeous,' Jenny laughed. 'However, I can't join you. I'm going dining and dancing with Rowley.'

They were all stunned.

Irrationally, Horacio felt a pang of sexual jealousy. 'Who is Rowley?' he inquired wonderingly. 'Who the hell is Rowley?' The name was familiar but he'd blanked out.

Arthur, oddly enough, felt a mild pang too. 'My handyman,' he said wryly.

'The dummy?' Horacio felt much as Jenny had when Rowley started handing her notes. What's going on here? Wait a minute, now.

'In a manner of speaking, yes,' said Arthur. 'Or, rather, in a manner of non-speaking.' His crescent smile creased his face.

'How extraordinary,' was Jess's comment. She really thought it was. She couldn't imagine anyone looking at Rowley, let alone going dancing with him. It made her want to go and take a look at him but, even if she did and he looked good, which he wouldn't, why would anyone want to go out with a handyman? Who was deaf! She looked at Jenny as if she were crazy. Then she reminded herself that Jenny *was* crazy. And she felt comforted. Of course, she thought, the poor woman's crazy, I'd forgotten. She acts so normal. She's quite a perfect, unobtrusive guest. Sweet, really. Suddenly Jess found herself prepared to be generous-minded to Jenny. One had to feel generous towards – even sorry for – anyone who would accept such a pathetic invitation. Jess warmed to Jenny. All her jealousy evaporated. And here's Horacio, she thought, whom a thousand women would give their eye-teeth to go out to dinner with. A man to die for. How queer life is. She began to laugh.

Jenny was surprised at the sensation she'd caused. There were Arthur and Horacio with their mouths hanging open and Jess with her eyes bugging out of her head.

Jenny began to laugh at the same time as Jess, and the men joined in. Everyone laughed for their own reasons and poured drinks with an air of festival.

Promptly at seven, Rowley arrived. He was clean-shaven, shampooed, his hair slicked down. He wore spanking-clean blue jeans, a red plaid shirt, boots.

But no amount of grooming, Arthur thought, could assuage the rough, common, handicapped look he had about him.

He carried a bouquet of dahlias in his big, calloused hand.

Jenny was wearing tan-coloured jeans that she'd removed the label from so that they looked ordinary except for their perfect fit. She also wore a shortsleeved blouse with white herons on a black ground. She looked elegant but, thought Arthur, she looked equally elegant naked.

He wondered if that was why Horacio was put off – he couldn't handle her elegance. He wondered if he should be worried about the boy. He was full of admiration for Rowley for pulling off this coup, but not as amazed as Jess obviously was. He knew Rowley because of their tennis. He knew he was surprising and, actually, for one of his condition, extremely confident.

Jenny accepted the flowers. 'Thank you, Rowley,' she said, remembering to look at him full-face as she talked. 'I'll just stop by my room and put them in a vase. What colours! Good-night all. Have a good French dinner!'

As Jenny and Rowley went off together across the lawn, the other three were quiet. None of them could have said why they felt so strangely moved.

16

Rowley was trembling with excitement. He had the evening all planned. They would play a game of chess, which was the way he could best express his intelligence, and he would win, and she would be pleased. He had prepared a supper of garden salad, steamed vegetables, spaghetti with a sauce made of fresh tomatoes and basil. She would be interested that he was a vegetarian. With supper they would drink a bottle of Wente blanc de blanc that he had chilling next to the two beautiful wine glasses he'd gone to Santa Rosa expressly to buy. After supper they would go on his motorcycle to the Always Inn, where he would introduce her to his friends and they would dance and smoke a joint if she seemed inclined. (He doubted she would.) He was a good dancer. He could respond to the vibrations, get the beat. It would be so noisy they wouldn't be able to talk and that would be fine. They could learn about each other nonverbally through chess and dancing. On the motorcycle he would feel her arms around his waist. Afterwards, when he took her to her room, they would talk a little together, but he would have to be careful that, with the floodgates so magically opened, he didn't overwhelm her with all the things he had to say – now that he had a listener. There had been a man in prison who could understand him, an old safe-cracker, and his teachers could. (Strangely enough, his parents couldn't, never even tried. They were ashamed of him. He'd run away from home when he was twelve.) So, he would just talk to her a little. Then, if it seemed at all possible, he would kiss her good-night.

Everything went as Rowley planned, even to the kiss. He walked her to her room. Standing at the french windows, with the light from her room streaming out at them, he bent his face to hers and kissed her lips. She was taken by surprise and blushed. But she didn't seem displeased. He looked at her carefully to see. Weren't her eyelids lowering, her lips reaching?

He embraced her, wrapped her in his arms, and kissed her again, holding her tight against his entire body. She responded with warmth and his answer to her response was alarming. 'Good-night, babe,' he said, and moved away.

'Good-night, Rowley. Thanks for a wonderful time.'

Rowley walked away, adjusting his swollen sex to the tightness of his crotch. So long since he'd felt this expansion. It hurt like hell, but what a great pain! What a night! Thanks for a *wonderful* time, she'd said. And she'd kissed him. God, she tasted good. Wow!

His happiness was uncontainable. What should he do? Go back to the Inn? No, he didn't want to see anyone. Someone might bring him down.

His motorcycle was still standing where he'd left it upon their return. It was a 1976 Ducati 750, a red and black café racer with a beautiful profile, lean and close to the ground. He'd paid only eight hundred dollars for it, a steal from a man who'd had a bad accident and didn't want to look at it any more.

Rowley kicked it to life and bounded off into the night. He drove a hundred miles to the end of the valley, over the hills to Lake Country, around Clear Lake, and home, establishing his happiness by shattering the tranquil night of two rural counties.

Unhelmeted, he felt the wind in his hair, on his face. He seemed to feel the stars there too, bouncing off him – stars in his eyes, in his hair, on his face. He had only to think of Beulah and he got an erection. Stars in my cock, he thought.

Coming down the hills from Lake County, swinging round the curves, the bike answering to his slightest body shift so that he never had to muscle it, he thought about not returning to Arthur's estate. Just riding on instead.

I know I'll ruin it, he thought. I'll do something wrong, something bad. I always do. I'll get in trouble somehow. I never learn, never change. I should leave while my life is the best it's ever been – before I ruin it.

You're only granted a few hours of happiness in a lifetime and I'm having them now.

No. I always run away. I'm going to stop running. I'm going to stay at Arthur's, love Beulah, learn, and grow. And when the time comes to leave, I won't run. I'll depart. I'll say goodbye and thank you and go on my way like – a gentleman. Like Arthur himself would do.

He thought of Beulah again, and again grew hot and stiff. Soon he'd have her between his legs, like the bike, and he'd ride her to the moon. He unbuttoned his fly and released his cock to the wind of his passage, to the night and the stars.

He blew. His sperms burst into the sky. He seemed to see them tracing through the air in effervescent lines, a meteor shower, an explosion of his uncontainable joy.

He went off the road and into a field. A bump sent him flying off the motorcycle. It was a hay field, so he landed fairly softly, while the machine on its side roared (vibrated) and spun its wheels.

He crawled over and turned off the key. He was scared. His heart was beating furiously. That was a close one.

He lay quietly on his back until he was calm, almost dozing.

It wouldn't have been a bad way to go, feeling so happy, he thought. He wouldn't have minded going like that. But think of being with Beulah, in Beulah – it would be so incredible. He couldn't go yet.

Also, this wouldn't quite be going like a gentleman. He smiled at the inconceivable picture of Arthur meeting his end in this way.

17

Early the next morning, Jenny plugged her ears with cotton and walked around the estate, seeing what it would be like to be Rowley.

Rowley, catching sight of her, called ecstatically, 'Good morning!' and couldn't understand why she didn't react to his call.

He felt upset. Was she ignoring him purposely. Why? Did she regret that kiss? (Oh God, what a kiss!) He'd better find out rather than suffer. He went after her. 'Hey, Beulah, why didn't you answer me just now when I called out to you?'

Jenny saw Rowley standing before her and could make nothing of his moving lips. The idea of removing the earplugs in front of him and revealing what she'd been doing, was extremely embarrassing to her, but there seemed no other course open to her since she couldn't hear him and did not wish to stand there looking stupidly at him another minute. So she removed the cotton and stood abashed, head hanging.

But Rowley understood at once and was immensely appreciative. He gently lifted her chin so that she would look at him. He said silently, moving his lips so she could read them, 'I love you.'

Jenny, surprised, alarmed, and touched, fled the scene.

★　★　★

In the dining-room, Horacio was reading the morning *Chronicle*. The story of the missing patient had faded to the oblivion of page nine. Police were stymied since learning that Maria Lopez was an assumed name and Fair Haven would not divulge, or did not know, her real name, which made it impossible to put a trace on her. Has anyone seen this woman? was the querulous caption under the same blurry distance shot of a thin young woman with hair.

Beulah sat down across from him with coffee, an orange, and a croissant.

'How was your evening?' he asked her pleasantly.

'Very nice,' she replied happily. 'Rowley cooked me a delectable dinner. Then we went dancing at the Always Inn, where I was the only one not flying high on coke or grass.' She laughed. 'But everyone was very friendly and I had a great time. Pure fun. I don't think I've been out on a date in, well – ever! I mean – well . . .' She recovered. 'And it was my first motorcycle ride too. I felt like a kid.'

'And Rowley?' asked Horacio. 'How did he feel?'

'He's so sweet. Do you know that in my whole life a man has never cooked me a meal. It was the most heart-warming thing. I was so touched. He seemed to have gone to such trouble. He seemed to want to please me. I think in all my relationships I'm usually the pleaser not the pleasee.'

'Is this a relationship already?'

'Well, no. And I hate that word relationship. It sounds so industrial somehow. But Rowley –'

'That's enough about Rowley.' Horacio rustled his newspaper, feeling suddenly grumpy.

'No, it isn't. I want to say more. You did ask.'

'OK,' Horacio sighed. 'He's very sweet. What else?'

'Well, I think he's been through an awful lot. More than we could ever dream. Because of his handicap, of course, but, as well, he's been in prison. I – perhaps I should not have confided that to you. He didn't tell me in confidence exactly, but Arthur may not know.' She looked anxious.

'Relax. I'll keep it quiet. I keep telling you secrets too. It's the cousinly thing.'

Horacio, against all actuarial odds, had not done time. He knew he was owing. He could quit now while he was ahead, far ahead, but he knew he wouldn't. Because he wasn't a thief to 'get ahead', he was an outlaw. He hated authority. He hated a banal existence. There was nothing else in life to do that was half so challenging, that could test him. He knew that everyone was a crook at heart. Diogenes, who went about with a candle during the day looking for an honest man, told the world that there was no such thing under the sun. Horacio believed him. And he liked it that he didn't have to pretend to himself to be honest, that he acted out his crookedness. In a way that made him honest.

As well, when he was in the act of a crime, he felt power. He felt a sense of self, of being unique and indomitable, a superman, one above and beyond ordinary existence. He'd beaten the system, had life knocked.

Until the last time when, teetering on the cornice, he'd thought, big fucking deal, and wanted to end it all.

Uncle Arthur was motivated differently. He really liked the bucks and the good life, needed to live like this. And, too, Arthur liked the planning of a crime. No one could touch him for his carefulness and originality. Arthur *had* done time. In England. He never talked about it. In the business, it was understood that you had to be prepared to pay. But it didn't bear thinking of. Horacio never thought about it. Until, like now, when he heard about someone who'd been inside. Then he thought, My time will come. How long can you beat the averages? Followed by the thought, Forever. As long as you stay cool and keep lucky.

Again he thought of the last job, the moment on the cornice, the mistake in the tree, the annoyingly persistent girl. It had been a close one. Damned close. 'What was Rowley in for?' he asked Beulah.

'Assault. But he said he was owing for lots of things. He was a hustler, a pretty all-inclusive word, I guess. But he doesn't seem to have been embittered by his imprisonment. I could learn from him – about how to handle adversity.'

'You don't look to me as if you know the meaning of the word.'

70

'I do know.' Jenny bristled at his condescending tone. 'I've known imprisonment. I, too, am handicapped in my way.' Then she blushed, thinking, Wow, he may be sounding patronizing but I am sounding ridiculous. I have known imprisonment indeed. Pin a rose on me. A de luxe sanitarium isn't exactly Soledad. Plus the fact that I'm telling Horacio much too much – as well as forgetting that I'm not Jenny. I'm Beulah Ludwig, and she isn't handicapped in the least. *I, too, am handicapped.* Lord! I sure wish I could erase that sentence. 'I'm speaking metaphorically, of course. I mean, adversity varies. It can be bad luck or utter calamity, losing at poker or having your house burn down.'

'Thank you for explaining it to me.'

'God, you're touchy this morning.'

'You're the touchy one.' He poured them more coffee. 'So you're not bothered that Rowley's an ex-con?'

'No, I can tell he's basically honest.'

'Bullshit. Nobody's honest. Just some are stupid enough to get caught. Rowley's been dealt some bad cards from the beginning, and I'm not talking about your metaphorical poker game.'

'He's living honestly now.'

'He's got a good set-up here. Give him an illegal chance for a better set-up and he'll grab it.'

'No, he won't. I don't think so. He's not greedy. He hustled because it was the only way he knew to survive. In prison he learned some useful skills with which he can now get jobs.' She scowled at him.

'You're an idealist, which is to say you're a fool. No wonder you can't get along in the world. No wonder nobody wanted to make love to you for a whole year.'

Jenny flushed. 'Boy, are you mean!'

'What are you two fighting about?' Jess asked as she and Arthur arrived at the breakfast-table. She wore a ravishing robe of yellow chiffon and a knock-out scent which, she'd told Jenny earlier, had been created especially for her. Jenny, in her black shorts and grey sweatshirt, felt incredibly drab and scentless. Jess's arrival, on top of Horacio's below-the-

71

belt remark (although she realized it was half in humour), took the spirit out of her. She'd felt absolutely exuberant when she sat down half an hour ago.

'Here I had such hopes for a romance between you two,' Arthur said to Horacio, 'then you let Rowley steal her away.'

'He can have her,' said Horacio.

'Now, now,' said Jess.

'She keeps saying she wants to change but she won't take my advice about it.'

'Which is?'

'To realize there are no such things as honesty, virtue, selflessness, or love – except between parent and child, and even that's rare; that's only until the kid learns to talk.'

'What a cynic,' Jenny squealed. 'Has believing that worked for you?'

'Has believing the opposite worked for you?'

'No, but I think I'm a happier person than you. In some ways you seem a deeply sad man to me. As well as a complete shithead.' Again Jenny blushed. She'd never uttered an obscenity before. My, she really was getting Beulahish. It felt good. She liked it.

Horacio liked it too. He laughed. They both burst out laughing, to the surprise of Jess and Arthur.

'Today,' said Arthur, when tranquillity was restored, 'in honour of the Harvest Festival, the townspeople of Sonoma will re-enact the wedding of General Vallejo's sons to the daughters of Count Agoston Haraszthy, the father of California's wine industry. Shall we go?'

No one looked terribly interested. 'Good,' said Arthur. Let's boycott it. I'm hurt that I wasn't asked to play General Vallejo.'

At a signal from Arthur, Jess said, 'Beulah, come for a walk with me, I want to hear about your evening with Rowley and tell you about ours.' The two women linked arms and sauntered out of the door and across the lawn.

Arthur and Horacio were left looking each other over cagily. Horacio sipped coffee and asked. 'Who is this Beulah

Ludwig, anyway? What have you got on?'

'Dear boy, I thought it was you who were trying to get it on – or up, as it were.'

Horacio laughed. 'I should have known you'd have a tape there, if only for the lasciviousness of it. More likely you were after some information she might impart to me in a vulnerable moment.'

'I'm surprised you didn't launder the room. Not up to snuff, Nephew.'

'You tell me how you make love to a woman and launder the room at the same time.'

'I think it will suffice if I just tell you how to make love to a woman.'

Horacio laughed again. 'Well,' he said, 'you won't get much bed-talk out of her and Rowley, just the sound of pencil on paper.'

'Curiously enough, they do talk together. She can make sense of his gibbering noises. It's amazing. Tell me, uh – do you know of anything unusual about Beulah?' As soon as he asked that he regretted the impulse. But he was crazy to know how much Horacio knew.

Horacio looked sharply at his uncle. 'Should I?'

'No, no,' he covered, 'just something that would explain how she understands Rowley – a lip-reader in disguise, someone who can talk in tongues, which is a phrase that always amuses me.' Good, he thought, Horacio doesn't know who Beulah is and he has come on this untimely visit quite by chance. Now to convince the lad nothing is on and, hopefully, to have him on his way before Laveen arrives. I don't dare ask him his plans, for fear he'll linger on here purposely, out of contrariness.

Arthur assumed a serious mien. 'Beulah's father was my dearest friend. I asked her up here to get to know her better. I guess I'm at an age when I wish I had some children of my own.'

Horacio, not taken in for a minute, said musingly, looking equally serious, 'Yes, you always knew who the best abortionists were.'

73

'Which, alas, *you* didn't,' Arthur needled him back without missing a beat.

They both laughed heartily. 'You can have some of my kids if you want,' Horacio said.

'What are you doing about all that?'

'Oh God, don't ask. It's the grief of my life. I really like the little bastards. I'd like them to live with me. But what do I do with their mothers? I wish I could knock them all off. The bitches.'

Arthur shivered. 'You sound like you mean it. What a complicated person you are.'

Horacio looked at Arthur. He wanted to say, to ask, what can I do, Uncle, to keep from wanting to die? I don't care any more. Life's gone flat. It's a struggle to get up in the morning and put on my clothes. Help me.

But Arthur was musing aloud, 'I would have liked to have had a child with Jess. Of course we're too old now, and ten years ago I never guessed I'd love her so long and so much. Between you and me, I think she did have a baby once. She has the stretch marks − one of nature's almost imperceptible clues, delicate, touching traces of the most soul-, body − , and heart-rending experience nature hands out. But she's never spoken of it. It would be like Jess to bury it so deep that she herself had truly forgotten.' Arthur looked searchingly at Horacio. 'I've never spoken of this to anyone.'

Horacio felt that Arthur was trying to help him. By reveal-ing this about Jess, he was asking him to forgive the bitches, who were, after all, the mothers of his children. He was saying that Jess, too, might have had a bastard for some man and that this was not an easy thing.

The conversation, which had begun in a jousting way, their usual style, was now intimate. Horacio cherished the moment.

Then Rowley came to the table for his day's instructions.

Arthur led him outdoors and described the work he wanted done. At the same time, feeling paranoid, he was wondering if Rowley could possibly know who Beulah was. Maybe his interest in her wasn't as touching and romantic as it seemed.

But no. He doubted it. Rowley lived in his own world, was not a media buff, didn't read the papers or watch television and, even if he did, he might put it together about Jenny and Maria Lopez but he could not know about the painting. That was inside dope.

But Rowley was smart. One tended, wrongly, to assume that a handicapped person wasn't working with a full deck.

But everyone was missing something, were they not? Even if it wasn't as apparent as sight or sound or limbs. Jenny, periodically, was missing her mind, Jess her self confidence, Horacio his spirit, (this was beginning to sound like the Wizard of Oz) Laveen his humanity (he was a monster). And what about himself? Good question. Probably his backhand. Yes, the only thing he was really missing was a good backhand. And, of course, his youth. But that wasn't as serious. And it certainly was not as recoverable.

18

During the next week, Jenny allowed herself to be wooed by Rowley. She basked under the sun of his adoration, flowered under it, burst into bloom and scent so that bees and butterflies came to her presence, winged about her, alighted in her hair.

Twice a day, Rowley brought fresh flowers to her room. He wrote poems to her, cooked fragile pastries for her.

He tidied himself up, shaved each day, cut his hair, washed it frequently, changed clothes when they got dirty or sweaty, which was constantly, exhibited his body to its best advantage (6' 1", 155lb., 29" waist, 45" chest, 14" biceps).

Nevertheless, despite all this effort, Rowley always looked unkempt and seedy. His hair was unruly. His body, although slender, sculptured, and strong, was without grace or the beauty of fine proportion. Compared to Horacio who, alas, seemed always on hand for comparison purposes, Rowley had no grace, style, wit, or beauty.

But what are those, thought Jenny, compared to the ability to love, to give, to please, to reveal oneself, be vulnerable, risk all?

She was thrilled, entranced, and every day had a stronger sense of self – for if Rowley loved her, there must be someone there for him to love.

As the days passed, Rowley progressed as well with his kisses, reaching into her mouth, under her lips, to the tip of her throat. His lips clasped hers. His tongue searched her mouth, drew her tongue into his. His kissed her nose, ears, eyelids, ever so gently licked her brow.

He bowed to her breasts which rose and swelled to meet his swollen lips. What pleasure! The sweetest kisses she had ever known. He lingered, gazed, dwelled ages on her bosoms.

Of course, with all this rising and swelling and sighing and sweetness there was nothing for it but to come together wholly, which, in a few days, they did. And for two who had abstained so long, they accomplished this with such ease it was as if their bodies had known each other from birth.

So wet and slippery and swollen and scented were they, so dazed and enraptured, that their clothes simply fell away from them one evening and he entered her as they lay on their sides, face to face, and there was a stunning sense of recognition as if his body were hers, hers his, as if they had been twins once, in the same womb, in the same fluid, joined by the same umbilicus, and now were reunited at last. So their joining was not a discovery so much as a recognition, a rediscovery. Rowley and Jenny had found each other after a long time lost and apart.

Three and four times a day they met for this fabulous joining. They had only to spy each other across the lawn for this persistent swelling to begin and to long to be eased. It was like an allergy. They were so sensitized to each other that to be near, to smell, or even to see each other was to occasion this marvellous swelling.

Marvellous if the antidote could at once be applied, that is, and it could be. In Jenny's room, Rowley's, in the pond, behind the bushes, under the trees.

Which is not to say it was an in-and-out proposition – they had too much respect for the love act and for themselves for that. They must give it their full time and attention, bring to it all the artistry they could summon, cherish each other.

Like Arthur's definition of a good tennis game, there must be craft, wile, strength, and surprise. Each time they would offer each other a new gift of the senses so that their love-making was even better, ever more deliriously, chimerically, empirically splendid and moving.

For them both there was a gather-ye-rosebuds-while-ye-may attitude underlying their passion although, for Rowley anyhow, it was a more desperate and doomed feeling than that.

There was always the knowledge that he was an escaped criminal. He wanted to live with Beulah forever, but how could he inflict his situation on her? He felt safe here, lying low, but he couldn't ask her to lie forever low with him. His mug must be hanging in every post office and his handicap marked him worse than any facial scar. Even if by some wonder he could go back into society, he didn't do well there. He was deeply antisocial. He would get into trouble.

Jenny never thought a day ahead in any case. She, long ago, had taught herself not to lest she be overwhelmed by the infinite possibilities of disaster.

She too was hiding out, on the run, not who she pretended to be. Here, under wraps, she was a model of sane behaviour. Back in society, even in her small town, she couldn't trust herself to behave normally or in any kind of acceptable fashion for very long, never knew when she might one day start gathering her rocks – or worse, as Damon always feared, start throwing them.

She felt safe in Rowley's arms. It was tempting to dream of

77

his looking after her forever. But this was not fair. It would be making of him a bodyguard, a mindguard. That would not be good for him and she herself would be weakened thereby.

Better not to think of any kind of future together. They must simply be glad of their love for now; each day, each hour, take nourishment and strength from it. For them both, for now, and for their love, Arthur's estate was a refuge.

For Horacio, too, Arthur's was a refuge. Not only was there Arthur, with whom he could enjoy the luxury of being himself, but there was Beulah with whom, for the first time, he could enjoy a relationship that made no sexual or emotional demands. She was a pal. His first female buddy ever. They could talk, laugh, fight, about anything. He could say or do whatever came to mind. What a novelty. At the same time, he could see and appreciate that she was a lovely, desirable woman. But they were friends, friends! Hemingway said, 'If two people really love each other there can be no happy ending.' But friendship was different. It simply didn't end at all. You took it with you to the grave, still cuddling it to you, thinking how it had enriched your life. With a friend, you could come and go with no explanation, live or die. A friend would never make you feel guilty or make you feel like a rat. A friend would not get her hooks into you and, above all, never on any occasion, no matter how pressed, no matter how big an asshole you'd been, would this friend *ever* make a scene!

When he thought of his big, barren, unfinished house and the women he was involved with one way or another, and his criminal career that seemed so suddenly meaningless, he felt grateful for this time-out at Arthur's, for the sense of being replenished.

What it came down to was that he had lost interest in his life. Here he was not regaining it. No, but here, at least he felt interested in this time-out life, in the people in this place now: Beulah, Jess, Rowley, Arthur, and what was transpiring between them and what Arthur had going.

For once, he merely observed – but only until the day

78

when he could and would participate.

It didn't get him up early in the morning but it kept him going.

Arthur was reading the very poem by Herrick:

'Gather ye rosebuds while ye may,
Old Time is still a-flying:
And this same flower that smiles today
Tomorrow will be dying.'

He closed his book and sighed. He had a premonition that, just as Jess was his last love, this was to be his last crime.

He saw Rowley coming with the tennis rackets and balls and felt the old joy rise up in his bosom. Smiling, he thought, last love, last crime – that's all very well. Just as long as this isn't anywhere near my last tennis game.

Arthur, too, had a feeling of everyone else's happiness right now, of his estate being almost Shangri-Lalian.

It made it seem rather a pity that the malevolent Laveen was on the verge of arriving and that the crime must go on. As desperately as he needed the money, and including Laveen *assured* him of success, was it wise, even briefly, to associate with anyone so terrible?

Laveen was going to be very upset to find Horacio here. Arthur sighed. He did wish Horacio would go away.

PART II

19

Arthur, Jess, Jenny, Rowley, and Horacio were all up at the tennis court when Laveen arrived.

Horacio was in a large wooden chair, Jess and Jenny on a rustic bench. They were drinking lemonade and watching the game. It was fun to watch, lively with long, full-court, rallies since Arthur and Rowley rejoiced in hitting the ball right to each other instead of putting it away. Sometimes they amused themselves by seeing how many feet into the air they could lob the ball, although it wasn't as amusing for the person on the sunny side – Rowley.

They both had powerful serves and in their service showed no quarter, striving for the elusive ace each time. Arthur kept up a running commentary for himself and for his audience, much of it at the expense of Rowley, which didn't matter to him since he was immune to the eavesdrop.

'Holy mother of pigs!' Arthur exclaimed gleefully. 'He thought he'd put that one by me but I staggered him with my return. Just watch the english I'm going to put on this next ball. He'll be confounded when he gets ready for a forehand and it gives a leap over to his backhand. What? He got it. How the devil did he do that? I think the boy keeps another ball up his sleeve. I know he's got some big ones in his pants. But not a word to Beulah. You know how easily aroused she is. Hey!' Arthur ran back for a ball, missed it, and shouted, 'Out! Wasn't that out?' he appealed to the gallery. 'What do you mean, no? It was out by a mile. A foot? Look at the mark. Oh, very well. Game to Rowley. I don't want to play any more. I want to sulk a while. It's hotter than a pig's patooti up here. Let's hie us to the pond. Get that, will you, Jess?'

The phone, which hung in one corner of the court, was ringing. Jess ambled over to it. 'It's Laveen,' she said. 'He's at the gate.'

'Curses. Who will let him in? Horacio, be a good lad. This fellow Laveen always drops by unannounced, out of the blue. Haven't seen him in years. Wonder what he's doing in the area?'

'He's got luggage,' Jess reported.

'Hmmnn, I wonder if I could have invited him here or whether, like Horacio, he's just thrust himself upon me and is prepared to stay endlessly. Well, maybe Rowley should go down if there's luggage.'

'I can take his bags in if the man's feeble,' Horacio said. 'Finish the set.' He strode off the court and down to the gate, thinking, Laveen eh? The plot thickens. I wonder who he is?

He opened the gate to a man of his own age, body type, and size. He had to look two or three times at him before he could assuredly say, 'Cousin Harry, greetings!' and then he wondered if he shouldn't have pretended to be deceived. Clearly he should have.

'Laveen's the name.' He gave him a look that made his blood run cold. 'Remember that, Horacio.'

Horacio would remember.

The plot hadn't simply thickened, it had congealed. If Laveen was here, this was big-time stuff, was out of Horacio's league and even out of Arthur's. International in scope at the very least, more likely inter-planetary.

'What do you mean, you haven't seen him for years?' Jess asked when they were alone together in their room and Arthur had come out of his shower.

'Now, Jess, you know not to ask questions.'

'Well, I hate that Laveen. At least you could have told me he was coming. Ugh! He gives me the creeps. All those clothes he wears. I have the feeling that if he took them all off, he'd be covered with hair, every inch. Or worse, no hair. Not one hair. A hairless slug-like body.'

'You're right,' Arthur said blithely, towelling himself.

'He's hairless.'

'Really?'

'Yes, but not slug-like. Surprisingly, there are muscles. Being a distant cousin, he has the great Huntington torso genes.'

'What about the beard?'

'False.'

'Is it a disguise, then?'

'No, people born without hair do look rather freaky so they wear wigs to look normal. He goes overboard and wears a beard too. He had his eyebrows implanted. But the give-away is no lashes. That's why he wears tinted glasses. Laveen is a master of disguise. He can look like almost anybody if he wants to – having such a blank canvas to work with. But that's not all. He can assume a person's walk, voice, mannerisms. In fact, you may think you're talking to Arthur right now, but I'm actually Laveen.'

Jess laughed but went over to hug Arthur to reassure herself and to forget the momentary involuntary shiver of horror his remark occasioned.

'He would have been a great actor. Or would he? It would be hard with no soul. Yes, I think he'd have needed a soul.'

'I've always thought you had just the right amount of body hair,' Jess said admiringly.

'Why, how kind! Yes, I always thought seventeen chest hairs was just right. Not too excessive but enough to work with.'

She laughed again. 'Come and let me stroke them,' she said throatily, lying down.

'Very well, but don't lose any. Promise? And try not to muss them.'

They made love together. Afterwards, as always Arthur felt deliciously sleepy and Jess felt talkative, needing mental strokes. They'd had this post-coital exchange hundreds of times. Each time it was fresh and new to Jess, inexpressibly boring for Arthur. He could keep up his side of it in his sleep. Which is what he did.

'Was that nice for you?'

85

'Wonderful!'

'Do I make you happy?'

'More than anyone in the world. Only you. My Jess. My one in a million.'

'You're not bored with me?'

'How could I be bored with the best lover in the world, the most beautiful woman.'

'You're not just saying that to please me?'

'I'm saying it because I love you.'

'I'm so glad. Because I love you will all my heart. I'd die for you. Or with you. If you died I'd take my own life right away so I could be with you. I'm so lucky to have you. You're so handsome, so brilliant. What do you see in me, a poor little nobody?'

'The most beautiful woman, best lover, one in a million . . .'

'Every time we make love, doesn't.that make us ever closer? Don't you feel a special closeness after we've made love together, darling Arthur?'

'More than anyone. One in a lover. Best beautiful. The most million . . .'

Happily, by then, Jess, too, was snoozing softly.

20

Jess *was* one in a million, Arthur reminded himself when he woke up and quietly began to dress. Granted a person who loves does not see straight, but even before he loved her he saw that she was the most beautiful woman on earth. Her exquisite bones, her vibrant hair, her woeful femininity, along with those eyes that lowered their lids to no man but confronted the world fearlessly, despite the fact that it intimidated the hell out of her. Her touching insecurity preserved her from the arrogance her beauty might have handicapped her with. It allowed her to be open, loving, adorable. But the arrogance in its best form was there – the eyes proclaiming that she knew she stood alone in the arena that mattered most in this world – personal beauty.

But never mind that; she was a good companion too. She cheered his tennis, laughed at his jokes, humoured his flaws, complied with his every wish and, above all, rarely asked questions. Uninquisitiveness was essential to him and rarely found in a woman. He understood why she had it. Unless any of his doings affected her personally, or their relationship together, she was simply uninterested.

As it was now five o'clock, Arthur went out to the patio for cocktails. Rowley had set out the bar but only Laveen was there.

Not only had he come without his beard, but he now had blonde curly hair and eyelashes too! Also curly. He looked totally different, young and insouciant. He had eschewed the suit and tie and was dressed *a la* Arthur, in shirt and slacks, only sandals instead of the old white bucks. Like the white bucks, Arthur had touches that were inimitable. He always wore a ratty old leather belt with an elegantly wrought silver buckle. Everyone appreciated that it must have been hard to get the leather to look that ratty, that warped and discoloured, with its width varying every few inches. The end protruding from the buckle was too long and, having no loop to hold it, flopped down over his fly. This belt truly held up his trousers, the waists of which were always too big since he liked his clothes full and loose. It often amused Arthur, particularly at stuffy parties, to have the belt buckle unaccountably give way so that his trousers dropped right to his ankles. He wore no skivvies but, being Brooks Bros., his shirt-tails were long. How he did this trick none of his intimates could figure, for he never touched the buckle when it happened. Rather he would be gesturing expansively with both hands, perhaps giving a toast, when squeals, shrieks, and giggles would arrest his attention. He'd look down at the puddle of trousers at his feet to murmur, 'How shocking!'

'Tell me, Laveen,' he murmured now, 'to what do we owe these golden curls?'

'I told you I'd be changed. I didn't want the dummy to remember me. Even though he's mute, he might talk.'

'How wise you are,' Arthur said admiringly. 'For he and Jenny have formed rather a close alliance and they seem to be able to communicate quite well. I still believe that with lip-reading he must miss many a nuance and she can't possibly get every word of his incomprehensible utterings, but they seem to operate on a wavelength of their own and to have a perfect understanding. When you think how two people from the same background with the same schooling in the same language often can't communicate worth a damn, it really gives one pause. Jenny, uh, Beulah will be here shortly. I assume she sometimes saw you at the sanatarium.'

'Yes. I made the rounds once a week. But she won't know me in this guise. However, Horacio knew me. What is he doing here, Arthur?'

'I'm sorry to say he surprised me with a visit. He could easily become a fly in the ointment, but so far so good, he suspects nothing.'

'Get rid of him.'

'Laveen, to try to get him to leave would be to cleave him even closer. Be cool. Trust me. Everything's under control.'

'You have your nephew here, the dummy in the mark's pants. Where is it written that this is an under-control situation? It stinks.'

'I beg of you not to concern yourself. Here, I laid in some Glenlivet especially for you. An excellent scotch.' Arthur handed him a glass and watched him sip. 'Do you like it?'

'It's foul.'

'Beulah, darling.' Arthur walked forward to meet her. 'Come and meet my old friend, Laveen.'

I've seen this man before, Jenny thought, as she shook hands with Laveen.

Laveen almost did not know her. Her hair! Her hair was gone! He could not have said why it disturbed him, angered him. He felt deprived, cheated. Maybe he had wanted to cut it off himself. Or did he have an erotic fantasy of lying with her, letting her hirsute profusion cover the wilderness of his skin from head to toe? No. More likely he simply had hated her hair and now didn't have it there to hate. He turned away from her and walked over to the pond to collect himself.

Jenny took the wine, a Smith-Madrone Chardonnay, from the bucket of ice and poured herself a hefty goblet. She was getting to like the cocktail hour a lot and couldn't imagine how she'd gone her entire life without participating in this fabulous custom. Of course it rather knocked you out for the night, but that was all right, you just tried to get more things in during the day, which was good because that made the time pass quickly until the cocktail hour.

One of her great pleasures had been reading for an hour or so before falling asleep, and it did look as if she would have to relinquish that. She found that with wine at the cocktail hour and more wine during dinner, her eyes couldn't keep to the written line. It worked pretty well with one eye closed, but this was hard on the open eye, which got weary having to go it alone. She would get into bed, pick up her book, close one eye, read a page, close the other eye, and close the book.

All this sex made her sleepy too. But there was nothing *wrong*, after all, with being sleepy. That's what bedtime was for, wasn't it? Sleep? It wasn't as if sex and wine were causing her to do something she shouldn't do – like steal or murder. It was only making her sleep.

It would be a shame *never* to read another book, she thought, trying to feel guilty, but if she had to choose . . .

Really, what it all came down to was that she was relaxed for the first time for years. She was totally contented.

Or she had been until a minute ago, when she met that man Laveen. She felt like a rabbit who had just scented a fox, if she had her predator right, because if she felt she knew him from somewhere, mightn't it follow that he was feeling he knew her?

89

Jenny watched Laveen walk over to look at some lilies Arthur was encouraging to grow at the edge of the pond. He looked even more familiar from the back. The way he carried his shoulders. Hmmmn.

The sanatarium! Surely she'd seen him around Fair Haven just out of the corners of her eyes.

Another patient? Was Arthur's old friend another escaped patient, perhaps disguised, which is why he looked more familiar from the back? Another escaped crazy here at Arthur's, incognito? Perhaps another like herself, who actually hadn't even been at Fair Haven when she escaped from it. Maybe any time we aren't at Fair Haven, we're escaping from it, and therefore the news story about Maria Lopez is essentially correct. Because we *will* be back. Eventually we'll be captured and returned, Laveen and I. Recidivism, it's called.

Already Jenny was pouring herself another glass of wine. It was delicious.

How comical, she thought, if gradually the loony bin emptied and one by one the patients fled to Arthur's, following Maria's own original route – that is, the route she would have taken if, as the news story said, she'd really escaped from there. Maria could lead them from Fair Haven to Arthur's as Harriet Tubman did the slaves from the South to the North. The path to Arthur's would become more and more worn and defined with use. There would be worry in the valley about erosion because of this scar in the earth from the bin to the estate, until some wise land management man suggested they use it as an irrigation ditch to water the vineyards.

'What are you grinning about?' It was Horacio in crisp white pants and jade green shirt.

'I was having such a funny thought. I wish I could share it with you but I can't.'

'You can tell me anything, you know that.'

'It's a comfort to think so. I do tell you quite a lot. But, although I feel we are friends, I know nothing about your life. You release a smoke-screen of intimacy, giving the impression of being confidential without actually revealing a thing. While I am always spilling the beans to you, your life remains totally mysterious.'

'My life? It's an open book.'

Jess arrived, looking gorgeous, causing a stir. 'How do you do, Laveen,' she said graciously. 'So sorry I wasn't here to greet you when you arrived, but I understand you've made yourself comfortable in the east wig – I mean wing.'

Arthur was gratified to note she showed no surprise at Laveen's change from a swarthy, bearded, draped creature to the blonde, remote, California-androgynous person he'd become. He wasn't so gratified at her pretend slip of the tongue, but Laveen didn't seem to pick up on it.

'Now, Beulah.' Jess turned to Jenny. 'I do hope you're going to dine with us tonight and not go off with Rowley. I can't possibly handle all these men by myself.'

'You could handle twenty men, but I will dine with you. Rowley is helping out at the Always Inn tonight. They needed a busboy desperately so he bailed them out. He's so nice.'

While Jess and Beulah talked, Horacio eyed Laveen, a.k.a Hairless Harry Huntington, fully fledged member of what is romantically called the underworld, a man for whom Interpol had hunted frantically for years, master of disguise. No one had ever seen him as he really looked.

Horacio almost hadn't known him. Those eyebrows looked so real, they must be implants. The lashes were false. (How did he find blonde ones?) But he couldn't have shaved that close. His cheeks and hands were as smooth as a woman's. Maybe Laveen *was* a woman. No one was who they seemed, especially here at Arthur's.

Laveen still stood aloofly by the pond. Horacio felt awed by him, frightened of him. The man was a legend. He was jealous of him too. But Horacio knew that what it took to be that good, he didn't want to have.

He was tempted to go and push him into the pond – just to see if he'd get wet. Probably he wouldn't.

'Where shall we dine tonight?' Jess was asking Arthur.

'What shall we wear?'

'Let's eat in. I'll cook,' said Jenny. 'It's my turn to cook.' She appealed to Laveen since he, too, wouldn't want to eat out and be spotted as a real or imagined escapee.

Laveen shrugged.

'It's silly to go to so much trouble,' said Jess, 'when we can hop in the car . . .'

'It isn't trouble. It will be fun.'

'It's a good idea,' said Horacio. 'I'll make the salad. We'll call you when it's ready.' He took Beulah's arm and led her off to the kitchen. 'I hate to cook but I'm a mean salad-maker.'

In the kitchen, Jenny looked through the shelves. 'I think I'll make a pizza. Did you ever have a home-made pizza? Let's see, there's cheese, tomato, black olives, green peppers and, oh goody, they even have some Linguica sausage.' She got going on the dough.

'The thing is,' Horacio said, washing lettuce. 'You don't want to go out to a restaurant because you don't want to be seen. You haven't left this place since I've been here – almost a week.'

'That's not true!' Jenny squealed, feeling unjustly accused. 'I went dancing with Rowley. I go walking every morning while you're still deep in the sack, mouldering away.'

'No one can see a person in a disco, or walking in the hills at break of dawn.'

'Who cares if I'm seen? Anyhow, I like it right here on the estate. I'm so happy here at Arthur's. Haven't you noticed?'

'Yes, I have. You are a very happy person. What's the secret?'

'Some salad,' she said scornfully, changing the subject. 'That's nothing but lettuce. What a pitiful salad.'

'I'm a purist,' he said defensively. 'Anyhow, you're putting every other ingredient on your pizza.'

'Here, give me a hand and grate this mozzarella and stop looking at me like that, like you're waiting for me to satisfy your curiosity on some point. I'm not confiding in you any more. Here, grate.'

She shoved the grater at him roughly. Horacio feigned

being knocked off balance and fell to the floor, pretending to hit his head on the counter as he fell. 'Ohhhhh!'

He lay on the floor in a mock swoon.

Jenny bent over him, 'Are you all right?'

Silence. Horacio kept his eyes shut. The familiar words reverberated. Now he was not just pretending to be stunned. He opened his eyes and saw her sweet face bending over him, all concern, and the scene on Pacific Heights came back to him full force. 'You must have cut your hair the next day,' he said.

'What?' Jenny made a grab for her hair as if just learning it was gone. All she could think was: He knows I'm Maria Lopez and thinks I've escaped. Her eyes burned into his.

Seeing her blanched face and eyes like coals, he asked tenderly, 'Are *you* all right?'

She's afraid I think she's escaped, he realized, for this all means that she is Maria Lopez. I'll have to puzzle out that business later.

'You look awful,' he said, 'as if you just fell from a tree.'

'For heaven's sake!' Jenny exclaimed. 'Are you . . .? Could you be – the man who fell from the building?'

'The tree. I almost fell from the building but, come to think of it, thanks to you, I didn't. You snapped me out of a very bad moment.'

They were both silent, remembering. Jenny sat down on the floor beside him as her crouch was getting uncomfortable.

'I could tell it was a bad moment, even though I couldn't see you very well. I knew. I could almost palpably feel your unhappiness.' Without thinking, she touched his forehead, stroking back a lock of hair that had fallen. 'Poor Horacio,' she said vaguely.

Horacio eased up to a sitting position. 'I never realized it was you until just now when you said, Are you all right. What a difference hair makes. Of course it was dark there under the tree. It's quite an amazing coincidence!'

'You never said a word that night, never made a peep. Because your voice is so distinctive, right? So boring and droning.'

'Right. I'm going to change that. I'm going to get a voice-lift.'

Jenny laughed. Horacio laughed. Then they were quiet. Suddenly, sitting so close together on the kitchen floor seemed unbearably intimate. Jenny leapt to her feet. 'Do you live in that building you were standing on?' she asked, putting the pizza in the oven.

'No, I live in Mill Valley.'

'So do I!' She smiled. 'More coincidence.'

Horacio stood up and hoisted himself up to sit on the counter. 'What's your real name?'

'Jenny Hunt.'

Jenny was amazed at herself. Why had she said that? So that he wouldn't think she was Maria? No. No, she'd said it because she wanted to. It felt great. She'd never felt so free as she did that minute. 'Jenny Hunt,' she said again, really going for it. 'I live in Mill Valley, California. I'm an artist. I'm also the richest young single woman in the country.'

'My!' said Horacio, while thinking, What a liar – believing her to be Maria Lopez. And yet if she was Maria, she was crazy and could believe she was Jenny Hunt like some crazies believed they were Napoleon. But if she was the girl who helped him, and she was, he knew she had not escaped Fair Haven on the day they claimed and therefore could not be Maria. He was pretty sure she was Maria.

As happens with ecstatic moments, Jenny returned to earth with redoubled anxiety. 'But do keep calling me Beulah,' she urged him.

'I will,' he assured her, 'when I'm not calling you honey-pie.'

21

During dinner – home-made pizza and lettuce salad, which Arthur elected to have not in the rose garden or patio or dining-room but in a small and not very clean gazebo at the furthest end of the pond – Horacio whispered to Jess, 'Do you think Laveen is a woman disguised as a man?'

He could see her transformed by this wild surmise. The green-eyed monster, who'd been hiding under the picnic table, lashed its tail gleefully, having Jess once more back in its coils.

'If so,' Horacio added, 'Arthur's getting pretty sneaky in his old age.'

There, he thought. That will cause a little trouble around here while I go off to Mill Valley tomorrow. Jess won't relax until she actually sets eyes on Laveen's penis – if he has one. Even if he's not a woman he may not have one. I'm beginning to think I may not. I'd better see one of my ladies tomorrow. It's so great to be free of them and all their demands, their needs. If only I was equally free of my need for them.

Horacio had decided to go to Mill Valley and check out the existence of Jenny Hunt, to see if Beulah was Jenny or was only Maria wishing she were Jenny.

Arthur could see that Horacio was trying to figure something out. If he had a pencil he'd be chewing on it, Arthur thought fondly. Figuring is not Horacio's strong point. Obviously he's learned something that's biting him and now he's busy drawing wrong conclusions.

Laveen was thinking about Jenny and Rowley, but he wasn't

trying to figure it out. He never wasted time figuring. He saw. He saw that Rowley was ordinary. He was the sort of man who, if he could speak, would be loud and obnoxious. Jenny felt drawn to him and kin to him because of his handicap. The fluke of her understanding him helped create the bond. Also, sensually deprived, her physical need was served. Somehow, Rowley had broken through her very significant tactile defensiveness. Jenny was not ordinary. She was extraordinary. And quite remarkably beautiful. Even in the gloaming, even knowing she was no longer rich, she was dazzling to his eyes. He wanted her – much more than he wanted the picture. He saw now that that was why he was drawn into this ridiculously minor scam in the first place. Getting *her* would be the challenge. It was her innocence that excited him. She was as good as he was bad, as simple as he was complex. He would like to have her and hurt her. Hurt her badly, see her weep. He would like to have control over her. He grew excited thinking about it.

Yes, Horacio, he did have.

After dinner, Jenny went down to Rowley's gatehouse to await his return from the Always Inn. The one room was cluttered in a young man's way – dirty clothes on the floor, bed unmade – but was essentially clean and ordered. There was a Franklin stove and a neat stack of small-cut wood. Washed dishes stood in a rack beside the sink. On a shelf were a few dozen paperbacks. Those that weren't science fiction were by Somerset Maugham, his favourite writer. A fine story-teller, Jenny thought, and a handicapped person too. She wondered if Rowley knew that Maugham's novel, *Of Human Bondage*, about the young man with a club foot, was really about himself and his stutter.

Thank goodness Rowley had all his lovely body intact. He was so physical, so energetic. But he was risking it all with that motorcycle, 'The Duke,' he called it. Well, risk went hand in hand with youth. Sometimes, when she and Rowley were together she felt so – so careful, so set in her ways, like an old lady.

She tidied his room as she thought these things, made the bed, turned it down.

Rowley stood in the doorway, his face dazed with joy at seeing her. 'I was afraid you wouldn't be here.'

'Why? Of course I'd be here if I said I would.'

'I'm always afraid I'll never see you again, that you'll realize . . .'

'Realize what, Rowley?'

'That I'm not good enough for you. I'm not, you know. You should have a fine strong man, a good man. I'm weak. But, do you know what?'

Jenny smiled, 'What?'

'A friend offered me a snort of coke tonight and I said no, I said my lady wouldn't like me to have it. Anyhow, who needs cocaine when they have you?'

Jenny felt a little guilty at the thought of her wine. They embraced and kissed. They danced slowly around the room to some tune in Rowley's mind, kissing and caressing each other. They took off their shirts and danced flesh to flesh. More clothes dropped to the floor. Jenny rubbed his torso with hers, circling around him.

When she was at his back he picked her up, piggyback, and she put her breasts on his shoulders.

He craned his neck around to kiss her nipples. He could feel her fluff on the small of his back.

When they got in bed, aroused though they were, they talked together before combining. Face to face, eyes on lips, they conversed at length because they were careful not to let each feel that physical pleasure was the keystone of their attachment – though it was.

They inquired minutely into each other's day – the few parts of it they'd been apart – and hung on every word. Or tried to appear to. They gazed earnestly at each other, listening with eyes and heart, but their hands were reading the braille of their genitals so that their speeches became parenthesized with sighs as they felt each other swell and seep. Jenny reversed herself and gave him her other lips to read.

As she kissed him, she stroked his behind and felt for his spincter, which seemed to her to be man's most tender and vulnerable spot. She thought how funny it would be if a man's buttocks were different sizes like his testicles, or as women's breasts often were.

Now his sex was too big to hold and she released it just as, with her mouth free, she let loose an astonishing yell engendered by the kisses he'd been impressing on her as well as her glossal feel of his own desire. It was wonderful to be able to express herself this way and not be embarrassed by her noise, for she knew some men were horrified by such sounds. Why they let a woman scream on a roller-coaster and not in bed, she didn't know. Sex was very much like riding a roller-coaster, she thought, in terms of excitement and feeling out of control. But she knew Rowley could feel the reverberations of her sounds just as he could with the music he danced to – and that he was glad of them.

He drew her up to him and they embraced heart to heart. As she received him into her body, she seemed to enter a maelstrom that made the roller-coaster image only child's play. She clung to Rowley with all her might as they whirled off together into the dazzling cosmos.

'Beulah, my darling, my sweetest angel,' Rowley said later when she returned to herself. 'Won't you stay the whole night with me tonight?'

'I can't, Rowley, I'm sorry.'

'Please?'

'No.'

'Are you ashamed?'

'Of course not. Everyone here knows I care for you. I'm not ashamed at all; I'm proud.'

'Then why?'

'I can't say.'

'Then you don't love me.'

'Rowley, please, we've had such a nice time tonight, why –'

'Spoil it,' he finished for her. 'But can't you just tell me why?'

'I need time to be alone,' she said begrudgingly, a thin explanation. She tried to embellish it. 'I need to wake up alone and lie thinking about my work and what I will paint and how I will paint it. I need to go for my morning walk alone and –'

'I wish I could walk with you too.'

Jenny felt an unreasonable panic at the idea of not being able to have her morning walk alone. It was a time for her mind to be quiet – long, tranquil strolls through vineyards, pastures, fields of wildflowers, wooded glens.

'Go to sleep now, Rowley. You're tired. I'll stay with you until you fall asleep.'

He fell asleep in her embrace, embracing her. When she tried to leave she could not. Even in his sleep he held her tight, so tight she could not extricate herself. He held her desperately close, an octopus grip. Finally she had to wake him so that he would release her, and he had to grow all sad again watching her dress and go.

Back in her own room, Jenny rushed to release the valuable painting from its box so it could take the night air and be free to greet the morning. She searched it anxiously for any signs of malaise due to its long confinement, but it was vivid. Rose tones predominated, as if it, too, was all ablush from a night of love. Again, Jenny undressed. She lay luxuriously in bed with a book by Borges, whose stories were so short she believed she could read them entirely before sleep stole her consciousness. Each one was like a description of a condensation of a longer story he had invented and pondered. They had all the allure of Chuang Tzu's poems, which gave rise to the same intense and fabulous feeling that she was just *about* to get them, and that when she did, everything (in life) would become clear.

But what with all the wine and sex she read a paragraph of *The Circular Ruins*, closed one eye, read two more lines, and closed the other.

No epiphany tonight.

22

Saying he'd return in time for cocktails, Horacio set off the next day for his reconnoitering trip to Mill Valley.

He put the top down on the white lady, and stayed on the country roads. He admired the hand-tailored round edges of his car: unibody construction, no bolts. It was a lean, hard, quick car that hugged the road, a hill-climber. He felt one with the landscape and had a keen sense of his passage through it. He loved his old Porsche, aesthetically, and ascetically too, for it was damned uncomfortable on any long-ranging road trip, hard riding, hell on the kidneys, so that he had a keen sense of passage in more ways than one.

He stopped at the Marin Civic Center, Frank Lloyd Wright's final masterpiece and still more modern and more poetic than any building built since, went to the County Recorder's office, and looked in the property rolls to find Jenny Hunt's Mill Valley house, if any. It existed. Three thirty-eight Hillcrest Avenue. The assessed value, after Proposition 13, was a hundred and four thousand, which meant it would probably command three hundred and fifty on the market, not unusual for Mill Valley, a beautiful town, a desirable place to live, but not a town of mansions, just houses – until his own.

As he entered the town he could look up and see his house gradually emcompassing a hilltop a mile or so away. It looked gloomy to him, a crouching monster clasping the crest of the hill, enshrouded by surrounding pine trees he'd purposely not disturbed. It seemed to him he'd created a cave instead of an aerie, that he was living in the hill instead of on it.

Comparatively, Jenny Hunt's house, an insubstantial,

intricate construction on a similar site, seemed airy and charming, like a bird that had dropped down from the sky for a minute which would be taking off again presently – much like Jenny herself. That is, if Beulah and Jenny were one.

Getting into the house was, for Horacio, no problem, and an hour later he knew quite a lot about Jenny Hunt, but not whether she was the same person as Beulah. There were no photographs. However, her clothes were the same size. She, too, read books and painted pictures. He studied the paintings. He would compare styles when he got back to the estate. He liked the pictures a lot. They gave him something, tranquillity maybe. They seemed to tell him that life could be quite bearable, even nice, if he just looked around and saw things as Jenny saw them.

Or if he happened to have a hundred million dollars. No, it would be easy to think so, but such an inheritance could make life unendurably difficult and forbidding. It was different when you made it yourself, went after it, accumulated it, wanted it, understood it.

Of course, that was assuming that Beulah not only was Jenny Hunt but was *the* Jenny Hunt. And where the heck did Maria Lopez come in? And why?

The house was extremely pleasant. Horacio found it hard to leave. It consisted only of a kitchen, dining-room, living-room, bedroom, and studio. Her desk held none of the detritus of one who managed her own affairs: no account books, bills, stubs of incoming or outgoing sums, so he could not see if her auto insurance was for an Alfa Romeo. A painting over the mantlepiece of a World War II flyer seemed to be her father as a young man.

Back at the wheel of his car, Horacio fell into such a deep, brown study about Beulah, Arthur, and Laveen, that he didn't notice he was heading back to the valley without having vented his libido on one of his chicks.

Maybe I'm just plain disinclined, he thought when he did notice. This whole Helena Hot Springs set-up is so interesting. I can't wait to get back. Who needs sex when the game's afoot?

101

I wonder how much they're going to take her for, and how?

Shortly after Horacio set off on his scouting expedition to Mill Valley, Arthur rang up Jenny saying he would like to get together with her for a serious talk. Would she please come to his study?

Jenny had just set up a still life of an old pair of Rowley's jeans, thrown down on a table. It had all the fascination of doing a drape, complicated by bits of stitching, buttons, belt loops, leather, and worn places. The denim was old and soft and lay in seductive folds. She had done many quick charcoal studies of it the last few days and now was set to paint.

She was loath to leave and go to Arthur, but her concentration had already been broken by his call. So she hastily shed her smock, put away the valuable-painting-by-the-great-contemporary artist which she always took out while she worked, giving it its exercise as it were, and trotted through the house to Arthur's study, which surprisingly, was not book-lined with leather chairs and crackling fire but was more like a Zen meditation room, white and stark, furnished simply, almost brutally, not Arthur's voluptuous style at all. It was his own sanctum and, he thought, conducive indeed to study, with just a hint of the cell about it to keep him alert, to cause him to calculate any action so finitely as to never wind up in a real cell again. This room was also sound-proof.

Jenny entered and sat cross-legged at Arthur's feet.

'You're looking extremely well,' he began. 'The ten days here has agreed with you, Jenny. You have more colour, more flesh, have lost that dry, pinched, haunted look. Your juices are flowing.'

'Creatively as well as physically,' Jenny agreed. 'Emotionally too. I'm feeling strong in every way.'

'That's what I was hoping. Now you are fit to hear some rather dramatic news I have for you.'

Jenny fixed him with her large eyes and waited expectantly.

'You are no longer a rich woman. The reason Damon Carner resigned his post with you is that he lost all of your

102

fortune. He was ashamed to tell you this himself and asked me to do so. He mishandled all those millions. You have your house, your car, your bills are paid for a year, and that is it.'

'Oh.'

Arthur remained quiet while she assimilated this.

'The money was always intangible,' she mused aloud. 'I don't know if I ever really thought of myself as such a rich woman – except that I was the only person I knew who had an adviser. The loss of my adviser seemed more important to me than this news of the loss of my money. I felt very alarmed. And yet there was relief, too, at the loss of Damon. Also a kind of excitement, if you know what I mean, the excitement of change, of – winging it. Damon was always so – afraid. He acted as if people were after my life, not my fortune. Going incognito everywhere. Absurd, really. You know, Arthur, one of the first things that comes to my mind now is that I won't ever have to go back to Fair Haven – because I can't afford to.'

Arthur cleared his throat uneasily. 'Actually Damon included that in your bills for the year, three months at Fair haven. He was so afraid you might have a breakdown and have no recourse.'

'Afraid to the last.'

'He really did believe it was a haven for you.'

'It was a hell for me.'

'You don't think it was ever necessary?'

'I don't know, Arthur. I do get terribly afraid, and much of my fear is of myself, of what I might do, not of what someone else might do to me. I gather the rocks. What if I threw one and hurt someone? I know I am repressed. Going crazy allows me to act up, I guess, get out of myself, be wild and peculiar instead of the good little girl, the obedient one. Maybe if I could once have followed it through and become violent instead of being tamped down, drugged, shocked back into normalcy, I'd be all right.'

'Except that in the meantime you might have hurt somebody.'

'Yes, and how could I ever live with that? Then I might go

over the edge and never come back.' Jenny shook her head, dumbfounded. 'I wish I could figure it all out. God knows, the psychiatrists can't. As for my fortune, money means nothing to me. I have no concept of it at all. I don't know what money is any more than I know what time is, or death.' She smiled ruefully. 'I guess I'm about to learn.'

Jenny went back to her painting, Arthur commenced his usual, easy-going day, Rowley did chores, and Jess devoted herself to finding out if Laveen had a penis.

Pursuant to this, she was following him (her?) about and spying on him, particularly when he was with Arthur, because of the possibility that he didn't have one.

Presently she was under a bush by Arthur's study window. It certainly did appear that he and Arthur had an intimate relationship of some sort, one which involved secrets, for they'd had several private conversations during the morning which, unfortunately, she'd been unable to overhear. Not even murmurs reached her now. Oh, to read lips like Rowley.

At noon-time Laveen had not joined Arthur in his nude swim, and when Jess urged him to do so, Laveen began to act as if she were after him, so she had to back off. A simple way to find out would be to make a pass, but it would be too gruesome. Ugh!

She knew by now that Arthur, salaciously, had set a bugging device under Beulah's bed, and it occurred to her resourceful mind to remove it from there and place it instead in Laveen's bathroom. If she heard the toilet seat go up before he peed, she'd have her answer.

But Beulah was putting in a long day's painting and she always locked herself in during her work time. Jess would have to be patient. She backed out of the bush, got up, and wiped her knees.

She saw that Rowley was also on his knees, weeding the rosebeds. Jess shook her head. What a tramp that boy was. He always looked as if he was just off the freight car. What on earth did Beulah see in him? She was so refined, so ethereal almost. Love was certainly blind as a bat. Or sex was. She should try to open Beulah's eyes a bit – now that she was so mysteriously unjealous of her, even fond of her.

Ah, there was Beulah now, coming from her room, going over to see Rowley. She hoped they wouldn't get carried away and fall to fornicating among the roses. Those thorns were hell on the skin and Beulah's skin was so lovely now with its apricot tan.

Jess slipped into Beulah's room for the bug and self-contained tape-recorder. She found a place for it in Laveen's bathroom.

23

Arthur, meanwhile, was urging Laveen to have his interview with Jenny in her own room. It wasn't that he didn't trust Laveen to do his part impeccably, but it was a comfort to know he'd have it all on tape.

Their plan depended on two interviews, the first of which – Arthur's with Jenny – had already taken place.

Laveen agreed to talk to her in her room, and, of course, after leaving Arthur, and previous to his conversation with Jenny, he laundered her room and satisfied himself it was clean. He was surprised at Arthur and a little disappointed in him. The old man was losing his touch, he thought, not realizing the tape had been transported to his own bathroom for an audio-genital check.

Jenny was returning to her room from her encounter with Rowley in the rose bushes when Laveen appeared from behind a tree. 'Excuse me,' he said. 'I would like to talk with you in your room.'

'All right,' she said amiably, although she felt immediately apprehensive. To be anywhere near Laveen was to feel apprehensive, like being with an alien; not from another land but another world, someone whose system, processes, modalities, internal organs, mind, needs, were so different that there could not possibly be any meeting on any level, any affinity, connection, relationship, or exchange.

With this man, Jenny knew she could never share orgasm or laughter, but she supposed she could talk to him in her room.

'This is a big day for talks,' she muttered, entering the french windows.

'I suppose you realize that you are dripping with blood,' said Laveen, going to the green velvet chair.

'No, I didn't. Dear me. Well, it's all quite superficial, I assure you. Just a few scratches from thorns. I bleed easily.'

'Doesn't everybody?'

She went to the bathroom to stanch the blood, then returned and sat down on the bed. She gave him all her attention. 'Yes?'

He looked at her fixedly. 'It's hard to know how to begin.'

She doubted his opening remark extremely, feeling he knew exactly how to begin, middle, and end, and that he was only meaning to scare her, which he had.

'You see,' he said, 'I know who you are. I know that you are Maria Lopez and that you have escaped from Fair Haven Sanitarium. I know that you are being hunted . . .'

Jenny envisioned ravening bloodhounds. Slavering ones, rather, since it was wolves, not bloodhounds, who ravened. Laveen ravens, she thought. Raven is Laveen spelled backwards – almost.

'And when they catch you they will lock you up again.'

Her blood ran cold. It wasn't just the horrible words but the way he said them. The man was gifted. She said nothing.

He continued, 'You seem to be well and happy here. I don't suppose you want to be found – and returned.'

Her voice came, small but courageous. 'You seem to be very happy, too. Very well and happy.'

106

'I beg your pardon?'

'Arthur's place suits you very well too,' she repeated, in stronger voice that was still little more than a whisper.

Laveen was baffled. He felt he had suddenly, inexplicably lost control of the conversation. The woman seemed to believe she was holding a high card of some sort.

'Aren't we lucky to have discovered such a – a port in the storm. I almost said haven. That place should be called Dread Haven. Or Dead Raven. Raven, that is, as in ravening beasts.'

Now it was Laveen's turn to be silent. He observed her.

'Maria Tubman,' she said inconsequentially, losing him entirely.

They were both quiet and still.

'Was that all?' she asked. 'I was just about to go and –'

'No, it isn't all.' Laveen had an uncontrollable urge to jump to his feet and hit her in the face, but he controlled it and in fact leaned back in the chair looking more relaxed than ever. 'You don't understand,' he said. 'I have discovered you and I mean to turn you in.'

'But I have discovered you, too. So it seems to me we're quits.'

Laveen had an appalling thought that she knew his true identity. But that was impossible. Unless Horacio . . . 'What do you mean, you have discovered me?'

'Well, you were at Fair Haven too, were you not? Although you are disguised now and look different, I know that I saw you there.'

'Of course I was there,' he recovered at once. 'That's how I know you and recognize you for who you are.'

'Right. That's what I just said.'

Laveen was once again baffled. He reminded himself that he was dealing with a crazy woman.

Then he saw. 'You think I am an escaped patient, too. That is funny,' he said, not cracking a smile, although he was truly amused. 'However, you are deceived. I was an administrator there. The administrator. You see, Fair Haven is my place. I took it over two years ago for a friend who is on sabbatical.' (On Sabbatical was Laveen's term for dead. He had in fact replaced the friend, assumed his identity.)

'Does Arthur know that you work there?' she asked keenly.

'No, he doesn't. When I saw that you were here, I decided to use my knowledge for my own purposes and not involve poor Arthur in any way. I'm on my way to Europe, but I haven't the fare. It's a shame. I need fifty thousand dollars by tomorrow.'

'I haven't got fifty thousand dollars.' She smiled. 'I learned today, from Arthur, that I have lost my entire fortune.'

'My sympathies. Perhaps there is some way in which you could, shall we say, realize the sum? It's a small amount to pay for freedom, for being able to continue in this idyllic place, with your Pan-like lover, happy at your work, amusing company for your idle hours . . .'

'Yes, it is all that and more, but you make it sound hateful. It is as if you hate to see someone happy.'

'I do. But allow me to make my point. I was going on to say – what a difference from Fair Haven, where you were locked in your room, had no lover, no friends, were unable to work, and really weren't getting well.'

He waited but she was silent. For a woman, he thought, she had an extraordinary gift for silence and for attentiveness.

'When I last heard,' he reminded her, 'you thought you were a penguin.'

One time at Fair Haven, Jenny had tried to persuade the doctor that she collected rocks in the same spirit as did the female penguin who prepares her nest with them. She had waddled about his office, picking up objects (ashtray, paperweight, etc.) in her mouth (beak), then dropping them in a pile (nest) on the rug.

Jenny stared at Laveen coolly. 'I *am* a penguin,' she said.

Once again he wanted to hit her, but controlled himself and made do with a scowl. 'Enough fooling.'

'What was the point that you were so proudly making?' she asked.

'That fifty thousand dollars is a small price to pay for your sanity as well as your freedom.'

Inwardly, Jenny collapsed. 'Put like that, it's certainly true.'

'I am making a propostion to you, clear and simple. Fifty thousand for my silence. Can you say no?'

'I can't.'

'Do you have something to sell?'

'I do. I shall have to go to San Francisco.'

'To get it?'

'To sell it. To realize it, as you would say.'

'It's only money. Don't look so dismayed.'

I wish it were, Jenny thought woefully. But it's my beloved painting I shall have to give up in order to get only money for this beastly man.

'I'm not at all convinced they would lock me up again,' she lied. Her voice quavered pathetically. 'I think I could prove I was well now.' She had never sounded more feeble. 'Certainly I can prove that I didn't escape.'

'Your word against mine,' he said. 'I would be believed, not you. How do you explain, for instance, your hiding here incognito?'

'I'm not hiding.'

'You could have fooled me.' He gestured, opening his hands. 'I would see that it hit the papers. Your friends would learn the truth about you.'

'They should know, anyhow. It's not such a guilty secret – to sometimes go mad.'

He smiled malignly. He was a villain, Jenny realized. Here was an actual classic villain and she was in his clutches. She used sometimes to imagine that she was in her adviser's clutches, but she saw now how silly that was. Damon Carner was such a mild, well-meaning man. This man wanted to hurt her, could hurt her. And it wasn't just the mortgage falling due on Christmas Eve, it was her whole life falling due. She had to do what he said to preserve her freedom and sanity. What if, she wondered, I had to marry him, like in the old melodramas. I know I would rather die. Because there is more going on here than just blackmail. He is enjoying it, this having me in his clutches. Even though he scares me, I must try not to show it and give him the satisfaction of his dominance. I must speak up boldly and not be frail and tremulous.

'Yes, I would be considered the authority on your mental state,' he was saying. 'Especially when I vouchsafed that you had become violent once again. With rocks. Rocks. That is your Achilles heel. Do you remember the old saying, she's got rocks in her head?'

'You'd better decide,' she said dryly, (by talking dryly, she effaced the vocal quaver somewhat) 'whether they are in my head or my heel. It is what we artists call confusing our metaphors. As for your incorrect use of vouchsafe,' she said wearily but still dryly, 'I'll let it go.' She sighed deeply, almost a groan. 'Tell me this. If you are not an escaped patient, why are you in disguise?'

'That is a private matter.'

'How do I know you will go to Europe and not turn me in or bleed me for more?'

'It's tempting, since you bleed so easily. But you can trust me.'

Jenny was quiet and thoughtful. She felt stiff with weariness. She felt that this conversation had gone on for hours and that she'd been physically tortured the whole time. She narrowed her eyes at him, 'You are one of those ravening Great Skua gulls that eat baby penguins,' she said. 'You descend with beak and claw and angry wing and scoop them from the beautiful stone nest their mother has laboured so hard on, a nest not of straw and threads and feathers and lichen but of rocks, where she thought her babies would be so safe – so safe.' Tears filled her eyes. So much for boldness.

Laveen was silent, and then he mused aloud. 'You really are quite amazing. Truly eccentric.' He shook his head in mild wonder. He stood up. 'Pull yourself together and make the appointment in my hearing for this business you will transact in San Francisco tomorrow. There's a directory there on the shelf.'

110

She called Smith. 'This is Beulah Ludwig. I have been commissioned by Jenny Hunt to sell the item you have expressed interest in. Could I meet with you tomorrow on that matter? Good. Two o'clock. I'll be there.'

'Jenny Hunt, eh? So that is your real name.'

'No, it isn't. That is yet another incognito.'

It could have been worse for her, Laveen thought as he left Beulah's room and headed for Arthur's study. She could have had to sleep with me. And nothing would be worth that. And yet, the day will come when we will fuck together. How that will surprise her. Especially when she enjoys it.

Laveen actually smiled, feeling flattered, as he remembered: That is rather a nice image, the Great Skua. I like that. I like it a lot.

24

From the tape, Jess felt convinced that Laveen was genitally equipped as a man and also that he had bowel problems.

Even if he had been the other sex, Arthur wouldn't have anything to do with a woman with bowel problems.

Jess herself, promptly at nine-ten every morning, released one perfect poo into the bowl the minute she sat down. It was so perfect, she didn't need to wipe herself. But of course she did anyway, so as to pay obeisance to society's hygienic and ablutionary rules.

Arthur marvelled at these perfect poos. To him it was a sign that her entire system was in sublime tune, that she ate, slept, and exercised in the way that was exactly right for her. And it was true. Being in physical tune was obviously, she personally thought, what retarded the ageing process with her. But the foundation of it all, she knew, was her love for Arthur. That was what gave her the harmony of her life. Without that there would be discord, sickness, and oldness.

She returned the tape-recorder to Beulah's room intact, since she didn't know how to erase it.

Therefore, when Arthur retrieved it and played it with the object of hearing Laveen's blackmail proposition to Jenny, he was astounded to hear instead a cacophony of bathroom sounds.

Presumably, this was Horacio's idea of a joke.

Arthur called Laveen on the house phone and Laveen came to his study. He gave him a verbatim report of his conversation with Jenny.

Arthur was delighted that she had thought Laveen was an escaped patient, and carried on boisterously about it while Laveen observed him dourly.

As well, he was very pleased it had all gone so smoothly. 'Now, Laveen, let us rehearse the plan from here on.'

'I'll go up to the city just before she does, disguised as Smith. I observed him carefully when I went there to query him. I'll arrive at his office at one-thirty, trusting that he will have written out the cheque for Jenny by then. If he hasn't, I will urge him to do so.'

'No violence.'

'Right. I'll bind him, gag him, put him in another room. When Jenny arrives, I, as Smith, will take the painting and give her the cheque for three hundred and fifty thousand dollars. Everybody's happy. She'll bank it and write me a cheque for fifty. I'll take the painting to our client in France and we'll soon have in hand five hundred thousand, which we'll split down the middle. I'll keep Jenny's fifty as agreed since I am more at risk.'

'Good. It's terrific. We are actually stealing from Smith, not Jenny. The only person who's hurt is Smith, and he's really only annoyed since he's bound to be insured to the gills. Jenny is out fifty, but still way ahead of her original investment. This is a very pretty caper. And if, by any chance, through Jenny, say, Smith comes to learn of your blackmail and suspects you, I shall vouch for your being here all day. But Jenny is bound to insist she gave the painting to Smith, because of your disguise.'

'In any case, after tomorrow, Laveen will no longer exist.' Laveen walked to the window and balefully gazed out upon the grounds. As usual, his expression seemed to find everything wanting. 'What about Horacio? I still worry about him. Why did he go off for the day?'

'Not to worry about my nephew,' said Arthur. 'He's completely in the dark.' He spoke confidently but admitted to a mild uneasiness in his heart. How very much he would like to know the contents of Horacio's mind. High time they got a sensitive enough bugging device to hear a man's thoughts.

He wondered if he should put a bug in Horacio's room, but decided it would be futile. He'd find it, and Jenny's room was still the hub.

He was damned annoyed at Horacio's trick with the tape, but now he'd bugged her room again, with an even smaller device, cleverly concealed. He didn't want any more tricks.

'Now I really do know who you are.'

It was Horacio, now, saying this to Jenny. They were in her room. He was lying on her bed. She was feeding a fire with small sticks of kindling to hasten the blaze. It was evening of the same day. They were both giving the cocktail hour the go-by – Horacio because he wanted to talk to Beulah, Jenny because she didn't want to socialize with Laveen.

Jenny did not turn to him but remained kneeling at the hearth, her back to him.

He had arrived back from Mill Valley and come straight to her room. They had embraced, happy to see each other, as if after a long absence, for they'd been living so closely for a week, and so away from the rest of the world, that an unnaturally rapid intimacy had grown between them.

Indeed, Jenny felt deeply attached to everyone at Arthur's, except for the hated Laveen.

The very words Laveen had said, she thought despairingly: *I know who you are*. But Laveen didn't know who she was at all. He, least and last of all, knew her, even if he did have access to her records and files. *I know who you are*. Words at once threatening and thrilling. Oh, to be fully known by someone and still be loved, forgiven.

Darling Rowley knew her not at all. He loved a fantasy woman that he invested in her. But he loved so ardently, she was willing and happy to be his fantasy, to respond gratefully to his adoration, never experienced before.

Horacio knew her as Beulah. As Beulah, she'd been honest in her conversation with him except for the basic deception that, after all, was only in a name. She'd still been Jenny in essence. Perhaps not entirely, since she had wanted to change, be more Beulahish, which had come to mean for her more like other people. Now he thought he knew who she really was, Maria Lopez the hunted, who didn't exist at all.

She stood up and turned to him. Trying not to look too defeated, she asked, 'Who am I, Horacio?'

'Jenny Hunt, a damned wonderful artist.'

Jenny was staggered by surprise – and joy. Her heart warmed to him forever. From now on he could do no wrong. All Rowley's I-love-yous were powerless next to Horacio's estimation of her work. Horacio *did* know who she was. Her heart was so full she couldn't speak for a moment. She went and sat by him on the bed, just feeling happy.

'I went to your Mill Valley house and snooped.' He told her about his day. 'But I still can't tell for sure whether you are *the* Jenny Hunt and I'm confused about the Maria Lopez angle. Is someone setting you up as Maria, or is that another incognito?'

'I was *the* Jenny Hunt, but my fortune has since been lost, mishandled. All I have left of any tangible worth, aside from my house and car, is a painting which I must sell at once to raise money for Laveen, who knows me in my incognito of Maria and threatens me with a return to Fair Haven.'

'Don't pay him. I'll go and kick his ass.'

This was pure braggadocio. Horacio wouldn't dare to kick

Laveen's shadow. Still, Jenny looked at him admiringly and he felt like a dragon-slayer. At the same time he was thinking, painting? Aha!

'It won't help me to kick his ass and it might hurt. There is something you could do for me, though, that would be a help. In fact I've been miserable trying to think how to get around this.'

'Name it.'

'Take the painting to town for me. I'm scared to go myself. What's the good of going to get the money to preserve my incognito, only to be recognized by someone else on the way to do it?'

'Why pay Laveen? Screw him. He can't do anything to you.'

'Yes he can. The money doesn't matter to me as much as what I'm accomplishing by being here.' She began to spill it all out to Horacio, imagining his warm sympathy and compassion. 'I couldn't bear to go back to that place, to be locked up again, and I believe Laveen could see to it that I would be. I want to keep calm and give him the money and have him go away. I don't want to undo the good I've done by being here. I feel so well. I'm working well. I'm growing up. I do have this propensity for violence, you see. I have come close to really hurting someone. If I did – if I ever did harm someone, I couldn't go on, Horacio, I couldn't live with myself.

'Now I feel nothing but peace, a peace that is beyond price. And I do have the money, or I will have once this painting that I have is sold. It kills me to sell it. I love it. I revere it. But, oh well, I won't go into all that. It's worth much more than the fifty thousand Laveen is asking. In fact, I've been offered three hundred and fifty for it and I've been told it's worth half a million. So I'll still have plenty left over. He doesn't know what it is I'm selling.'

I bet, Horacio thought.

'Where do I take this painting?'

'To the art dealer, Smith, who's made an offer for it. I have an appointment at two tomorrow. I'll call and tell him to expect you instead of Beulah.' She clasped his hands. 'Oh,

115

will you do it for me?'

'Of course.'

'Thank you, Horacio, with all my heart, for everything.'

Horacio felt aroused. Maiden in distress. He the bold knight, the gallant. He shifted his position, wavering whether to clasp her in his arms and really show her what the old boy could do – or keep to the role of family friend.

No, much as he wanted to, as lovely and appealing as she looked right now, it wouldn't be right.

There was Rowley to consider, after all, although he wasn't a big consideration, almost negligible really. But there was the element of destroying poor Jenny's already tenuous peace. She could never handle two lovers.

Mainly, what deterred him was the fact that it wouldn't be fair to make love to her one day and steal from her the next. One had to have some integrity in these matters.

For that is what he would do – steal the painting before Laveen did. Obviously the blackmail was just a dodge to flush out the painting. The painting was what they were after.

Now, how to accomplish the theft without losing his nice sinecure here, without losing Jenny's faithful cousinship or Arthur's loving unclehood? Pretty damned challenging, all in all. And imagine being one-up on the legendary H.H.H.! Of course, it wouldn't do for him to find out. It wouldn't do to be murdered for his insolence.

25

Arthur was sensitive to anything happening around the estate, and when he realized that Horacio and Jenny had been closeted together for over an hour, he was burning to hear the tape of their conversation. Since Jenny was in the room when Horacio arrived, Horacio would not have had a chance to look for the newly-placed bug, but he might try and look for it afterwards. That must be prevented at all costs.

Rowley was riding the lawnmower over the grass at the front of the house. Arthur hailed him. As he didn't have to shout over the sound of the mower, he just mouthed his message to Rowley. 'Do me a favour. My nephew is in Beulah's room, talking with her. When they leave, which they will, shortly, for dinner, go into the room and stay there until I come. Don't let anyone else in. Especially don't let Horacio back in. Go now and wait for them at the french windows. Just leave the mower where it is.'

Arthur took his Anejo and lime to a chair in the living-room where he could observe the hallway to Jenny's room. That door, then, was also covered.

Rowley went to the french windows. He waited. He grew unhappy. He began to grieve. Why was Horacio in Beulah's room? What were they doing? Talking, of course, nothing more, and yet the idea of their talking companionably together at great length, and perhaps in depth as well, was painful to him. Talking and probably laughing as well. Beulah always seemed to laugh a lot with Horacio, and he with her. It was curious that although he could imagine the sound of her voice and the way she said her words, there was no way he could 'hear' her laughter.

Laughter was just a grimace to him, a contortion of the face and body. He did not understand it. He himself had never laughed. In fact, it seemed to him that until coming here to work for Arthur, he had never seen laughing.

Jess and Arthur, Horacio and Beulah, were often engulfed by laughter. Their bodies actually doubled up at times: shoulders shook (Arthur's stomach shook), eyes closed tight, skin blushed. Beulah leaned forward when she laughed and Horacio leaned back, throwing his chest out, his head back. Jess covered her face when she laughed, sometimes with both hands. Rowley thought she didn't like to show how her face

117

creased up, but he liked the look of it when it did. Laveen showed his teeth, but if it was laughter, it just came from the mouth, did not inhabit his body, wrinkle his face, or move his blood.

Rowley, waiting for Beulah, felt more and more tortured at the idea of the two of them together in her bedroom. If she did not come out within one more minute, he would have to burst into her room on some pretext.

It wasn't until the end of his conversation with Jenny that Horacio recollected the tape Arthur had placed under her bed. He actually blushed at his stupidity. He would have to get the tape, erase this talk, and put something else on it, something so silly that Arthur would suppose right away that Horacio was playing a joke on him.

Horacio relaxed, and the blood that had rushed to his face subsided. Yes, that would do it. And if Arthur guessed that the joke on the tape was a red herring, that would be all right too. Arthur would feel outfoxed but, perversely, he would feel proud of his nephew for the good move. Horacio knew he couldn't approach Arthur for sheer genius, but he did have some good moves and he was about to unleash the lot of them.

Not only was he going to be three hundred and fifty thousand dollars ahead tomorrow, but he was going to have the pleasure of throwing a spanner into Arthur's scam. The pupil outgrows the master.

'We should be getting on to dinner,' Jenny said. 'We've already missed cocktails. Excuse me a minute.'

She ducked into her bathroom. Instantly Horacio gathered himself up from his lounging position on the bed, catapulted himself off it, and on to his hands and knees to look and feel under the bed for the bug.

As Arthur had changed its location, Horacio did not find it.

At that same minute, Rowley burst into the room through the french windows. He saw no one there. And yet no one had left. Beulah always used these doors. He was confounded. 'Beulah!' he called almost desperately, such a state had he got himself into. 'Beulah!'

She came out of the bathroom. 'Rowley, what is it?' She looked around with puzzlement. 'Where's Horacio. Did Horacio leave?'

Horacio, abashed, rose up from his position on the floor beside the bed. 'Here I am.'

'Why were you hiding?' Rowley scowled at him.

'What?'

'He wants to know why you were hiding.' Beulah interpreted. 'Why were you hiding, Horacio?'

Horacio went through an elaborate pantomime with highly exaggerated motions for Rowley of how he had been sitting on the bed and his comb had fallen out of his pocket, so he had got down to look for it and found it.

Now he began combing his hair.

Rowley was furious at this charade.

'He reads lips perfectly well,' said Jenny, gently reproaching him.

Horacio knew that. He smiled at her. 'Shall we go in to dinner?' he asked her.

Again she felt sensitive for Rowley. She rebuffed Horacio. 'I'll be right along,' she said, 'you go on ahead.'

So Horacio had to leave the room.

She tried to kiss away the fury from Rowley's face.

'What was he doing in here with you so long?'

'We were talking. He's a good friend to me, Rowley.'

'I am your friend.'

'Yes. And my lover,' she smiled.

'I want to be your friend.'

'You are.' And yet, she thought, I could not have asked this favour of Rowley. I could not have trusted him not to harm Laveen. Nor do I feel I could have laid the responsibility of delivering the painting on to him. It would break his heart if he knew I had asked Horacio to help me, and not him. But it's true. Horacio is such a man of the world, such a cool, dependable, fellow. Rowley is all raw emotions: young, passionate, and wild.

'He didn't drop his comb,' Rowley said.

Jenny didn't think so either. But why on earth would he be hiding from Rowley?

'He's scared of me,' Rowley answered her thought.

I can't imagine why he would be, she thought. I can't imagine Horacio scared of anyone. But she didn't say this, because Rowley looked so pleased with his idea.

'I must go, Rowley,' she told him.

'Will I see you after supper?'

'Yes.'

'We'll play chess,' he said. 'I'll wait for you here.'

'All right.' She kissed him lightly, fleetingly, on a few interesting places, then eluded his grasp and fled the room.

Horacio, poised behind a tree, was exasperated to see Jenny leave her room without Rowley. In five more minutes he was going to be conspicuously late for dinner. He had to get that tape. Now.

Once Jenny had disappeared round the side of the house, he eased over to the bedroom window. Rowley was adding fuel to Jenny's fire, which meant he was probably going to wait for her there. Damn. He would have to bop him.

Once Rowley sat down in the armchair, he could enter through the hall door and neutralize him from behind.

Unlike his uncle, Horacio was not averse to violence; he often relished it.

Rowley sat down in the armchair in front of the fire.

Horacio hurried into the house and through it to his room, being careful not to run into anybody. He got a sap. He proceeded down the hallway to Jenny's door. He opened it. Rowley was relaxed in the chair, almost nodding.

Horacio took three large quiet steps (forgetting he needn't be quiet) and sapped Rowley behind the ear. He searched the room rapidly and thoroughly, but found no bug. He could only assume, hopefully, that Arthur, knowing Horacio knew about the bug and realizing Jenny was always alone in her room or with Rowley, who could make no comprehensible contribution, had given up using it.

Also, he remembered with relief, Arthur already had all the information he needed. Arthur had established in Jenny's mind that she was broke, then Laveen had hit her for fifty thousand so that she would reveal the painting's whereabouts.

Now Horacio had only to figure out his part in diverting the action of the game. He was beginning to form a nice idea.

He went back down the hall and entered the patio from the living-room door. There he encountered Laveen. They said good evening.

'I think we are both late for dinner,' Laveen said.

'Yes. The big question is: where is dinner to be? Arthur is always so impulsive about where he wants to eat.'

'Let's try the dining-room,' Laveen suggested.

'What a novel idea,' said Horacio.

Arthur, Jess and Jenny were indeed assembled in the dining-room, where Jess was serving out sweet corn, cheese fondue, and lamb chops.

'Jess, dear,' Arthur had said, just before dinner, 'I shall be leaving the table a few minutes into our meal. Please see that nobody follows me, Horacio in particular. I'll seat him next to you and, after I go, you must fix him and hold him with your most glittering, ancient-mariner eye.'

'All right, darling.'

So it was that, a few minutes into the chops and corn, Arthur took a sip of the Pouilly Fuissé that Laveen had brought as a house present, and pronounced it 'Unimbibable! I don't mean to be rude, Laveen, but this wine is an insult to Jess's culinary contribution. In a word, Ugh! I must descend to the furthest reaches of my wine cellar and replace this filthy frog fare with a decent Napa Valley number. I do hope Rowley fixed the light down there; I'm afraid of the dark.'

'Let me go for you,' said Horacio.

'My boy, I wouldn't dream of it. I count on you to keep the conversational ball rolling until my return.'

Arthur hotfooted it to Jenny's room. Entering, he saw

121

Rowley asleep in the armchair.

He jiggled his shoulder, 'All right, old son, off you go now. Say, Rowley old fellow, what's this?'

He saw that Rowley was out cold, with a swollen bruise behind his ear.

Arthur pressed his lips tightly together, not pleased. Violence, here in his own house! By one of his own guests. Not good. Not good at all. Someone else had come looking for the tape. Laveen? Or Horacio? Or, could one of them have been looking for the painting? Laveen, perhaps, now that he was certain it was here? But it was not entirely certain it was here, since Jenny might plan to stop for it somewhere en route to Smith's. Meanwhile, the bug.

He had placed it in the vase of roses, above the water-line, actually on the stem beneath the flower of the rose. Anyone thinking to look in the vase would pull out the flowers and scan the inside of the vase (which is what Horacio had done).

He pocketed the device, and as he looked at Rowley, he thought sadly, this has to be Horacio's doing. There must be something extremely interesting on this tape. Laveen's conversation was much earlier and he would have checked the room out first, before he talked to Jenny. Probably he had, and did not find it because Horacio had already placed it in some bathroom. Or did Laveen find the tape afterwards and cover his conversation by doctoring it with bathroom sounds? I rather think now that those amazing noises weren't Horacio's little joke, Arthur decided. I think Horacio had this conversation with Jenny unexpectedly, then remembered about the bugging device after the fact, but couldn't look for it with Rowley here, so he neutralized him, and then looked unsuccessfully for the bug.

Poor Rowley. He won't be ready to do favours for me again. I must get back to dinner, hot as I am to hear this tape. What about Rowley? He looks all right. His colour's good. Pulse steady. I could at least make him a bit more comfortable.

Arthur picked him up out of the chair and laid him down on Jenny's bed, unfolding the afghan at the end to cover him.

Arthur picked up Rowley, who was one hundred and fifty-five pounds, without thinking twice about it because, although he was in his sixties (no one knew how far in) he was still immensely strong. His arms could have modelled for Michelangelo and it had nothing to do with weight training, just God-given musculature. His pecs weren't too shabby either.

So, he picked up Rowley as Rowley might have picked up Beulah, and as he laid him down on the bed he felt something give. It wasn't a pain exactly. No, he certainly wouldn't describe it as a pain. Just that something deep inside him – gave. It was as if his body, his system, stopped for an instant and started again not quite as efficiently. Oh my, he thought, I don't care very much for that.

It reminded him of a friend, a fine athlete in his forties, an ex-Olympian. He was racing his young son along a beach, and when it came near the finish, when it was time to pour it on and surge ahead, he went to draw on that last burst of energy, his famous kick, and it wasn't here. He reached down for it and it simply wasn't there. His son beat him.

Arthur knew now that he would never again go to pick up a hundred and fifty pounds without thinking twice about it. What a shame. How sad it was to grow old. How unfair.

Then his mind got back to business.

Hurriedly he left the room, got the bottle of Clos du Bois he'd sequestered earlier in the hall closet, and returned to the dining-room. He checked his Casio: a seven-minute absence.

'My dears, forgive me.'

'Quite all right,' said Laveen. 'We've drunk the Fuissé regardless. Come and have some cold corn and tell us how everything is in the wine cellar. Are the rodents well?'

26

Jenny, not eating and drinking with her usual gusto, seemed to think that at one point Arthur, while dipping into the peach ice-cream which he had a passion for, called her Jenny instead of Beulah. In the entire time she'd been here it was his only slip-up. The interesting thing was that no one at the table reacted to the misnomer. Then she realized that no one had reacted because everyone – every single person at the table – knew she was Jenny Hunt.

They all know who I am! I only remain incognito now so that the others won't know that the others know. Because Laveen, Arthur, and Jess don't know that Horacio knows. Arthur doesn't know that Laveen knows. Jess, if she knows and I assume that she does, doesn't know that Horacio and Laveen know.

It is so absurd. Why is an incognito still a disguise if everyone has penetrated it? Who am I fooling now? Towards what end. This seems like the deepest conundrum or most elusive paradox.

Everyone, except Rowley, knows who I am, but I still travel incognito (from one room to another) for appearance's sake. Arthur can call me Jenny and no will notice or admit to noticing because it is understood, it is a house rule, that I am Beulah – just as Arthur is our host, Jess his wife, Laveen his friend, Horacio his nephew, Rowley his handyman. All their identities could be as false as my own. We all have escaped from somewhere.

But, in the end, what does it matter who we are? It is how we feel about each other that is essential, unless feelings are based more than we realize upon identities, upon biographical information. Unless we are in fact only the sum of what has happened to us: who we've loved, the things we have, what we've accomplished and not accomplished.

Still, it does seem maddening to think that I remain incognito so that the others won't know that the others know. It diminishes my incognito. It is nowhere near as grand, important, and fortifying as it was. It is like a crown prince going off incognito, and while he is gone someone seizes his throne so that he isn't crown prince any more and his incognito becomes absurd and meaningless.

It is actually quite a lot like that, since my fortune has been seized in my absence, in the eighteen-year absence of my mind.

There's probably some fine, Borgesian truth buried in all this, but I can't get ahold of it. I must go to Rowley.

'Excuse me, everyone, I've promised Rowley a chess game.'

At the mention of Rowley, Arthur glanced at Horacio and Laveen, but neither face disclosed that he was the attacker of Rowley.

Arthur saw that Jenny was happy to get away. It must have been hard for her, sitting down to eat with Laveen. She'd been very silent.

Jenny walked slowly through the living-room and down the hall of the wing, still pondering her humoured disguise.

If I am remaining incognito for them and no longer for me, doesn't that mean I'm being manipulated?

What if I was manipulated into the incognito in the first place?

Why?

So that Laveen could blackmail me!

Not a very Borgesian truth after all.

Thank God.

If it were, I wouldn't understand it.

Rowley was reeling around her room when Jenny entered it.

'What happened?' he was saying, 'What the hell happened? Beulah! Where's Beulah? Oh, Beulah, thank God!'

He embraced her wildly. 'I was afraid they had got you, too. I was so afraid you were hurt. Oh, my baby, my poor baby. My sweetheart! My angel!'

'Rowley, what on earth are you raving about? Here, sit down. Be calm. Tell me what this is all about. Won't you please sit down and stop rampaging about?'

'I was struck. Here. Look. I was out cold. I just came to a minute ago. I was on the bed. Covered. Yes, I was covered. Wait a minute. I was fixing the fire. I sat down in the armchair. That's the last thing I remember. That was right after you left.'

'Since then we've been at dinner – all of us. Do you think it was a prowler?'

'I don't know. Arthur told me to come here, to stay in this room. Maybe I was supposed to be guarding something. If so, I've let him down, failed him. Oh God.' He hung his head in shame.

'But guarding what? The only thing I have of any value, Arthur doesn't know about. Oh dear, I'd better check that it is here. I pray that it is.'

'Shall I leave the room?'

'Of course not. I'd like to share it with you, anyhow, since it will soon be gone. If it's here, that is.'

Anxiously, Jenny went to her paintbox, lifted the section holding the tubes and found the painting within. She smiled and drew it out lovingly. She sat down on the bed and pulled Rowley down beside her.

'This painting,' she told him, 'is by an artist who recently died. Since then it has come to be worth a great deal because he didn't leave many canvases.

'You may not see its beauty at first. It took me a while, but it is strangely alive, reflective, responsive. I see so much in it. It seems to have so many stories to tell, so many moods. I've had to keep it hidden. I should have it in a vault. But I couldn't bear to lock it away and not enjoy it. I love it. But I take it out as often as I can. While I'm working. And during the night. That's why I couldn't spend nights with you. I had to release the painting. I believed that its colour and content

126

would become stifled and lost if it were always in the box.'

In her enthusiasm, Jenny had been chattering heedlessly, but now she saw that Rowley was deeply shaken and that it wasn't due to his sore head. 'Oh, Rowley, I'm sorry.'

'You wanted to be with this painting more than with me, a human being who loves you.'

'Please don't feel unhappy or resentful. It is art, Rowley. It must be cherished and cared for. I think the artist must have been such an extraordinary person – amazingly sensitive, with a unique vision –'

'It's not art, it's you!' Rowley burst out. 'You invest it with all those things. It's just a picture. You are giving it a personality, a humanity. It is just a piece of canvas. It's not right to care so much for a – a thing!'

Jenny faltered. 'Yes – I know. You're right, but . . .'

'It's a crystal. You look in there and see all that is wonderful to you in life, in art, in people. You are just looking into your own heart.'

'But the artist, well, even if he accomplishes that crystalization, isn't that remarkable, Rowley? It is not for nothing that it is worth so much, after all.'

'If I told you this – this . . .' He looked around the room and grabbed up a porcelain animal. 'This blue dog was priceless, would it become remarkable to you? Would it suddenly bark!'

Jenny laughed nervously. 'Oh dear, I hope not.'

'Or that painting there. It is a nice painting of the vineyards in the spring when the mustard is all in flower, making a yellow ground for the design of the grapes. It is a much nicer picture to me than the one you hold. It means something to me.'

'But, Rowley, it is nowhere near as wonderful as looking out of the window to that same scene. My painting doesn't try to reproduce a given place. My painting –'

'It's an illusion!'

'Well, yes, all right. It is.'

My painting is incognito, Jenny thought happily.

'What it comes down to,' Rowley said wretchedly, 'is that

you care more for that painting than for me. You left my embrace to take a piece of canvas out of box. Because it's worth a lot of money. And I'm worthless.'

'That is a terrible thing to say.'

'But it's a true thing.'

'It isn't the money. It has nothing to do with the money at all. I believe in this painting.'

'You worship it? You have religious feeling for it?

'No! You don't understand. I don't know why you are being so mean.'

'Mean. I could never be mean to you. I would slit my throat first. But put yourself in my place. Imagine if it were reversed for us.'

Dutifully she imagined it. She put herself in Rowley's place and duly her actions appeared questionable.

Reversing their situation, she imagined him leaving her embrace one night, even though she clung desperately to him and begged him to stay with her. He detached himself from her octopus grip and went to his own room to take a painting out of a box, so it could breathe, so it could take its exercise. She saw him moon over the painting then go to bed to read half a page of some book with one eye before falling asleep all by himself, when he could be sleeping with her.

Yes, that would hurt. It would be incomprehensible too.

She wondered if she should tell him that she was considered by experts to be crazy. In that light her behaviour would not seem so amazingly strange and hurtful to him. He wouldn't take it personally.

But her behaviour wasn't *that* odd. It wasn't as if she put the painting on the pillow next to her to kiss it or anything. There was no ceremony involved, no blood rite. It could be worse, her behaviour.

But did she leave Rowley's side to be with the painting, or did she perhaps use the painting to preserve her freedom so as not to be utterly possessed by Rowley night and day?

She *did* want to sleep alone. She wanted to wake alone, walk, and work, and be alone a lot. She wanted to have her aloneness and when she saw him, greet him with a glad heart.

128

If she never left him, how could she be glad to see him?

But the painting, too. She loved the painting. And tomorrow it would be gone.

'It's a talisman, I guess,' she said unexpectedly. 'A symbol, an icon, an illusion. All those things. I don't know, Rowley, but there's no getting around that it means a lot to me. Maybe the money does too. It's all I have in the world now. My art won't earn me anything. I'm sure to be an incompetent at any job I undertake. I don't know. Let's not talk about it any more. Your poor head. How can you even think straight? Shall I get you some aspirin?'

'Yes. And I'm staying with you here tonight. In case they come back. I'll sleep on the floor.'

'You will not, you'll sleep in my arms. Should I tell Arthur what happened?'

'Yes, do.'

Jenny went in search of Arthur. She found Jess, who told her, 'He's in his study and asks not to be disturbed for any reason.'

Jenny told Jess about Rowley being unaccountably bashed and asked her to pass it on.

Arthur was in his study, listening to the tape of Jenny's conversation with Horacio re: Laveen, the painting, and her true identity.

27

'So that devil Horacio has wormed his way into her confidence and he, not she, will take the painting to Smith.'

It was early the next morning and Arthur was in Laveen's

east-wing bedroom. They were both unshaven (but of course only Arthur looked the worse for it) and clothed in bath-robes, terry and silk respectively. They sipped hot black coffee, and if anything they seemed energized rather than dismayed by this new problem. 'Which means,' said Laveen, 'it will never arrive.'

'I have an idea how to dissuade her from having any trust in Horacio,' said Arthur. 'But, failing that, we must have an alternative plan.'

'Which will be to rip it off him en route.'

'Exactly. You said you had a man if we needed one. A guard at Fair Haven?'

'Yes, he went there with me. He's worked for me before. Moe Bates. He's an ex-con. Loyal.'

'I doubt that one will be enough against Horacio.'

'I will be the other, disguised as a thug,' said Laveen with, for him, relish.

'No one says thug any more,' said Arthur disapprovingly.

'It's a San Francisco word.'

'No, it originated in India, a Hindi word meaning a robber who strangles his victim. You are thinking of the equally archaic word, hoodlum.'

'Right. That's the one that originated in Frisco to describe men who made mayhem on the Chinese population during the 1860s. I wonder why no one makes mayhem on the Frisco gay population now. At least on the lesbians. We should bring back the hoodlum, Arthur. And the thug too, why not. I'm afraid crime is in the doldrums. The only real violence is on TV.'

'My, you're chatty this morning, Laveen. You almost seem cheerful – although I know such a thing is impossible.'

'I'm looking forward to foiling Horacio. Tell me about your nephew.'

Arthur poured more coffee and stirred in lots of sugar. 'Well, the thing about Horacio,' he said, 'is that he's un-accountable. There's an unknown quantity, so you can't predict what he'll do: an impulsiveness to his nature. He might commit a crime at a moment's notice and create the caper as he goes along. That seems to add zest for him. His ability to make split-second decisions, and to do the mad, impulsive thing, makes up for a lack of intelligence and careful planning. He doesn't like anything too tame. The great Wallenda said, "to be on the wire is life, the rest is waiting." Horacio likes to be on the wire, to take a caper to its limits. He should have been a racing-car driver. Which reminds me, he drives that Porsche like a bat out of hell.'

'We'll need a road-block,' Laveen planned aloud. 'I will rent a truck.' He paused to glare at a bird that was singing outside the window. 'Which I will be in, blocking his way. Moe will tail him, so as to box him in from behind when Horacio finds me blocking him in front. Of course, if Jenny takes the painting, we'll continue with the original plan. It would be a shame to abandon it. I wouldn't get my fifty thousand, my perk, and unless Damon insured the painting . . .'

'I will do all I can to set Jenny against Horacio so that she won't entrust him with it. You'd better call this Moe character to come right over, and I'll have Jess get hold of Rowley to let Moe in and keep him out of sight. I'll talk to Jenny now.'

'Watch out. She has a way of turning the conversation into a maze. You should have heard ours.'

'I had every intention of doing so but the tape was missing.'

'Yes. It had been put in my bathroom. I had some fun with it.'

Arthur laughed. 'You certainly did. But who put it there?'

'I was naturally curious to know who did, so I put a substance on the bug that would show up on the fingers of the person who came to collect it.'

'And?'

'It was Jess.'

'Jess! Why?'

'You tell me.'

'Talk about labyrinths, how that woman's mind works is ever a puzzlement to me. She continues to surprise me. What

131

a woman.' Arthur felt proud of Jess for surprising him – hard to do after ten years. 'Do you have a lady, Laveen?'

'All women hate me instinctively.'

'Surely not,' said Arthur kindly, although he believed it. It was hard to imagine Laveen's own mother taking him to her bosom.

'They're quite right to. They know I haven't an ounce of human feeling or compassion.'

'Poor fellow.'

'Don't pity me. I wouldn't have it any other way. Except that it is hard to satisfy my – well, not my lust, since every woman has a price, but my yearning for sexual satisfaction, fulfilment. Bought women are as dry as cuttlebone. I've never experienced entering a woman who was aroused, who wanted me.'

Arthur thought all this was awfully sad. He knew Laveen was not unique in his lack of human feeling, but his was a singular coldness which indeed he seemed to nurture and preen himself on.

But if people stopped recoiling from the fellow and instead leaned towards him, mightn't that change his effect? Mightn't he warm up in response? Arthur tried to imagine Laveen being even a tiny bit affable, and failed.

Oh nuts, he thought, I have a crime in hand here. I can't be bothered with Laveen's psyche.

He got up, retying his robe. 'By the way, Laveen,' he said as he downed the last of his coffee and marched regally away, 'let me reiterate: no violence! You will have to carry guns, but don't use them. He's my nephew and I love him. Even if he were a stranger, I abhor anything more persuasive than words and symbols. Respect my feelings on this, even if you haven't any yourself. And lastly, Horacio has a secret compartment in his Porsche, which doubtless is where he will put the painting.' Arthur described it to Laveen.

Laveen nodded.

As he showered and shaved, Arthur pursued the subject of Laveen's psyche. I suppose, he thought, that if I'd been born freakish or impaired, I'd have trouble relating too. But look at Rowley! Impaired as all hell, but what a sweetheart!

And look at Jess, dealt a perfect hand of cards, but she still feels she has to lie and cheat and connive whenever she plays.

The thing is, a person's small flaws can endear them to us because their flaws humanize them. Laveen is all flaw, which is unacceptable. His total defectiveness does not endear.

I myself can't stand the man. But I suppose I respect him.

Jenny was telling Rowley, 'I almost had to go to San Francisco today on some business. Now Horacio's going for me and it feels like such a reprieve! I don't even want to work, I just want to play.' She moved gaily about the room.

Rowley felt suddenly full of gloom. This was happening more and more often with him in his dealings with Beulah. 'I keep forgetting you have another life,' he said. 'You're just visiting here. One day you'll go to the city on business and never return. What will I do then?'

'Sweetheart, let's not think about it. Let's just take each day as it comes and be glad of each other for now. I want to stay here a good deal longer if I can, if Arthur will have me, and I think he will.'

'To think of you even going out of my sight. I worry even when you go walking off in the morning alone. If anything happened to you . . .' Rowley looked anguished.

'If anything happened to me,' Jenny said sensibly, 'or if I went away, you must just say to yourself that we were lucky to have been together for a little while, and loved each other so well. I will always feel grateful for the love and tenderness you have shown me, Rowley. They have enriched my life.'

'I have so much caring for you.'

'I know. I feel it every minute.'

'Sometimes I think of your going from me and I feel such an emptiness, such hunger and sadness.'

'Don't think of it, then,' she begged him. 'Be happy. Please be happy.' She began to feel frightened of the enormity of Rowley's love.

'Some poet said, She walks in beauty. I always repeat that

133

line to myself whenever I see you. She walks in beauty. You are the most beautiful woman I have ever known or seen. This beauty is in you but it also surrounds you.'

Jenny tried to make a joke. 'Actually I put it on each morning. It's not easy to get. I saw it in a classified ad. and sent away for it.'

He was not to be jollied out of his mood. 'Oh Beulah, I feel so lucky to have you but I have this terrible fear that I will do something to ruin it, that I will drive you away, because even though you are making me a better man every day, I am not a good man, not anywhere near good enough for my angel. You should have the best. A king. Someone like Arthur. Only younger and even richer.'

'I am content with my Rowley.'

There was a knock on the door. Jess's voice called, 'Beulah, is Rowley there?'

'Yes,' Jenny opened the door.

'Tell him Arthur wants him down at the gate to let in some man who's coming to see Laveen. The man is to await Laveen in the gatehouse, to go no further.'

'OK, Jess.'

'And Arthur wants to talk to you; he's on the patio.'

Jenny gave Rowley the message and walked on with Jess to the patio. Now it was Jess's turn to look miserable. 'What's the matter?' Jenny asked.

'Arthur never wants to talk to me. He never sends for me because he has something special to talk about.'

'But he doesn't need to. You're always with him. You wake up together, do you not? Eat together, spend the whole day . . .'

'But he never really talks to me. You two will sit down and talk together intently for almost an hour. I've seen you before. What do you talk *about*?'

'Why, I don't know. This and that I suppose. I imagine he's sent for me because he has something on his mind that he particularly wants to discuss. He has taken it upon himself to advise me on some matters – for which I'm very grateful.'

'I would like you to tell me what you talked about.'

'I can't promise you any such thing.'

'Arthur has no secrets from me.'

'I'm sure he doesn't. But I might have.'

'I'll tell you something in return,' Jess said, her voice heavy with promise. 'Something you'll be very glad to know.'

'I don't want to know it,' Jenny said, as gently as she could. 'I'm sorry. I just – don't like to play games, Jess.'

'But life is a game. Everyone knows that.'

'Not to me.'

'What is it to you?'

Jenny laughed softly, flushed, and said, 'A desperate matter.'

'Dear child,' said Arthur, 'I'm sorry to take you from your painting, but something is preying on my mind and I want to unburden myself.'

Arthur was still in his terry robe. On the glass-topped table was a large bowl of blueberries and cream, a cup of coffee, and the morning *Chronicle*.

'I find myself in a terribly awkward position. You see, as host, I like to feel that I have here at my estate a felicitous community. I usually choose my guests carefully so that there is a pleasant mix. But then comes some guest un-announced and one has to make do and hope that this casse-role of personalities . . .'

Jenny wondered if he knew about the terrible Laveen and his blackmailing of her. He would hate to know it. He would feel so badly, to have invited her here to his home and submitted her to blackmail by a fellow guest under his very roof! But no, he couldn't have learned about it. He didn't seem that distressed. Not from the way he was eating those blueberries.

Jenny sat, in her way that was so quiet and still, waiting for Arthur to come to the point, and was surprised when he said, 'Horacio, you see, is not all that he seems.'

'Oh?'

'Yes, I tell you this because I see that you are growing fond of the lad.'

135

'I like Horacio very much but –'

'I think you are falling in love with him. It's hard not to. My nephew has great charm.'

'Actually not, Arthur. I mean, yes he does have charm, but we are just pals, Horacio and I, cronies.'

'Ah, that's what you tell yourself, but I can see more. And nothing would make me happier than to see the two of you together. Believe me. I love you both. But you must know that Horacio is by profession –'

'Wait! Before you go on. I really must make it clear that I am not falling in love with Horacio. It is Rowley I adore.'

'Well, yes, I can see that you are having a little fling with Rowley. Horacio let you down, I'm afraid, let himself down, stayed down, didn't come up.'

Jenny laughed and blushed and wondered how on earth he knew.

'It isn't because of that. Not at all. *That* was the fling. Rowley is dear to my heart. Horacio is my friend. A good friend – up or down.' She laughed.

'Jenny, if you'll only let me say –'

'I don't know if you should say. I mean, I would not want you to tell me some secret of Horacio's any more than I would want you to tell Horacio my secrets. Although, dear God, I did tell Horacio one of Rowley's secrets and that was indiscreet of me. I do regret it. I wish I could take it back.'

Now Arthur was dying to know that secret. Well, he would get it out of Horacio. But, damn the woman, she kept leading him astray and he couldn't get his message across. She'd practically made it impossible for him. He must take another approach.

'Here I am, needing someone to confide in,' he said plaintively, 'and you won't oblige me. It seems I have obliged you in some ways, some small ways, and that now you might help *me* a little in return.'

Jenny looked stricken. 'Arthur, dear friend, of course. Forgive me. How horrible of me. What a bitch I am. Please speak. Tell me anything.'

'Thank you. Thank you.' Arthur cleared his throat and

blurted out, 'Horacio is a thief.'

'You mean a kleptomaniac?'

'No. By profession, a thief. I thought you should be fore-warned.'

'But surely he wouldn't steal from his friends.'

'He wouldn't think twice about it. Not from me, of course, because he knows that I know about him. But he finds certain thefts irresistible. It's hard to explain. In a way he does it for the fun. To make life more interesting. You and Horacio are two extremes. Nothing bores you. You have fantastic inner reserves and you find everything and everyone a source of infinite satisfaction. You are the most easily delighted person I have ever known. One has only,' he added dryly, 'to watch your inexplicable enchantment with Rowley.'

'But Rowley is wonderful! You have no idea. In my whole life I have never encountered a more gentle, sensitive –'

'Never mind that now. I beseech you to let me talk. I am comparing you and Horacio. Horacio is always bored. To make life more interesting he must have a hand in crime or a sexual exploit. But he is never happy or satisfied with any woman or crime. They always disappoint him. So he races on to the next one hoping it will be different and, of course, it (and she) never is. It's always a let-down. He keeps on because for a time excitement makes up for feeling. But the cumulative effect is bad because it gets harder for him to get excited. The crime must be more dangerous, the woman more beautiful, more difficult, and more than one at a time.'

'Poor Horacio.'

'Yes, I suppose one can say poor Horacio. At any rate he has seemed quite content here, quite amazingly content, for him. But it can't last. He will break loose any minute and do something awful without warning. So I am warning you.'

'Thank you for telling me. I do appreciate it and I will be most alert.'

They talked for a little longer, then Jenny kissed him and went back to her room. He could tell by the way she walked that she was very disturbed in her mind.

I have succeeded, Arthur flattered himself. Granted I did

137

not start out auspiciously, but I brought it off. I was convincing because I hit on saying to her what I honestly thought about Horacio. How innovative! Presently I will learn that Jenny is going up to the city. She will never trust 'poor Horacio' with the painting now.

Ho, ho, Horacio! You thought you'd outsmart your old uncle.

Where is Rowley? Damn, he's at the gate waiting for Laveen's ex-con. This crime is getting in the way of my tennis.

28

At the gate, meanwhile, Rowley let in the man who had come to see Laveen, and recognized him as a graduate of Soledad. He had one of those hard, hidden faces that Rowley himself had once assumed, but it had become so habitual with this man that he could now assume no other. If he smiled, his whole face would crack and fall off. His expression was graven. He'd left the prison, having fulfilled his term, a year before Rowley escaped. He hoped the man would not remember him. They'd had no contact to speak of. Rowley only recognized him because he never forgot a face. He could conjure up the whole yard of Soledad faces before his mind's eye, that entire legion of society's lost and damned.

He showed Moe Bates into the gatehouse and went to tell Laveen he had come.

Arthur waited all morning to hear that Jenny was going to San Francisco. But the morning passed with no such word arriving, and when, at twelve, a car came out of the garage, he was astounded to see that it was Horacio in his white lady. Jenny stood in the driveway, blithely waving him off.

Jenny waved him off but not so blithely as it appeared to Arthur's aggravated eyes. She had wrestled and wrestled with her decision – her very first big decision made all by herself. She desperately hoped she'd made the right one and that her motives were decent. It seemed the only thing to do. How could she tell Horacio, friend and cousin, that she did not trust him – especially after he'd been so kind? And yet, after what Arthur had told her, she did not trust him. How could she?

So she had decided not to give him the painting. This was the scenario: Horacio had borne away a painting wrapped in brown paper, tied in twine. He believed he carried the valuable painting, but in fact she'd given him the crummy one of the vineyard from her bedroom wall. Then she called Smith and said that her messenger had taken the wrong painting, but to give him the cheque post-dated, and she would have the correct painting in his hands by tomorrow. This was in case Horacio truly delivered it.

If, on the other hand, Horacio did steal the painting, she could honestly tell Laveen that it never got to Smith and therefore she could not possibly pay him.

Shockingly, she rather hoped that Horacio would steal it so that she could disappoint Laveen and still have her painting! There was no getting around that she was obsessively attached to it, and that if she looked into her heart she would see that she had seized happily on Arthur's news of Horacio's criminality so that she could have a powerful motive not to relinquish the painting.

She did not like to think of the moment when she would have to tell Laveen she didn't have the money, but Jenny was very good at not thinking ahead.

Anyhow, the decision was made and taken and she would soon find out how it all turned out, and no harm done either way.

She walked over to the pond and gazed into the silken

water. There was a moment of stillness and of remarkable light from the high noon sun. She felt a deep pleasure in her surroundings, especially poignant as her stay was threatened now and might end at any time. This, along with the release she felt now that the decision was taken, made her feel good. A strange peace enfolded her. Again she experienced the sense that she was on the brink of understanding – everything! The secret of life itself was almost in her grasp! An imminent revelation was contained in this uncanny moment.

But no, no, she didn't have it after all. It was gone now; it had eluded her. But she'd had it almost – almost! And that feeling itself was so splendid that epiphany itself would have to be a let-down.

Rowley, seeing Beulah by the pond, began to walk towards her. He stopped. He looked at her, touched profoundly by her beauty. He felt her peace. He felt connected to her, bonded – as close as the pond was set into the land, the tree into the ground, the rock into the earth. They were one. Forever. At this moment he knew that the love he felt for her would be with him to the grave, that it was as vital a part of him as any life-sustaining organ in his body, that it was the very breath of life itself. This was it. Right now. All in her. His life.

Arthur, watching from the study window, was distracted from meditating the consequences of Horacio's departure by the picture of the two young people. There was Jenny, apparently in some mystical state, on the verge of becoming airborne and wafting off across the pond. And there was Rowley, suddenly transfixed by her, entranced.

Jess came up behind him. 'What are you looking at?'

'It's funny. Time seemed to stand still for a moment. But now it has just started up again with a vengeance. This entire day isn't going quite as I planned. What to do now? Well, there's really nothing to do, but wait.'

'Have a game with Rowley.'

'Excellent idea.'

'And I'll watch you play. Just see. It will be like the old days. Before Beulah.'

'You don't really mind having her here, do you, Jess darling? It's done her a world of good. Think what a poor, frightened-seeming, exhausted little thing she was when she arrived.'

'True, but now I feel she has such – power. Everything seems to turn around her somehow. I can't explain it. But now it is I who somehow feel frightened and exhausted. Worried. I'm worried about you.'

'Nonsense.'

'That terribly hard-looking man who came to see Laveen has just gone madly chasing after Horacio.'

'That's all right. He was supposed to.'

'Do you know what he told Laveen?'

'Oh dear, you've been spying again.'

'He said Rowley was in the same prison as he was.'

'Is that so. I rather suspected Rowley had been in the joint.'

'He was. And, about six or seven months ago, Rowley escaped.'

'My goodness. That *is* news.'

'Arthur, we are harbouring an escaped criminal!'

'Not really. We'd have to know he had escaped to be actually harbouring him, to be aiding and abetting the boy.'

'But we do know now.'

'It's only hearsay. Laveen's friend could be wrong. And, in any case, I wouldn't send Rowley away for the world. Why, how could we possibly do without the boy?'

'Which simply means that Beulah will have to stay here too, because he obviously can't live without her. One has only to look at him to see that.'

'Yes, that's actually what I was looking at when you asked. Ah youth!'

'Ah age!' said Jess. 'For it is exactly how I feel about you.'
He hugged her.

'Is everything going to be all right, Arthur?'

'Everything's going to be splendid.'

141

PART III

29

Horacio held a gun to his own head.

It had taken him fifteen minutes to shake the man following him. Then he pulled off the main route on to a dirt road sheltered by live oaks. Nearby some black and white ruminating cows made him feel he should think the matter over some more before proceeding.

Because this was going to be very tricky. The bullet would pass a hairsbreadth, literally, from his temple. And it was going to hurt. And it was going to bleed. A lot. Maybe deafen him. Still, if a part of him had to go, the ear was a good part. It wasn't an organ or a muscle or a bone. It was just a piece of flesh. If only it weren't so close to his brain!

I'd sure hate to miss with this thing. Or would I? Maybe there's a little game of Russian roulette going on here. Once again I'm on the cornice. Will I fall? Does it matter? What else is there to do in life, after all, except grow old?

But this is good – a priceless painting for a piece of an ear. Can't beat that. I return to the ranch screaming, 'Foul! Foul! I've been robbed. The painting is gone. Forgive me, Jenny, I've failed you.'

'But thank God you're alive,' she'll say (assuming I am).

'I tried to stop them,' I'll say, going for more credit.

'You shouldn't have risked your precious self.'

'They thought they left me for dead; I thought they did too.'

'Oh noble Horacio! What does the painting matter,' etc. etc.

Without another thought, Horacio lined up the gun, held out his ear as far as he could from his head, and blew it off.

Later, his head ringing and reeling, drenched in blood, he drove very slowly back towards the estate.

A truck swerved in front of him, cutting across the road. He pressed the breaks, turned the wheel, and screeched into a U-turn. But there was another car behind him. He was cornered and his reactions were not at their swiftest.

A bleak, swarthy man pulled open his door, dragged him all bloody from the car. He looked as horrified and surprised as a face that dead-pan could look, without falling off. He spoke, but Horacio did not hear, could not hear. He lay on the ground, looking into a magnum barrel as big as a sewer pipe.

Another man was searching his car. Horacio let himself appear to fade. He closed his eyes, went limp and, at the same instant he pulled the bleak man's foot from under him. Down he went. Horacio leapt to his feet. Or, rather, he gave himself the message to leap but, in effect, pitifully staggered to his knees.

He grabbed the gun from the fallen bandit.

Then there was a blinding pain in his already deafened head and his face was suddenly deep in dirt.

He had bit the dust and couldn't taste it. Couldn't see, hear, or feel. He was senseless.

Arthur was in a fury. He had expressly forbidden violence, and here was Horacio beaten, shot, possibly stabbed.

Horacio had dragged himself back to the estate (if one can use the expression dragging oneself to describe driving a Porsche) seeming more dead than alive.

A doctor was called, and although he assured Arthur that Horacio was much more alive than dead, he ordered bed-rest for several days to mend the concussion. As he dressed the side of Horacio's head he suggested to Arthur that Horacio should see a plastic surgeon, in time, about fashioning him a new ear.

'Meanwhile, this robbery and gun injury must be reported to the police.' He patted Horacio's shoulder. 'His hearing will return; it's traumatized now.'

Horacio didn't hear him and didn't care. He'd forgotten for the time being what this was all about. He thought he'd failed at something for the first time. A new experience. But he wasn't experiencing it. He didn't hear. Or care. He slept. He commenced his bed-rest for his concussion.

Laveen, ostensibly on a shopping trip to San Francisco, returned at six with several Brooks Brothers boxes, having shed his hoodlum disguise a mile from the estate.

He rang Arthur to say that he was back, and Arthur stormed into Laveen's bedroom just as he was pouring himself a Glenlivet. Neat.

Normally Arthur would have heard Laveen's explanations before lashing out, but he was too angry.

'I love that boy. Next to Jess he's my dearest friend in all the world. And kin besides. That bullet came as close as one can come to killing a man. Obviously it was shot with intent to kill. I won't hear you first, Laveen, because nothing, *nothing* you can say – oh!'

'What is it?'

Arthur turned pale and sagged into a chair. Laveen rushed to his side.

'It's all right,' Arthur said, 'Just a little – uh, discomfort. I've over-excited myself. This has all been a terrible shock. Truly can't stand violence, you know. I'm in the wrong business. Hate it. Mild fibrillations is all. Pour me – No, I'll just sit quietly. Or perhaps I'll lie down.'

'Shall I call Jess?'

'Good God, no. She's already in a terrible state about all this.'

'Let me relieve your mind. Neither Moe nor I shot Horacio. He was wounded when we boxed him in and held him up. But not so wounded he couldn't put up a struggle. I had to knock him out, but it was a mere selective tap. He'd grabbed Moe's gun, so I had to do it. I do believe the other was only a flesh-wound, a scalp graze which will always bleed a lot. But, as you say, awfully close. Awfully close.'

'Who did shoot him then? This is a mystery.' Mentally

147

stimulated, Arthur revived. 'How extraordinary. Am I to believe what you say?'

'Yes. You know me. I never need to justify myself, let along invent some silly tale. The man was already shot when we found him. He was driving slowly along. Moe had lost him in the beginning. He came upon me where I was set to block the road. I knew Horacio hadn't come through. We drove back together to find him heading back to the estate, weaving all over the road. We sandwiched him, pulled him out of the car. He went for Moe and I sapped him. The painting was in the secret compartment. Do you feel better?'

'Yes. Yes, I do.' Arthur mopped his brow, sat up with his old élan.

Laveen asked, 'What's his story? Has he said what happened?'

'No. He was out of it. Blood loss, traumatic wound. Deaf. Amnesiac. The doctor put him out. It's a wonder he got back here.' Arthur glared. 'You should not have left him.'

'You're being ridiculous. How could I possibly stay? His pulse was strong, I assure you. And what does it matter, anyhow? I don't understand these emotional attachments of yours. It's no way to operate.'

'We should have called it off once Horacio was involved,' Arthur said regretfully, cursing himself. 'Or we should have included him. I am not myself. My powers are not at their height. Well, let it be. What's done is done. And we do have the painting.' He decided to cheer up. 'A little rum would be in order now, my boy, if you'd be so kind. Don't neglect the squeeze of fresh lime.'

Laveen had to leave the room to go to the bar, and when he returned, Arthur was delving into the blue dark boxes, looking much improved. He withdrew the painting and gave it to Laveen to unwrap while he settled back to savour his drink.

Laveen carefully untied the string and unstuck the brown paper. He removed three layers of paper and exposed the painting. 'That's curious,' he said, looking at it intently. 'It's quite familiar. Could it be that we didn't discover it because it was hanging in plain sight on her bedroom wall? Could this

148

possibly be worth half a million dollars?'

Arthur sighed and said dryly, with words no amount of rum and lime could moisten. 'That is *not* the painting.'

30

Jess *was* in a terrible state, weeping and irrational.

Jenny, in trying to soothe her, seemed to enrage her further. This scene had gone on seemingly for hours. It occurred to Jenny that Jess was trying to sustain it, was tripping on it, while she herself, with real reason to be upset, was feeling more and more drained.

'But you act as if it were Arthur himself who was hurt,' Jenny exclaimed, feeling bewildered.

They were in Jess and Arthur's bedroom, which was done up in hues of green and rose. A Chinese carpet covered the floor, while the bed, canopied in softest blue, was like a reproduction of the pond, with its covers of watery silk bordered with a lily design. Spidery-legged tables were covered with pictures of the two of them taken over the years. The room was sensual, luxurious, and heady with the scents of Jess's powders, perfumes, and unguents.

'Arthur *is* hurt,' she shot back. 'He is profoundly upset. To hurt one of his own is to hurt him. Just as I would be hurt by any pain of his and,' she added rather over-dramatically, Jenny thought, as well as unconvincingly, 'just as his death would be my death.'

'Really, Jess? Surely not.'

'He is my life. Life without Arthur would be meaningless to me. If I lost him the pain would be so intolerable that the only release would be death.'

Jenny was dubious but interested.

'You are young, and so beautiful. Suppose Arthur did die. You would grieve dreadfully, of course, but, in time, in a year or so, you would take on life again.'

'If I lost Arthur, I wouldn't recover. And,' she added mysteriously, 'I am not so young.'

'But we are being morbid.' Jenny tried to smile. 'It is Horacio who is hurt, and not mortally.'

'Before you came here, Arthur and I were as happy as we've ever been. Life was so peaceful. There were just the two of us. Rowley didn't count. Just us two here on our own island, safe from the world. Now there is all this trouble and this is just the beginning. It will get worse. This is only a harbinger of the horrors to come.'

'Do you blame me for what's happened? If you do, then I certainly won't remain here.'

'Yes, I do blame you, but it's not good saying you'll go. You mustn't. I forbid you to go. Arthur would be furious if he knew I had talked like this. He wants you here, and what he wants, I want, even if I can see that it is bad for him, that no good will come of it.'

Jenny couldn't help but say, 'If you are looking for the real source of trouble, try Laveen.'

'Laveen is an old friend of Arthur's,' she said reprovingly. 'Arthur's friends are my friends.'

'Then why don't you consider me a friend of Arthur's and therefore your friend?'

'Because you are a woman.'

'Oh, Jess, what a terrible way to think, to feel.'

'I'm not a fool.'

'I know things were different in your day, when women competed ruthlessly for men. But now we are sisters. We help each other in love and business.'

'Ha! What do you know about either? You are a child. You've never worked or loved.'

Jenny hung her head. 'That's true.'

Jess took pity, forgot herself for a rare instant. 'Maybe that's why you're so nice. Maybe that's why I think you're quite the nicest woman I've met.'

Jenny smiled. 'Thank you, Jess.' They hugged each other with real affection.

'Go along now,' Jess said, 'you're spoiling my mood, I didn't want to feel good this soon.'

Jenny left Jess, went outside, dropped her clothes on the patio and dived into the darkling pond. A lowering sky was creating a false dusk at seven o'clock. Jenny swam briskly, trying to energize herself. Her passage with Jess had left her limp, following as it did so soon upon the harrowing incident of the return of Horacio.

She was not a good decision-maker. Horacio had been robbed. And hurt.

But she still had the painting!

And because he was robbed and hurt for all the world to see, Laveen could not expect her money. That part had turned out OK.

Maybe she *was* a good decision-maker, since Horacio was not hurt badly. The definition of a good decision, as far as she could see, was for no one to get hurt badly.

She churned the waters with a vigorous crawl, then gradually eased into a breast-stroke, sliding frog-like through the water, emptying her mind with each breath she bubbled out, until she felt collected from her mental and physical disarray of the previous hours.

Now, if she could just get to her room without encountering anyone, and light a little fire for herself, and be allowed quietly to think, then she would know how to proceed. She would have supper alone in her room and just think.

This was not allowed her.

Laveen was waiting for her at the outside door to her bedroom. She had nothing on but her open shirt, carrying her skirt and underthings, and she was repelled by the look he gave her, which seemed to leave tracks on her body like snail slime.

'Excuse me.' She brushed by him rudely and went into her room and from thence into her bathroom, where she wrapped a towel around her hair, a robe around her body.

When she came out, he was still at her door.

'What is it you want?'

'To conclude our business.' He walked in. 'I've come for the fifty thousand dollars.'

'I don't have it.'

'Why not? You made the appointment in my presence. Didn't you keep it?'

'No, I didn't. I was afaid to go to town and be discovered. So I asked Horacio to go for me. Surely you have heard that he arrived back in a cruel state. We none of us know what happened exactly, but he did say he'd been robbed.'

'Have you looked in the car or on his person to see if the money is there or the item which he was to translate into money for you?'

'Why, no. I haven't.'

'That is very strange.'

'It's not in the least strange. I've been so concerned about him i forgot entirely about your blackmail. Then Jess was in a terrible state and I had to deal with her. I simply forgot!'

He raised his brows. 'Forgot about such a large sum of money?'

Jenny got mad. 'Yes, forgot. I forgot. Money is not uppermost in my mind. I know you find that impossible to understand since it is the very breath of life to you.'

She began towelling her hair to vent her rage in some physical action. Love is the breath of life to Jess, she thought, and to Rowley. What is the breath of life to me? Creativity, I guess. My work, my art, the spirit that resides in the valuable painting. And yet that creative force dies in me when I lose my mind. I guess it is my mind that I need to survive. The breath of life to me is having my mind.

'Don't you think you'd better look for it?'

She raised her head and threw back her hair. 'For my mind?'

'For the money.'

'No, I don't think so. I am certainly not going to disturb poor Horacio now. And I would be very surprised if you had not looked in his car already. Meanwhile, what it comes down to, Laveen, is that I can't give you money which I do not have. We will have to wait to hear Horacio's story in the morning. I only pray that my business was not connected with his being injured, but I believe that it must have been. I feel dreadfully responsible. Good night. I want to be alone now.'

'Not good night. I'm afraid I can't leave feeling so very unsatisfied with your explanation.'

'Get out.'

'No.'

At this point, Rowley entered through the french windows. He saw Beulah, looking angry and upset, mouth the word 'out' to Laveen. When he saw Laveen refuse, Rowley immediately made a move to eject him forcibly. Laveen fixed a baleful eye on Rowley, saying quietly, 'Don't you dare to lay a hand on me,' and it stopped Rowley cold. Even without hearing the tone of voice, there was something so dangerous in Laveen's whole aspect at that moment that it would have stopped a battalion of Rowleys.

Jenny herself felt so frightened that she actually stepped between the two of them, throwing herself on Rowley's breast, hoping it would appear she was clinging to him for protection, rather than trying to prevent him from engaging with Laveen.

Laveen turned on his heel and sauntered out of the doors.

'That son of a bitch,' Rowley said through his teeth. He felt humiliated. He put Beulah aside and went after Laveen. He grabbed his shoulder, pulled him around and punched him in the face.

Quick as a flash, Laveen had his knee up and into Rowley's balls. He left him on the ground, doubled up in pain. Rowley vomited.

Jenny bent over him, trembling, her slightly secured peace from the twilight swim utterly shattered, and along with it the calm and sanity of the preciously happy foregoing weeks at Arthur's.

When she awoke the next morning, she saw that some time

153

between when she had tried to ease Rowley's pain and when she went to her bed or, who knows, maybe while sleepwalking during the night, she had got a large rock from the garden and set it on her bedside table.

31

One deafened ear, one black eye, two tender balls, three sore hearts, and a partridge in a pear tree. The score of walking wounded and lying-down wounded was mounting. How could there be so much violence among so few people in this most sylvan, tranquil place of all, Arthur wondered. My proscribing it doesn't seem to matter one whit. No one pays the least attention to me. And I'm forgetting Rowley's battered head, the first blow struck. And Horacio has one of those too, a similar sap-type wound. Hmmmn.

Arthur was walking around his property, deep in thought. It was the next morning and he was first up. Everyone had taken supper to their rooms the night before, in separate secret forays to the kitchen, wanting to keep to themselves.

Except for Jess, who had ladled him out an exhausting night of ardour, tears, and anger. Although she claimed she yearned for their days of peace and quiet, she certainly did seem to revel in all this excitement, in flaying his house guests up and down and sideways.

Wow, what a mean tongue that woman had between such adorable lips, convinced as she was that the only way Arthur could like her best was to have pointed out to him the hideous flaws of every other person he was in contact with. How could she understand him so little? How could she be such a fool as to think his mind had such a paltry grasp of human affairs that in order to love her he had to hate everyone else? It was insane, really. Jess loved him insanely. She was an obsessed woman. In all other aspects of her life, she was in control, superior. But in regard to her love for him, she was a blithering idiot. How did he live with it, with her? He guessed in his own way he loved her insanely too, or else wanted, needed, to be loved insanely by someone so beautiful. It was, of course, damned flattering in its way.

But, damn it, he hadn't meant to waste this time in thoughts of Jess. He had to do some serious thinking about Laveen. Was he to be trusted? What about the painting? Did Laveen have the real one? Or did Horacio? Did one of them hide the valuable one and arrange the other as a red herring? Did Laveen? What about the violence? Had Laveen shot Horacio? He'd been peeved about Horacio all along. Did he shoot Horacio and leave him for dead, because Horacio knew Laveen was double-crossing Arthur, knew somehow about the painting switch? What about the missing tape, the tape that would have disclosed Laveen's entire interview with Jenny? Maybe something else had developed during that talk besides what Laveen reported.

He says Jess planted the tape in his bathroom, but I only have his word for that, Arthur reasoned. I never did ask Jess about it. I'd better do that now. For that's what it comes down to: if Laveen lied about that tape, he is lying about everything else. If he didn't, then I am wronging the poor fellow and between us we must figure this thing out.

Arthur went back to his room and woke Jess up. She was fully alert at once, one of the nice things about her. She was never groggy in the morning, never in a stupor.

'Jess, I have an important question to ask you and I want you to be completely honest with me. Many things hang on your answer.'

'How exciting. It makes me feel so important. Fire away, my darling. Can I wash my face first? I hate to have you see me all puffy-eyed.'

'You look gorgeous. Your eyes are like lamps.'

'Oh well, then,' she smirked. 'In that case, carry on.'

'It is about the –'

'But do at least pass me my brush so that I can untangle my hair while we talk.'

'Jess, I am passing you the brush and then I want your full attention. Not another word about how you look.'

She gave him her full attention.

'I placed a tape in Beulah's room. Three days ago when I retrieved it, there were only bathroom sounds on it.'

Jess moved uneasily.

'Laveen says you had placed it in his bathroom.'

'Oh!'

'Yes. There is nothing, absolutely nothing, one can put over on Laveen. Now, tell me please, did you put the tape in his bathroom?'

'Well, I, er – yes.'

'And then, without erasing it, you returned it to Beulah's room?'

'Yes.' Jess was blushing uncomfortably.

'How much time was it gone?'

'Let me think.' She put an exquisite finger to her brow to illustrate the thinking process. 'That was the day Horacio went to town. It wasn't until the afternoon, when Beulah came away from her writing that I was able to get it, and I guess it was before dinner that I put it back. Way before. I'm sure that it was only a couple of hours that it was gone – a time when Beulah is rarely in her room – so that I thought it would be OK. I do apologize for interfering. It was wrong of me, I know. It was only out of love for you.'

'Of course,' said Arthur wryly. 'What other reason could it possibly have been? But tell me, because I confess I am baffled, how was it out of love for me that you put a bug in Laveen's bathroom?'

'To see if he had a penis.'

Arthur was silent.

'You see, the tape would declare whether or not the toilet seat went up. Wasn't that clever of me? It's too bad I had to hear all those other disgusting sounds as well. Ugh!' She shivered with distaste. No one could do a distasteful shiver as

156

well as Jess.

'And did he have a penis?' Arthur asked.

'Why, yes, he did.'

'That must have been a great relief to you.'

'Enormous! Not his penis, you understand – my relief.'

Arthur laughed heartily. 'You stand alone, Jess. You are one in a million.' he bent over and kissed her and she pulled him down on the bed. She smiled beguilingly. 'Just kiss my titties for two minutes and then I'll let you go.'

He did. He kissed her breasts for two minutes, then left them to suckle her for half an hour, giving her absolute paroxysms of pleasure.

'Now I must go to Horacio,' he said. 'I want to be the first to talk with him when he wakes up. So you only have thirty seconds to tell me how wonderful I am.'

'But it would take me thirty years!'

'Just make a beginning.'

He was surprised to see her grow profoundly thoughtful and then say, in all earnestness, tears standing out in her eyes, 'My darling Arthur, there are no words, especially from *my* mouth. Let me for once just be silent for half a minute.' She took his hand and looked gravely at him for thirty seconds.

Arthur went away smiling, feeling quite touched. How charming, he thought. How clever she is. He completely forgot how she'd exasperated him all night long.

And Jess lay back, feeling pleased with Arthur and with herself. Why can't I be that nice all the time, she thought. I guess being silent is the key. It's easy to be nice with your mouth closed. That's why Rowley is so extremely nice. But boring. Beulah will end up with Horacio, I bet. I think that's apparent to the meanest eye. Of course, if Horacio's going to be deaf too, then he'll be boring. I simply couldn't bear for a man not to hear me. But that was a lovely silent moment between me and Arthur. It will make him forget my bad behaviour in the night and he will only think how charming I am. But it is true that I couldn't find the words to describe his wonderfulness. I've said them all a million times. I want new

157

words to express my love for Arthur. I'll ask Beulah. She's good with words. They seem to come straight from her feelings without going through all that short-circuiting in between, as mine do while I figure their effect. I wonder how she does that?

Jess went into the bathroom to do a perfect poo, then decided to sleep for another hour.

32

'Horacio, dear boy,' said Arthur, as soon as his nephew opened his eyes.

I've been ambushed, thought Horacio, referring not to the events of the previous day but to this moment of awakening with Arthur crouched by his side.

Arthur would have preferred him to awaken a little later, as he still hadn't figured how to ask him about the painting when he himself was not suppposed to know that it existed.

'How are you feeling? You look awful.'

'I feel awful. I want some sex. I haven't had sex in over a week. I haven't gone that long since I was seventeen. I'm getting hot flashes. Seriously.'

'It's your own fault. The lovely Beulah has been here the entire time.'

'She's too nice. Too happy. I want a mean, sullen bitch.' Horacio sat up and grimaced with pain. 'Why is she so damned happy?' he asked, figuring it was a good, safe subject. 'I really want to know.'

'Maybe she's happy because she's nice. And honest. Maybe honesty is the best policy, after all. Wouldn't it be a shame if we'd been wrong all along? Why, oh why, is Beulah happy? Let us say that she lives in the fullness of her potential. She does not ever diminish herself or her daily existence by − inimical acts or thoughts. Hmmm. Rather a nice definition.'

'Yes, yes, very good.' Horacio hadn't been listening very hard but encouraged Arthur. 'Is she never sad, then?'

'Oh yes. I think she is so deeply sad, essentially, that she grasps like a child for happiness, and like a child is easily pleased, easily moved to smiles and tears.'

'But didn't she have some trouble about throwing rocks at people which is why she was at Fair Haven? I call that pretty damned inimical.'

Arthur paused before answering to see if Horacio would realize that he'd blown his secret about knowing who Beulah was. No, he didn't seem to realize − so interested was he in the discussion. It's hard, Arthur thought uncritically, not only to remember what we know but to remember who knows that we know what we know (or don't know). Maybe that means I could ask about the painting and Horacio would not remember that I don't know about it.

'Take your time answering. I'm not going anywhere.'

'Yes, she did. I have a theory about that, admittedly a simple one.'

'Shoot.'

'It's an outlet. Anger, hostility, and their ilk go so against her nature that she is unable to give expression to them, can't get in touch with those feelings even when they're perfectly justified.'

'So, when they come upon her, her mind shuts down and her body picks up a rock.'

'Yes, afterwards she can't imagine why she did such a thing; if she even remembers. But, for the most part, the poor darling didn't even throw the rocks, she only gathered them.' Arthur scrutinized Horacio. 'How are you really? I'm glad you've got your hearing back.'

'Had I lost it?' I wish I'd known that, he thought. Then I could have pretended to be deaf still and not have been able to talk to anyone. Except Rowley.

159

'Yes, since your ear was shot off. The doctor says a plastic surgeon can supply you with another.'

'That's good. Well, I guess I'll have a little nap now.'

'I won't stay much longer but I want to know what transpired with you yesterday. Naturally I'm deeply concerned.'

Horacio said bitterly, 'I was robbed twice. Two sets of thieves. Twice set upon, I was. I thought there was honour among us. It's not right to steal from each other, is it, Arthur?'

'If you had stolen the item that was stolen from you, that would make three sets of thieves.'

'Item? Did you say item? Why not suppose it was cash?'

'Because you are a stealer of items,' said Arthur. There was a rare glint of anger in his eyes. 'Let's not play games. You are a guest in my home. You have been attacked. I want to know how this happened and I want to know now.'

'The first set of thieves shot me, the next set thumped me. I imagine the painting – the item was a painting – is gone. I had not stolen it but was honourably taking it up to the city to sell for young Beulah.'

Arthur thought he sounded pretty straight.

'I was being a good-hearted messenger-boy for her so she could keep her happiness intact. I'm embarrassed. I handled the thing stupidly. Really stupidly.'

If it had all gone right, Horacio thought grumpily, I'd have the painting myself, claim it was stolen from me, and Arthur would believe that Laveen had stolen it as planned. When Laveen claimed not to have it, Arthur would smell a double-cross. It would have been fine. But now Laveen has the damned thing and I don't. Or does he? Wait a minute. Apparently Laveen has claimed not to have it and Arthur does smell a double-cross. How interesting. Otherwise, Arthur would not be questioning me.

'Did you have anything to do with either set of thieves, Uncle?' he inquired ingenuously.'

'Do you think I would hurt you?'

'No, I don't.' Horacio suddenly drooped. Perspiration burst from his brow.

'I'm tiring you. Sleep some more. I'll see you later. Just ring one of us when you want anything.'

'I want a woman,' Horacio said desperately. He threw back the bed covers. 'I'll have to get up and go away from here.' He got out of bed, then staggered.

'No,' said Arthur firmly. 'I insist you lie abed as prescribed.'

'I've got to go. Where are my clothes?' Horacio began reeling around like a blind man. He flapped his arms meaninglessly. 'Sex,' he said. 'I've got to fuck.' His head fell on to one shoulder, his mouth fell open, and his tongue protruded. 'Pussy!' His body went into a jerking motion, fell to the rug, writhed horribly. Foam gathered at the corners of his mouth.

Arthur watched with interest, smiling. He'd seen Horacio go into his fit routine before but, even so, it was hard not to be taken in by it. Especially when it got to the foam. Such a nice touch. Convincing. The boy was good.

'All right now, get up and get back into bed. I've been many things to you: uncle, mentor, closest friend. Your procurer, never. However, I'll see what I can do.'

Horacio got back into bed. 'I'll be here,' he said.

'I know how he feels,' said Jess. 'Some people can't go two days without sex without going bananas.'

'I think it's particularly pressing for Horacio because of yesterday's fiasco. Horacio never makes a mess of things and yesterday, whatever happened, was a mess. So he's feeling insecure as well as thoroughly depressed. For some, sex is the best sop to insecurity. It makes you feel a man again, if briefly.'

'But haven't you said it's complicated with him, that he needs a sense of danger and excitement to make it all work?'

'Yes, but I don't think that's beyond us do you? He'd be jeopardizing his broken head to leave here now and, you see, it's terribly important to me that Horacio does not leave us just yet.'

'I see.'

'Oh, my, Horacio,' said Jess, coming into his room. 'You do look poorly. You have this terrible wild-eyed intensity, as if you're about to burst out of your skin. Arthur has confided to me your desperate need and I have thought to myself: if I have an ounce of family feeling, I should help the boy out. He'd do as much for me.'

'What?' Horacio was puzzled.

Jess began unbuttoning an array of tiny buttons on her blouse. She had chosen this blouse particularly. There were endless buttons.

'Are you kidding!' said Horacio, alarmed, as he got the message. (Alarmed and therefore aroused.)

'These buttons are maddening. Here, you do them.' She leaned over him to display her spectacular breasts.

Horacio leapt from the bed and clasped his head in pain. 'Aargh!'

'No, just be still.' She pulled him down. 'And let me do the work. See' – she pointed to his bulging pyjama bottoms – 'you can't say you're not getting interested.'

'I'm not going to fuck you, Jess.'

'Of course you are. Think of it as medicinal. I'm the nurse. I know exactly what you're going through and I won't have you suffer. It's nothing to me. You know I love Arthur. I'm just here as a friend of the family. To ease you.'

'Well, be a real good friend and hightail it out of here.' Horacio pulled the blankets up over his head and curled into a ball. Jess calmly finished undressing then started to tug the blankets off him.

He was so cleverly cocooned that she couldn't extricate him. She went, therefore, to the end of the bed to unpluck the blankets therefrom. She tunnelled into the bedcovers towards him and into the very cocoon itself. Her voice came muffled and chagrined, 'Oh, now you're all wilted. How disappointing. You've undone the effect of my entrance and my buttons. Also, I'm not at my best where I can't be seen. And where I can't breathe.'

'Wilted I will remain,' said Horacio. And he was right. Only his voice was firm. 'Go away.'

162

'Can't we have some air? I'm smothering. What if I die here all naked in your bed. What then?'

Horacio, moving slowly and carefully this time, got out of the bed. Jess had accomplished something in the meantime – his pyjamas were off. But his cock was still dejected.

She clambered out after him and embraced him.

'I don't want to have to strike you, Jess, but it may come to that.' Suddenly he froze as he heard Arthur's voice beyond the door.

'Ah, here we are.'

Here who are? Horacio wondered, stiff with the fear of discovery – cock getting stiff too.

'What a nice idea to bring Horacio his breakfast. Let me get the door for you,' said Arthur.

It must be Jenny, Horacio realized. Laveen wouldn't bring me breakfast. His sex was rising higher with every word. He spread-eagled himself against the lockless door. Jess was exuberant.

'Better knock first,' came Jenny's voice.

Good idea, Horacio thought. 'Jess,' he hissed, 'get the hell away and get dressed. Do something!'

She whispered into his good ear. 'See how you're rising and swelling, Horacio. All rosily rising and looking so swell,' she said admiringly. 'Let's quickly take advantage.'

While Arthur knocked, Horacio grabbed up Jess's clothes and tried to dress her. It was hopeless.

'His hearing is impaired,' said Arthur. 'Probably he can't hear us. Let's just go right in.'

The blood pounded through Horacio, coursing to *all* his extremities. He ran around the room like one berserk, Jess hot on his tail (literally).

'No,' said Jenny, 'I don't want to disturb him if he's sleeping.'

Good girl! Horacio applauded.

'I'll go round and look in the window,' said Arthur. 'You wait here.

Jess was pressing her body against Horacio's. 'Quickly now, before he's at the window. There's just time.'

'Let me pull the curtain.' He tried to pull away, amazed at her strength. Or at his weakness.

'No! I can't let you go. We must seize the second. Down here on the floor by the bed where we can't be seen from the window.'

'You're crazy!'

But it was Horacio who was looking crazed. She pulled him down on top of her, kicking one foot out from under him so that he fell to his knees.

'Horacio?' Jenny called. She must have heard the bump.

'Don't come in,' he choked out. 'I'll call you in a little while.' Whereupon he plunged fervently into Jess.

Oh dear, thought Jess, as the minutes passed. I'd forgotten what big, strong lovers young men are. There really is a difference. Ow!

Horacio's final release was explosive and Jess kept him coming and coming until he was drained of the last drop.

He collapsed down on her, semi-conscious.

All was quiet at door and window. Horacio had no idea how much time had gone by. It could even be the next day. Probably was.

Jess let him lie for a bit then roused him to return to his bed. She gathered her clothes and went into his bathroom. When she came out, neatly dressed, make-up reapplied, he smiled fondly at her.

'Thank you, Jess. You're terrific.'

She put a finger to her lips, winked at him, and left.

Pretty good for a 52-year-old, she thought smugly. Of course, Arthur had helped.

Horacio, invaded by a wondrous calm, deeply slept.

33

With Horacio thus succoured and replenished, Arthur set off for the sickroom a few hours later for another interview with him.

In the meantime he'd had a rousing set of tennis with Rowley and a mile swim. In this way, with the blood set coursing to his brain by the physical activity, he was able to explore further the puzzle of the wrong painting. He now felt that he could definitely continue to trust Laveen. That left two possibilities. One: that the other thieves had got the painting. Two: that there were no other thieves, that Horacio himself was the other thieves, that he had taken Jenny's painting and replaced it with the other to baffle Laveen and Arthur. This idea seemed the most convincing to Arthur. It was very much in keeping with what the police would call 'Horacio's psychological profile'.

Scratch Laveen, he thought. Scratch the other thieves. Horacio has the painting. I must make a deal with the lad.

But wait! What about the shot? If the other thieves were an invention, they couldn't very well have shot him. If I am to believe Laveen, and I've decided to believe Laveen, he did not shoot Horacio. Who, then? Would Horacio come that close to death simply to give credence to the invented theft? No. Even a week of stringent celibacy wouldn't make him that crazy.

But he has been depressed. The thing could have been a botched suicide attempt.

In the midst of a caper?

Yes. It could have been an honest suicide attempt disguised *to himself* as an element in the caper. Horacio is complicated enough for that.

Dear me, this is all extremely sensitive. Very tricky indeed.

Jenny lay in Rowley's arms, not being passionate, being fond. They were in his cottage, during his lunch hour, after his game with Arthur. He had showered, then they had eaten a salad together, and now they lay silently, her face pressed into his shoulder.

He has a delicate, stony scent, she thought. His skin is warm and smooth like a river rock that has lain in the sun. He is as hard as that rock from all his muscles, but smooth and soft feeling like a sun-scented stone. My Rowley. My dearest sweetheart. What a comfort to lie thus enfolded, to feel his caring. It's so simple, really. Just to love one another, man and woman, to do your work each day, eat your meals, talk together. Why has it all got so complicated of late, personalities so hagridden we can't make this simple basic connection to feel the caring and comfort we so desperately need. We fight it. We want to be free to do our work, to live, develop – as if love were an enslavement, not a resource.

No sooner did she think that than she began to feel restless and even physically uncomfortable. Cramped. She didn't want to move and disturb Rowley. She didn't want to talk to him or make love. She realized that she wanted to go to Horacio, see how he was, find out what had happened. He'd sounded so peculiar when he'd shouted to her to call him later in the day. What was going on in this bucolic setting? Why was everyone fighting, hitting, kicking, and even shooting?

Laveen, she knew, was at the centre, was the eye of the storm.

Suddenly she had a brilliant idea of how to get rid of Laveen. She saw that she should have done it at once and couldn't imagine, now, why she hadn't. Doubtless because of some misguided urge to protect Arthur.

She stirred with excitement and quickly sat up before Rowley misinterpreted it.

She was all aquiver. 'Rowley, love, I've got to go and talk

with Arthur. Thank you for the nice visit. I feel so refreshed and calmed. It has allowed me to think an excellent thought. I'll see you after work, Rowley, OK?'

'OK, baby.'

They kissed and parted.

Rowley stood at the door of his cottage watching Beulah traverse the lawn, which appeared blue in the light of the partly clouded day – except for the grass of her passage, which seemed to turn saffron-coloured from the sun through her yellow frock, or from her own wondrous glow.

He sighed with happiness. He had such a good sense of himself, of his own worth, since Beulah loved him. He, who had carried the double stigma of his handicap and of his social deviance, now felt purified. He felt, too, that he was acceptable in society's eyes as well as his own, that they would no longer look at him and see only a crook and a dummy, but a man of substance.

But he quailed, realizing that he still owed society, owed double now that he'd broken more rules by escaping. He saw that, as good as he felt about himself, he still could offer Beulah nothing more as a lover than a deaf, hunted felon.

He could turn himself back in, but how could he leave all this fullness of life for the cold, stupid ugliness of prison?

No matter. Whatever happened, he would have had this time. No one could take it from him. Whatever happened, he would continue to feel love for Beulah in his heart, and no matter how hunted, how captured, a sense of freedom in his soul. And, finally, no matter how thoroughly marked by disgrace he might be in society's eyes, to himself, because Beulah loved him, he could burst wide open, so full did he feel of her grace, which was not only her loveliness but her pardon.

Horacio and Arthur were at last laying their cards on the table and there were a lot of them to lay. The metaphorical table could have sat sixteen.

They had both come to the stunning realization that Jenny

herself still had the painting – stunning in its obviousness, once realized.

First, from the drift of Arthur's close questioning, Horacio was convinced that Laveen had not got it. It was then Arthur arrived at the understanding that Horacio didn't have it either.

Then they began to tell all. Arthur explicated the entire plan from the beginning, and Horacio was interested to learn that its origins were way back when Arthur, learning of the artist's ill health, had set out to ascertain who owned his few canvases – since their worth was bound to skyrocket posthumously – and was delighted to learn that his old friend Jenny had one.

'I can't believe she pulled a fast one on me,' Horacio said, shaking his head dolefully. 'What about all that childlike niceness of hers you were telling me about? I really had come around to feeling she was pretty special. I was suckered. Not only happy and nice, I thought, but also so impeccably honest that Diogenes himself would rejoice.'

'Diogenes would have been disappointed as hell,' Arthur scoffed. 'What would he have done then? How proceed? Of course all of us cynics are terribly vulnerable. Deep in our hearts we don't want to by cynical. More than anyone else we want to believe in honesty and goodness. That's why we look for it more than other people do. But we don't want to find it. We want to be ratified in our belief that it doesn't exist and that we are right to be cynical.

'As for Jenny, I don't think she was pulling a fast one, Horacio. She was continuing in her good-heartedness. I haven't told you yet how, after hearing the tape of your conversation with her, I tried to dissuade her from putting any trust in you. I told her you were a professional thief. I think, rather than hurt you by expressing any distrust in you, she elected to give you the wrong painting. If you'd made off with it, no harm done. In the unlikely event that you did deliver it, she could fix up the mistake.'

'Why not simply say she'd changed her mind about me taking it?'

'She was too scared to go herself. And she had Laveen to reckon with. She needed the money.'

'I still think we've been conned. Do you realize that she's in a fabulous position right now? She still has the painting, but she's released from having to pay Laveen, since I've said it was stolen and, because I've reported the theft, she could collect the insurance.'

'Where in hell does she keep that thing?' Arthur wondered. 'I've looked everywhere. She still trusts me, of course. Why don't I offer to recompense her for her loss so that she can own up to me all about it? She is so honest that she couldn't possibly take money for the loss of something she still has. Won't that force her hand?'

Horacio laughed. 'I remain cynical. It's too tempting for her. Then she could have the painting, the insurance, *and* the recompense money. She's caught up in a lie and could remain in it quite comfortably – a million and a half dollars' worth of comfortable.'

'I still believe in her,' said Arthur. 'I'll offer to make up for her loss with the sum of its worth, and she'll admit she still has it. You'll see.'

'Want to make a little bet on that?'

At that moment there was a knock at the door. 'It's me, Beulah,' she called.

'Come in,' said Horacio. He and Arthur raised their eyebrows at each other. They pressed palms. 'A thousand dollars.' said Horacio.

'It's a bet,' said Arthur.

As Jenny entered, she felt that Arthur and Horacio had a rather conspiratorial air about them. They seemed to be giving her funny looks. Not the fish-eye exactly, but something akin to it, as if they'd been talking about her, speculating about her, as if she were an over-the-counter stock they were in two minds whether to invest in.

She was struck by the resemblance of the two men that was both familial and affinitive. Arthur was a larger man. Horacio, from his Indian mother, was graceful, darker-

169

complected, also less aristocratic, less pure-bred. His face was not as vibrant as Arthur's, nor as handsome – until he smiled. He had that gorgeous smile, whereas Arthur's smile was a devilish, comical curve that tickled you just to observe, even if you weren't in on the joke.

'Hi,' she greeted them, feeling shy, feeling found out. But how could they possibly know? They couldn't.

'Hello. Come in.' They, too, seemed shy. It was as if they were, all three, meeting on a new footing.

'I'm so sorry about this, Horacio. I feel very much to blame. Are you going to be all right? Your head? Your ear?'

'My earlessness. Yes, I'll be fine. But your painting is as gone as my ear is. I'm sorry to have let you down. I just told Arthur that it was your painting which was stolen from me. I hope that was all right?'

'Yes. I don't care about the painting as long as you are all right. Have you really lost an ear? How horrible. God, I feel awful.'

Jenny looked faint. She sat down on the end of the bed. 'Is the whole thing gone?' she asked tremulously.

'Not to worry. They can make me a new one out of my elbow. No problem.'

'But it would cost so much money. I should pay for it.' (She was beating them to the offer of recompense money, Horacio thought humourously. Was it to find out if he really still had his ear?)

'Hell, no,' he responded. 'It is I who should pay you for the lost painting.'

(Here, Arthur glared at Horacio for jumping the gun. It was he, Arthur, who was to make this offer. They couldn't have all three of them wanting to pay each other recompense money.)

'Is it insured?' Horacio went on blithely.

'Why, I'm not sure. I imagine so. Damon never said, but it wouldn't be like him to neglect such a thing.'

'*I* should recompense you,' said Arthur. 'All this happened in my home. I am the one who is responsible.'

'No, you're not. But I'll tell you who is. It is Laveen,' said

Jenny. 'I have decided to tell you the whole story. Horacio already knows. Now I realize that you should know, that you would *want* to know. Laveen blackmailed me. He said he knew who I was and would see that I was locked up again in Fair Haven if I didn't pay him fifty thousand dollars!'

'Why, this is shocking!' Arthur rose to the occasion with magnificent umbrage. 'This is the most dastardly thing I have ever heard.'

'I had to sell my painting, which I love with all my heart, to raise the money.'

'But why didn't you tell me?' Arthur asked.

'I felt it was my business, that I shouldn't involve you in it. You had done so much for me already, inviting me here, helping me through my change of circumstance. All I wanted was to be able to stay a while longer – feeling well, growing strong. It seemed a simple matter just to sell the painting and give Laveen what he wanted. He said he'd go away immediately, to Europe. I confided in Horacio because I was too afraid to go to town myself. And now this horrible thing has happened to Horacio. He's maimed!'

(Maimed? thought Horacio for the first time. How ghastly!)

'We must report Laveen to the police at once,' said Arthur. 'Never mind that he's an old friend . . .'

'No, don't do that. He still might tell. I thought I would ask you, please, to tell him to leave here. I know he is a friend. Perhaps you feel that it is I who should go . . . I should go, really.' Her voice quavered. 'But I don't feel able to . . .'

'You certainly won't go. I wouldn't hear of it. He will go. I'll dispatch him at once. He's no longer a friend. He has forfeited any claim to friendship. What a breach of hospitality. It is positively vile.'

'He is vile, Arthur,' Jenny said heatedly. 'Truly vile. I don't think you realize . . .'

'I agree,' said Horacio. 'Vile.'

Arthur flashed him a warning eye.

At that moment, Laveen himself knocked and entered. Even with his dark glasses, the discoloration of one eye was apparent. 'What an interesting gathering,' he commented. Laveen never said anything, he commented.

He thinks he's such a big fucking deal, Horacio thought. Master criminal, wanted by the FBI, Interpol, probably the CIA to boot. Arthur says I'm jealous because I'm not wanted by anybody. I am. I'm jealous because he's a legend and I'm not. Hardly anyone, alive, gets to be a legend.

Arthur rose majestically to his feet. 'Laveen,' he said, 'Jenny accuses you of blackmailing her. She says you demanded fifty thousand dollars to keep you from divulging her identity and returning her to Fair Haven. Is this true?'

Laveen paused a moment then said, 'Yes.'

'Heinous,' said Arthur, managing to look deeply disappointed, even sickened.

'I needed the money. Blackmail is so much quicker than earning it.'

'I could have loaned it to you.'

Laveen shrugged. 'Then I'd have owed it. Tiresome.'

'I must ask you to leave the estate at once, and if I hear any outlying murmur to the fact of Maria Lopez lodging here with me, you will be in for much stronger recriminations.'

Laveen played the game. 'Very well, I'll be going in an hour or so. I have some clothes in the wash. I never pack wet clothes.' He turned and left the room.

Jenny gasped with relief, smiled, hugged Arthur warmly. 'Thank you. Thank you with all my heart.'

'I could do no less. It's a small thing. However, I'm afraid I will not be entirely happy until you allow me to replace the worth of the stolen painting. We can hope that the police will discover it, but I'll bet it is far out of the country by now. The money is nothing to me. It is everything to you. It's time you began to realize that.'

'Arthur, your letting me stay here is beyond price. It is worth more to me than a Rembrandt. Yea, a Dürer! I would *never* take money from you.'

'But I insist!'

She hugged and kissed him again. (Horacio was getting jealous. Why hadn't she hugged him when he offered?)

'You will insist in vain,' she said.
'But, damn it . . .' Arthur said querulously.
Horacio began to laugh. 'Give it up,' he said.
'Horacio's right,' said Jenny. 'Give it up.'

34

After she left, both Arthur and Horacio claimed they'd won the bet.

'It's clear that I won,' said Arthur. 'She wouldn't accept the money.'

'But she didn't come clean. That was inherent in the bet. That she'd come clean and say she still had the painting. You bet that she'd be unable to maintain the lie because of her goodness, especially when she heard your kind-hearted offer.'

'Why didn't she come clean?' Arthur honestly wondered. 'She loves us both, trusts *me* at least. She is, at this point, damned grateful to both of us. As well she should be. So why didn't she come clean? She *owes* it to us to tell all. Look at all we've done for her. And you practically lost your life for her. What if she *is* outfoxing us? Or what if we're wrong and she doesn't have the painting?'

'She has it.'

'Yes, I'm convinced that she does.'

'Heinous,' said Horacio, laughing. 'Pretty damned heinous of her, I'd say. Not to mention dastardly.'

'But who would listen to anything a maimed man would say?' Arthur asked. 'Who would even want to look at a maimed man?'

'How vile of you,' said Horacio.

The painting was out and about in Beulah's room, where Rowley was sewing up the split-open rear of a pair of jeans and Beulah was reading a book. There was a fire in the fireplace and Beulah looked up from her book to think what a pleasant domestic scene it was. She looked at the painting and observed that it did not reflect the spirit of her room but looked, today, rather menacing.

It certainly had a mind of its own, for her own mind felt entirely free from menace now that she had dealt with the Laveen problem so satisfactorily. He was going away. Out of her life forever. Hooray!

She looked again at the painting. Was it trying to tell her something? No, that was absurd. Bad enough to love the painting as much as she did and to anthropomorphize it so that she felt she had to give it air and light. Not food yet, thank God – although surely it did nourish itself from its environment even if it didn't reflect it. But now, if she was going to begin to think that it tried to communicate with her, she'd be in real trouble.

'What are you thinking about the painting?' Rowley asked.

She turned to him, laughing self-consciously. 'I was thinking it was trying to tell me something.'

'Tell you what?'

'Oh, well, I was feeling so peaceful here with you, both of us absorbed in something, yet being so close together in this nice atmosphere of the cheerful fire and the light of the day drawing in, and the tiny cheeping bird outside that manages to sound like an enormous baby chicken. It's all so nice . . . Then I looked at the painting and it seemed to tell me not to be fooled.'

'Probably you are feeling worried about something yourself. Why don't you try to talk to me about it?'

'But I'm not! I was worried about Laveen. But he is going away. I heard Arthur ask him to go. This is a great relief to me. I believe it was Laveen who hit you the other night, and I wouldn't be surprised if it was Laveen who hurt Horacio too.'

174

Because he was after the painting, she thought – but couldn't say, because Rowley didn't know that she had asked Horacio to take it to San Francisco for her. How very much she had kept from Rowley. It wasn't right. And yet, she had shared the painting with him. Only with him. But she had confided a whole lot more to Horacio.

'Why the rocks?' Rowley asked.

There were now three rocks on her bedside table and two on the bricks by the fireplace.

'I've been wondering about these rocks,' he said.

Jenny blushed. 'The rocks? Well, they're sort of pretty, don't you think?'

'No, they're not,' said Rowley. 'They're just rocks.'

'You're right. I guess it makes me feel good to have them here in the room with me. I don't know why.'

'You *are* worried then.'

'I really don't think I am – now that Laveen is going.'

Rowley came over to her and pulled her from the chair into his arms. 'You don't need rocks. You have me. Let me be your rock. I'll look after you. I won't let anyone hurt you.'

He looked so grave and sweet. He was big, strong, young, devoted. He would not let anyone hurt her. But he was vulnerable. He had been knocked unconscious and rendered helpless with pain. All his strength and youth and devotion were useless to her then.

Is that why she felt she had to depend on herself, on her rocks, or on whatever they stood for?

If only I did think I was a penguin building a nest, she thought. That would be so lovely and so simple.

'You're right, Rowley. Throw the rocks away. I don't need those stupid old rocks.'

He smiled happily and did as he was bidden.

As he left her room with the rocks, Jenny felt overcome by anxiety. I want my rocks, she thought. I need my rocks. I just said that to please Rowley, to make him feel important and needed. Why should I give up my rocks to please him? His love can't protect me like they can. His love can't protect me at all. It just puts more pressure on me if I have to worry about him and his feelings and make him feel needed and give up my rocks just to salve his ego.

But what have rocks ever done for me except signal to Damon it was time to incarcerate me once again?

How can one rock alter anything for me? For the better, that is?

Well, nothing can hurt a rock. A rock can't be kicked in the balls.

Rocks emanate power, make me feel safe. I have never thrown a rock. It is the most harmless thing in the world to have a few rocks around the house – for company. I would never want to hurt a human being. I could not live with myself two minutes if I ever really hurt someone.

And yet, how can you live, Oh, how can you live without hurting people and being hurt by them if you want to embrace life even a tiny bit, let alone fully?

She glowered at Rowley when he returned.

'What is it?' he asked.

She didn't tell him she wanted her rocks back. She would go and get them later. And hide them.

It wasn't Rowley's fault, she reminded herself. By taking her rocks away, he had only done what she had asked of him.

But he *made* her ask it of him.

'You look like you're going to cry. What is it, baby? Do you want your rocks back?'

She nodded dumbly. 'I'll get you your rocks,' he said. 'I'll bring them right back, OK?'

Oh dear, she thought, I'm not doing very well. I'm not doing very well at all.

He brought back the rocks and took her trembling self into his arms, comforting her. 'My poor baby,' he said, 'my poor baby.'

She felt revolted. I'm not your poor baby, she thought helplessly.

Before Laveen left, Arthur told him that he and Horacio would take it from here on, but that he would still get a third for the work he'd done.

176

'You can see,' he said, 'that there is no way we can include you now since she has forced me to drive you off. I am convinced that she still has the painting in hand. If I and Horacio can't get hold of it within twenty-four hours we might as well hang it up and get a job digging ditches.'

'I see that it is expedient for me to go,' Laveen said, 'but I don't want you to be blinded by your affection for Horacio. I have observed him. I'm sure he is a fine cat burglar where his most important strength,' he said with contempt, 'is the ability to walk silently. However, in my opinion he is of no use on a caper like this. He is unsteady and undependable. He is attached to Jenny. His is a man who will draw wrong conclusions at a minute's notice. He seems unable to correlate what his senses report to his mind.'

Arthur nodded. He thought Laveen was probably right.

'Use Rowley,' was Laveen's parting advice. 'Tell her you'll turn him in if she doesn't come up with the painting. Get tough with the little bitch.'

'That's just what I can't do, even if it were my style. I'm her trusted friend. You could have done that because you were playing the bad guy.'

'I didn't *play*,' said Laveen.

Arthur thought, That is the difference between us.

'Take my advice,' Laveen reiterated. 'Use the dummy. It's a natural. It's a much stronger hold than the threat of her own reincarceration since she's so fucking altruistic. I hate that woman.'

'Understandably. And I'm glad you said that because there you have your essential problem highlighted beautifully.'

'Problem? Are you kidding? I have no problem.'

'Your woman problem. I've been thinking about it. You've got to find one you won't hate even a little. You've got to get to know a woman and like her if you want her to respond to you.'

'Horacio has fantastic success with woman, according to you, and I'd say he likes them as little as I do. In fact, he can't perform with a woman he's fond of.'

'It depends upon what kind of success we're talking about.

Do you want a hundred women once? Or one woman often?'

'To begin with – one woman once.' He mused. 'Yes, and I would like it to be Jenny. I will do as you suggest. I'll get to know her. In another guise, of course. I will come back into her life as someone else entirely and get her.'

Arthur shivered. 'You don't understand, Laveen. We are talking about love here, not vengeance.'

Arthur dressed for dinner, pondering the caper, reflecting on Laveen's advice. He went to the bar and poured himself a rum, then wandered off to the kitchen thinking, Horacio will have to be the bad guy. I'm too much of a sweetheart.

35

Everyone was wandering into the kitchen. While the night before there had been individual, furtive forays to that room, tonight everyone was gathering there from some sort of herd instinct. There was an air of reunion, of celebration. The terrible Laveen had departed and *everyone* was relieved and glad.

Rowley was preparing a salad of snow peas, cucumbers, courgettes, and three lettuces. Two chickens turned on the rotisserie and periodically he basted them with wine, herbs, and their own juices.

While Jenny set out a board of cheeses and breads, Jess pulled the cork from a bottle of Château St Jean Gewurztraminer.

Rowley had brought in a patio lounger for Horacio so he could be at his ease, and he was much at ease, quaffing a Kirin and jesting with Jenny, who looked dressy for once in a blue silk toga-type dress that swirled and fluttered about her with any slight movement or gesture.

Jess raised her glass. 'I'm going to make a toast,' she declared. 'I came to a fantastic decision today, which was that I would befriend Beulah. I've never had a woman friend because if they are anything like me, and I must assume that they are, I simply can't trust them. The Indians say, Don't judge a man until you have walked a mile in his moccasins. I am a harsh judge of women because I have walked thousands of miles in their high heels and bedroom slippers. Beulah is different.'

But Jess didn't drink. Her hand faltered. She set down the glass. 'Now, at the last second, I shrink from the toast. It's too late for me to begin having women friends. My whole nature revolts. You must be my sister or my daughter to have my allegiance. So I will pretend that you are.' She smiled and drank. 'And, if you marry Horacio, we will be related: I will be your aunt.'

Jenny was touched but she felt hurt for Rowley. Even though Jess's back was turned to Rowley when she spoke, so that he couldn't read her lips, Jenny felt Jess was being insensitive. So she said, 'I'd love to be related to you, Jess, but certainly not if it means marrying Horacio.'

'Very well, then. I would admit to being your long-lost mother, except that I would have to admit to being years older than I am – and that I won't do. If I *were* your mother, I'd say, marry Horacio. Together you could learn to have fun, as Arthur and I do. When we are gone, you can carry on in our spirit.'

'I wouldn't have her,' Horacio said.

Again Jenny glanced unhappily towards Rowley, but he was absorbed in dinner preparations and not interested in their banter. 'Were you ever in love, Horacio?' Jenny surprised him.

'No. There was never a chance. Somehow there were always women in love with me that I had to deal with.' He shook his head woefully. 'I never got to seek out the one I wanted.'

179

'What one do you want?'

'I don't know. I used to know. I guess I don't care any more.'

'Maybe you never really cared, or you would have found her.'

'Oh,' said Jess. 'It was probably some impossible fantasy woman. His mother. That's who all these bachelor men are seeking, and then, as soon as they sleep with a woman, they know she can't be the one because their mother wouldn't do that.'

'Love is complicated,' Jenny sighed. 'I wish I understood it.'

'I understand it,' said Jess. 'My love for Arthur, and his for me, are perfect.'

Horacio had to roll his eyes at that, remembering what had transpired with him and Jess that very day.

She didn't miss his eye-roll. 'Yes, it is.' She stared at him. 'I would do anything for Arthur. *Anything*.'

It took a second for Horacio to realize what she was telling him. 'You are an amazing woman,' he said, when he got it. He marvelled, but also felt damned dismayed.

She smiled complacently. 'I'll suffer through any kind of horrible ordeal for Arthur,' she said, then winked to show she was joking. Although she wasn't entirely.

This exchange was lost on Jenny. 'But your love for Arthur is so possessive,' she ventured. 'I don't think love should stifle a person.'

'Yes it should,' said Jess. 'That is the nature of love. To utterly depend on a person. To be inseparable. A total bonding. So that just to be with that person is the most exquisite happiness on earth. Without them – the abyss.'

'But to depend on one person for your very existence! It seems sort of pathological to me.'

'Which is exactly how it should be. Anything else is some watered-down version.'

Jenny thought she could never love like that. Rowley could. She remembered a New Zealander she'd met years ago, a blond-bearded giant of a man, a world traveller, as different from herself as a person could be. They had talked about love relationships. 'My credo is,' he said, 'a rolling stone gathers no moss, a standing stone gets pissed on.'

It had shocked her at the time, but it had proved to be not unprofound. She bet Jess had been pissed on more than once during the course of her fabulous love for Arthur – and vice versa. But then, that was the name of the game, and games were to throw yourself into, not to watch. The blond giant was copping out from the difficulties and therefore from the joys as well. In the end he was opting for just sensation, which was great stuff but still a lowly feeling in the range of possible ones. Horacio had remained a bachelor but not a rolling stone. He, at least, had got himself entangled. He'd been in the game, body and soul. No sidelines for him.

Or for her either. No sir, sidelines were too close. She'd been way up in the bleachers, safe from contact. Her ten days with Rowley had been the longest love relationship in her experience. She was proud to have sustained it that long – a personal record. But, now, she could feel herself beginning to withdraw.

'There's a lot to be said for friendship. Jenny's my first woman friend,' Horacio said. 'I've had some good men friends, Arthur especially . . .'

'What's this about Arthur?' He wandered in with a full goblet of rum and lime.

As always, everyone smiled to see him.

It's true, thought Jenny, just to be in his presence is to feel more alive, so imagine if you loved him!

'Here you all are, my extended family. And look at those succulent chikabiddies. Is there corn, Rowley? Lots of corn? And multitudes of butter? Oh boy!'

Rowley passed a bag of corn to Jenny and she began to husk. Arthur watched critically to be sure she got off all the silk.

'Where shall we eat tonight?' he asked, 'How shall we dress? Let's have some fun. We need cheering up. At least I do. Everyone's been paying too much attention to Horacio. I'm jealous. I want this dinner-party to turn around me.'

'It's all arranged,' said Jess. 'We aren't dressing but staying just as we are, and we're eating here in the kitchen.'

'But how squalid!' said Arthur. 'How middle-America.'

'And Rowley is eating with us,' she added.

'We're eating with the help! In the servant's quarters! Well, then, let's go the whole hog and eat down at Rowley's cottage. We'll take Horacio down on a litter. A garlanded litter!'

And so it was arranged. Rowley and Arthur carried Horacio down to the gate cottage while Jess and Jenny strewed him with rose petals. Then Arthur pretended to be (or perhaps was) terribly envious so, to mollify him, they carried him down to the cottage on a litter too. Jenny and Jess took one end, Rowley took the other, while Arthur happily strewed himself with rose petals.

They ate in Rowley's place by firelight and candle-light. Arthur ate seven of the sixteen ears of corn and all four legs and thighs of the two chickens. No one else even got to *say* if they wanted dark meat.

After dinner, Arthur beat everyone at chess and Horacio beat everyone at draw poker. Every single person luxuriated in the absence of Laveen.

It was a time of grace.

Why, wondered Horacio later, did we go on with it? Why didn't we all live happily ever after?

But he knew it would never have occurred to Arthur, or to himself, not to go on with it.

PART IV

36

There was a hint of fall in the air for the first time, Jess thought. A certain morning briskness to the air, an underlying chill, although the sun shone just as brightly and bravely. Certainly the sweat was running off Arthur and Rowley as bountifully as on other days. There were in the midst of a seemingly endless rally that would decide the set and match.

Rowley was trying. If Arthur won, it would be the first time he had beaten Rowley when Rowley was trying to win. How happy that would make him. They would be in for at least a week of celebration.

She felt some anxiety, however, because Arthur was having to run for some of the balls. And that wasn't good for him. Playing tennis as hard as he did wasn't good for him, but running for balls was an absolute no-no. Ah, there, he had moved to the net now and maybe he could put one away. Rowley had to reach for that corner shot and the return looked pretty bloopy to her.

She leaned forward with excitement, thinking, This is the one Arthur's been looking for. Here it comes.

Arthur just tipped it over the net. Rowley, running like hell, by some miracle reached it, returned it, but then it was a simple matter for Arthur to angle it sharply to the left so that Rowley, on the right, still trying to regain his footing, let alone his balance, had no hope.

Game, set, match! Arthur was beaming. Rowley was peeved, but it was only a matter of minutes until he recovered his humour under Arthur's jollying influence. It was hard, Jess knew. Arthur was a good loser but a terrible winner. He exulted a little too much and too long.

They towelled themselves off. Jess thought Arthur looked pale.

'Wait a few minutes before you go for a swim. I want to talk to you,' she said.

She congratulated him at great length, citing certain well-played points, several blinding serves, until his colour seemed better. But still she detained him. It was easy to stay him by getting him to replay the game to her orally.

It was the game of his life, he said. The best game he'd ever played. It could be all downhill from here on and it would be all right by him, now that he'd played his ultimate game. But he rather thought he was on the uphill. It seemed pretty clear to him that he was getting better. After all, he had beaten Rowley, this very young, strong rival who, daily, was improving. It was amazing. Age, after all, meant nothing. One really did not grow old as long as one kept in the game. He wouldn't be at all surprised if he never died. The same was true with sex. There was no reason at all one couldn't get better at it all the time. The thing was to just keep doing it, keep learning, improving, searching out new possibilities, finding younger partners – Whoops, sorry about that, just joking . . .'

He fended off her blows and, laughing, they went down to the pond together.

It was the morning after the dinner in Rowley's gatehouse. Jenny was in her room, painting. Horacio was still sleeping. Rowley had taken a quick swim and was up on the roof doing some last shingling. Arthur and Jess swam together in the pond which, to Jess, also seemed chillier.

'Winter is coming. Where shall we go for the season, Arthur? Have you thought about it?'

Arthur thought that splitting the score three ways instead of two would alter his winter plans. In December they'd arranged to cruise with friends from Dar es Salaam to the Seychelles and stay there a few weeks. Then he thought of going to Bariloche, the beautiful Argentine lake district, for most of the winter. But now, what with paying Rowley to caretake the house in their absence and . . .

And, what if they didn't bring this off? What then? He wondered suddenly how much going from half to a third would alter Laveen's winter plans? He had taken it all pretty calmly. Of course, Harry wasn't a man to fuss and it was obvious he had to bow out the way things stood. Still, Arthur felt a strange uneasiness. Laveen had been awfully calm.

Jenny was unable to paint. She, too, was feeling uneasy about Laveen. It was only now when she took time to put it all together that she realized fully about Laveen. For, indeed, if he had stolen the painting from Horacio and hurt him, then Laveen *knew* she still had the real painting and that she had pulled a switch.

Yes, he knew that now for sure. Therefore he would come back for the real painting, would he not? Her hiding-place had proved safe. Probably he had searched for it unavailingly the night that he knocked out Rowley. But now she felt dissatisfied about its place in the paintbox. When Laveen came back, he would search more minutely, in all the places he had neglected before. What she must do now was take the painting with her whenever she left the room.

She couldn't package it and carry it around. That would be too obvious. Why not remove its mat and frame, then cover the loose canvas so she wouldn't sweat on it or otherwise soil it, and tie it to her back with ribbons, or, better yet, simply pin it to her bra straps. Yes, that would work. She wouldn't be able to go swimming, but those were the breaks. It was well worth it to foil Laveen.

That was why Horacio and Arthur did not find the painting that night when they searched Jenny's room. She had gone off to the Always Inn to dance, and Jess had gone to a dinner-party, so they had hours and hours to search. Expert searchers both, they came up empty-handed and utterly confounded.

'Jesus,' said Horacio. He lay down on the living-room couch, his head hurting. 'How can she be so good? How can she have found a place we can't find? How?'

'It must be somewhere else in the house. Here in the living-room, my room . . .'

'The goddamn potting shed, maybe,' said Horacio. 'We can't search the whole estate.'

'I know.' Arthur paced awhile, his hands linked behind his back, head down. 'We will have to go to Plan B. We will have to use Rowley. I'll have to work it out. Let's meet tomorrow morning in my study. It will be tricky. I don't want to lose either of them. I adore them both. It will be very tricky.'

Plan B? he thought to himself and smiled. More like plan E at this point.

Jess, who had been pushed off to dinner at a neighbours, arrived home in a bitchy mood. 'That was the most boring dinner I ever attended. It was unendurable. San Francisco society people. Yeuk! San Franciscans don't understand the meaning of the word society. I didn't hear an intelligent thought expressed the entire evening or even a stupid thought expressed grammatically. And every single one of them got drunk.'

Arthur had made Jess go to the party without him, saying Horacio shouldn't be left alone with his head still so fragile. Now he apologized, 'Too bad. I'm sorry Jess.'

But she was not to be assuaged that easily. 'I will never forgive you for shunting me off on those idiots while you and Horacio stayed here having a marvellous time.'

'Marvellous,' murmured Horacio. 'The very word.'

'I'm sick of being excluded. I should be privy to all . . .'

'That's enough, Jess,' said Arthur wearily, not in the mood for a scene. 'I'll meet you in the bedroom in a few minutes.'

'There you go shunting me again. While you and Horacio talk your secrets. Just like you were always doing with Laveen. I thought that was over with. I thought we were going to be peaceful and happy again. Instead –'

'Horacio has a penis,' Arthur said unwisely.

'I know. Don't I just know!' She glared at them both.

No one knew what to say next. Not even Jess. Horacio thought, if he were Arthur, he would hit her, even though he

188

had never hit a woman himself. He'd been hit by plenty though. Women are no damn good, he thought for easily the hundredth time.

Except for Jenny. He suddenly felt an aching sweetness in his heart for Jenny. Because she would not cause scenes. She was the nicest woman he'd ever known. She never raised her voice, or cried, or was bitchy. She made him laugh. She was kind, decent, understanding. And, boy, could she hide a painting where no one could find it.

'I'm leaving,' Jess said. 'I'm sick of being manipulated. I'm sick of jumping when you say jump. There are about fifteen men out there who would have me right this minute and who would let me be the jump-sayer – all of whom have been guests in your home at one time or another, who have seen how I love you, what a devoted lover I am to you, who would do anything in the world to have me for their own, who would treat me like a queen and not send me off to be bored while they talked secrets with a friend. Is that true or not?'

'Fourteen,' said Arthur. 'I can only think of fourteen.'

'I hate you!' She wheeled round and swept out of the room. They heard crashing sounds from the bedroom.

'She's tearing the room apart,' said Horacio. 'Maybe she'll find the painting.'

'She's also tearing herself apart. I'm afraid I'd better go and soothe her. Otherwise I'll have to spend all tomorrow looking for her as she pretends to make good on her fake threat to leave me. Goodnight, old son.'

'Goodnight, Uncle.'

37

Jenny and Rowley arrived home at midnight. They went to her room. He began to kiss her tenderly. Even though they'd been constantly together for so long, he continued to be seductive in the commencement of his lovemaking, as if each time were the first time for them. And truly he gave her to feel that it was. He was leisurely, sensitive, explorative, wooing. He still undressed her himself, took pleasure in the process, greeted each uncovered, redisclosed feature with wonder and delight, lingered over her loveliness, was excessively pleased by all that he saw and felt.

And so it was on this evening until he came to a feature the touch and sight of which did not please him at all – the painting.

'I don't believe this,' he said.

He'd removed her blouse, unhitched her bra from its front opening and slipped it off her shoulders, to find he was holding the attached painting.

'What?' Jenny was in a sensual daze.

'You have been *wearing* this painting,' he said. His accusative tone penetrated her languor. 'Next to your skin,' he said sadly and confusedly. 'Wearing it!'

'Well, I just had to have it with me, you see. I . . .' She didn't understand why he was so upset. What had she done?

'You had to have it with you. It means so much to you that you must have it with you every moment now. Must have it *on* you. I can't handle this. I accepted that you wouldn't sleep with me because you had to sleep with it. I accepted it because then you decided to let me sleep in this room with you. With you both! I understood that for some incredible reason the painting had a big importance for you. But now this! Wearing it!'

Jenny saw that he was angry. Furious. His face closed down as she had not seen it since that first day when he had asked her to go dancing and she had almost said no. He felt the same rejection now. No, not the same. This was ten times worse for him. And it was so silly!

He drew away from her, his body stiff, his face clamped. He looked almost catatonic.

She sensed that to explain, to tell all, would only make things worse, would be harder for him to handle, would release too many conflicts. This one conflict was simpler. So simple, it was idiotic . . .

'Rowley.'

But he wasn't looking at her. He couldn't hear her if he didn't look at her. Was he purposely not looking at her?

She took his face in her hands and turned him towards her. He shut his eyes.

Now *she* felt anger. If he would not even give her a chance to explain!

But it was also the anger one summons to tamp down guilt. She had hurt Rowley terribly. She could not bear to hurt this dearest of all persons and she felt angry at herself for doing so, unintentional as it was.

But she was angry at him too for being so thick-headed as to forbid communication between them at this crucial moment.

She had not meant to hurt him by wearing the painting. It was a stupid misunderstanding, but she knew that didn't make it any less painful. Still, he was drawing wrong conclusions and not letting her even try to explain.

He was wrong to close down on her this way, turn off all his senses, he who had been so open to her a minute ago, eager with sight, touch, smell, was now totally secluded from her. He had put himself in solitary.

He thought she loved the painting more than she loved him.

Or he thought it was a talisman that she had to wear now in

191

the way that a devout person wore a cross.

Or he thought that she believed the painting to be human and, contrastingly, did not think she loved him enough to 'wear' him, to have him with her every minute, flesh on flesh, in the way that she appeared to him to love the painting.

Jenny reached her arms around his rigid waist and hugged him. She pressed herself against him, hard, so he would *feel* her, since he would not look at her.

But his body was stiff, thick, unfeeling, unbending. He disengaged himself. He took her wrists and pulled her arms away. He put his hand against her chest and, still not looking at her, gently but relentlessly pushed her away from him. Then he turned away from her, left her, left the room.

And did she go after him then? Or did she go after him later? Did she creep down to his cottage and into his bed and love his body back to bending, his face back to seeing. No, she did none of these things.

Because it would mean leaving the painting. Or, worse, taking it with her.

She didn't go.

If Jenny had gone to Rowley's bed, she would not have found him there.

He never went to bed at all. Instead he wandered around the estate for hours, walking rigidly because his muscles were all tied up, walking around like a zombie, his mind rigid too, unable to form any clear thoughts, or unclear ones, gripped in a vice of blankness, dumbness. He was a walking dead man: unfeeling, unthinking, unbending. Rigor mortis had set in on his living body. But it still walked around, jerked itself around and around, like a clockwork toy slowly running down.

Gradually the terrible stiffness passed off, but it was three a.m. before he felt life and intelligence beginning to seep back into the confinement of his self. But that was worse, much worse. Because then he realized what he had done, how he had acted towards his beloved Beulah. He was horrified at his behaviour.

How could I be so mean? he thought. How could I think only of myself that way, be so selfish, so cold, to that sweet woman? What did she do to me? Nothing! Nothing at all. What does it matter, after all, if she wants to – to wear a painting?

Still his mind boggled at the idea, but then he thought loyally, She can do that if she wants. She can do anything. What has that to do with me or with our love? Nothing! It is only a piece of cloth that she – she . . . If she wants to wear it around, that's her business. Would I object if she wore a certain blouse?

Object? I didn't object: I turned on her viciously. I turned against her. I jeopardized our precious love by my stupid, mean, ugly behaviour. She can wear the thing. She can do anything she wants to. She can have her rocks. Why do I keep interfering with her? That's not how love should be. To interfere, to tell a person what to do and what not to do. To get angry because she likes a painting. It doesn't make sense that I did that. I could kill myself. Will she forgive me? What if she doesn't forgive me? What if she doesn't give me another chance? She shouldn't. I don't deserve her. What am I? Who am I? Nobody. Nothing. If I truly loved her I would go away from her, give her a chance to find someone fine who would treat her right and not turn on her like that.

Now Rowley's brain was as excited as it had been stupid before. He was all worked up. He wanted to go away forever to free Beulah from his dreadful love. Simultaneously he wanted to go to her and throw himself at her feet.

He went frenziedly from one place to another. To her window. To his motorcycle. He wrote her notes, tore them up, left them at her door, retrieved them. He picked flowers in the night, unable to see colours but remembering them, and formed gigantic bouquets. He stripped Arthur's gardens bare and left the bouquets at her door, funereal in their excess, flowers mounting higher and higher at her door with notes of love and apology among the blooms like wilting petals.

Then he would go to his motorcycle, the Duke, to go away

forever, to free her from his horrendous devotion once and for all. But he would not go away, would stay to pick more flowers, form bigger bouquets with notes that explained, pleaded, begged, abased, forgave.

And so the long night went for Rowley..

38

Arthur and Horacio met the next morning in the study for a meeting on tactics.

'The problem is this,' said Arthur. 'Jenny has the painting. We don't know where. We want it. But we don't want to estrange her. We don't want her to know we are thieves. Or at least not know that I am. She already knows that you are. But I think that you don't want to lose her friendship.'

'Why not? Why does this matter to us? Why can't we be ruthless? Why do we consider her feelings? We never have before. Or you haven't. In your line of work, the victim often has a pretty good idea that you are somehow involved. It never troubled you; it added to your fun.'

'But I have never stolen from my friends. I only elected to do so this time knowing that Jenny would be fully paid for the painting. Actually I was stealing from Smith. But now, if it is insured, and I am sure it is, she will still be reimbursed. The police know it was stolen from you, and she is sticking by that story.'

'Right. OK. So where are we? Jenny has the painting. We can steal it and she will not be monetarily wounded. But we can't steal it since we don't know where it is. So we have to prize it out of her. But to do so would be to acknowledge our interest . . .'

'Not only that, but we are supposed to believe that it has been stolen already.'

'So?'

'So we use Rowley,' said Arthur.

'How? Lay it out? Tell him we know Jenny has the painting and we want it? Why would he do that for us?'

'We tell him we know he's an escaped convict.'

'Is Rowley on the run?'

'Yes.'

'But the poor bugger! That's something you and I could never do, Uncle: send a man up.'

'Of course not, and especially not Rowley. We just use the threat. Or you do. You'll be leaving here and never see him again, whereas I hope to keep him here in my employ. You be the bad guy.'

'OK. I'll threaten Rowley with blowing the whistle on him if he doesn't come up with the painting – in the same way that Laveen threatened Jenny with a return to Fair Haven.'

'No, Horacio, we have to be more subtle than that. Rowley is a romantic. He would not steal from his one great love. He would go back to prison first.'

'Like hell he would.' Horacio could not imagine a man loving like that, least of all Rowley.

'Believe me. I understand people a lot better than you do. I have percipience.'

'All right, then, we tell Jenny . . . No, we don't want to confront her. We're stymied. There's no way out of this thing that I can see.'

'Why don't you just listen?' Arthur suggested mildly, but he was beginning to lose patience.

Horacio listened.

'You will tell Rowley that you want Jenny's painting. You will tell him about Fair Haven . . .'

'I get it. He'll get the painting for us so as to keep her free of Fair Haven!'

'Wrong.'

'What's wrong with that? That sounds good to me.'

'If Rowley felt you were threatening her happiness and

195

well-being, he'd take her away and we'd lose them both and the painting to boot.'

Again Horacio felt piqued that Arthur thought so highly of Rowley, cast him as such a noble character. He's just a punk, Horacio thought, a small-time punk.

'Horacio, you simply tell Rowley to bring you the painting. Assure him Jenny will get the insurance money. Say you would rather he got the painting for you than you going to get it from her by threatening to hand him over to the police if she doesn't relinquish it.'

Horacio shook his head. 'You've lost me.'

Arthur spoke slowly and patiently. 'We don't threaten Jenny with Fair Haven or Rowley with Soledad. We don't threaten Rowley with putting Jenny away or Jenny with putting Rowley away, but we do threaten Rowley with threatening Jenny that we will put him away.'

Horacio gazed blankly at Arthur, who felt he wasn't explaining it very well and that he himself just barely had a grasp of it. He wished he was back with Laveen's clear, calculating, cold-blooded brain. Horacio's strong point was not strategy. He was a man of action. Arthur had a real worry that once Horacio understood the plan – if ever – he would still do something unexpected, on impulse, and blow the whole thing.

'We don't want to send Rowley up,' Horacio reminded Arthur, 'or expose our bad-guy-ism to Jenny.'

'That is correct,' said Arthur patiently. 'And we won't. We only *use* the threat to get Rowley to do our will. He could not bear for us to put Jenny in that position.'

What position? Horacio wondered. He wondered why he couldn't understand Arthur's plan. Was he not listening? Was he too dumb? Was the plan beyond his powers to grasp?

What I'd like to do, Horacio realized, is just tell Rowley to give me the goddamn painting. If you don't give it to me, I'll say, I'll beat the bejesus out of you. Or, better, I'll kill you. Actually, I'll kill you even if you do give me the painting.

Every time Arthur said something nice about Rowley, Horacio wanted to go and kill the sucker.

'Rather than do so,' Arthur was saying, 'he'll get the painting for us. He knows she would give up the painting like a shot – to save him. But he doesn't want her to have to. And, for sure, he doesn't want her to learn that he's on the lam. So, to save her from all this upset and pain, he'll steal it for us.'

'So I tell him . . .' Horacio foundered. 'I don't get it, Arthur. I keep losing the thread.' Horacio got up and flailed his arms about.

Arthur sighed inwardly. Good God, he thought, Horacio is going into one of his acts.

Horacio staggered violently around the room, bumping into walls. He sobbed. 'I don't know what to tell Rowley.' He fell to his knees, his head bent at a hideous angle, and wrung his hands. 'I don't understand the plan.' He threw back his head and wailed, 'Who do I threaten and for what? If only I had percipience! If only . . .'

Arthur was not amused. He didn't smile. He was, in fact, concerned. Then he had a happy thought. 'We'll write it down, Horacio. It's better that way, in any case. We'll put it in a message from you to Rowley. We can't trust him to fully understand it through lip-reading anyhow, especially through your lips.'

'How insufferable of you,' Horacio said proudly. 'What cheek! I am a cheek-reader and I'll tell you, in my whole experience, I never saw a more insufferable, unreadable, damn cheek.'

'This is no time for fooling, Horacio.'

'Now you're giving me lip as well as cheek. I wish someone would give me . . . It reminds me of a joke, Arthur. This girl was telling her girlfriend how wonderful her lover was. "But he has dandruff," she said. "That's nothing," said her friend, "Just give him Head and Shoulders."

"Shoulders?" she replied. "*Shoulders?*"

'Horacio,' Arthur said grimly.

Horacio subsided, sat down quietly.

'Now,' said Arthur. 'Let's go through this one more time.'

39

Jess wandered round the grounds, dazed by the devastation of her gardens.

Jenny, opening her door to go to breakfast, was engulfed by flowers.

Rowley, on the roof, was called down (gestured down) by Horacio, and given a note.

A short while before, sharp-eyed Rowley had seen Arthur hand this same piece of paper to Horacio that Horacio was handing to him now, but Arthur never dreamed he was being observed. He had looked around but he had not looked up.

Rowley read the note:

'I want Beulah's painting and I believe you know where it is. Bring it to me. It is insured. She will not suffer any financial loss. The alternative is that I will go to her and tell her you are an escaped convict. I will tell her that if she doesn't give up the painting, I will turn you in. I think we will all three be happier if you just take it from her room and give it to me. You have an hour.'

An hour later, Rowley summoned Beulah to his cottage. His heart was heavy but he was also glad to be able to do something for Beulah. He had packed his few belongings and strapped them to his motor cycle.

She came into his cottage and into his arms. He held her close, close. He embraced her for the last time.

'I'm sorry about last night,' he said.

'I know you are. I have a hundred notes to prove it,' she laughed, 'and a thousand flowers.' She kissed him lovingly.

'You're crazy.'

'I know.'

'I'm crazy too,' she said honestly.

'And beautiful,' he said softly, sadly. 'The most wonderful woman in the whole world. Look, I have to show you something.' He gave her Horacio's note. 'This is from Horacio and Arthur. Horacio handed it to me an hour ago.'

She read it with amazement. 'I can't believe this. Horacio? Arthur? And all the time I thought it was just Laveen. Arthur, too? You're sure?'

'Positive. Horacio gave it to me but I saw Arthur hand it to Horacio.'

'This is a killer. My two friends. God! I feel sick. I could vomit.'

'Beulah, this is why I'm going away now. So that you won't be in a vulnerable position. They can't use me against you.'

'But . . .'

'I knew I had to go away, anyhow. This just gives me a good reason. This way I can save the painting for you. And save you from me. You see, I *am* on the run. There's no way we could make a life together. But at least we can be glad of the time we had. You'll have to go away now too. You don't want to stay here with these men. I was always so afraid of when you'd have to go away from here and leave me, knowing I couldn't follow and expose myself. Now this is easier because I'm going away too. Not easy, no. It's the hardest thing I've ever done. Much harder than escaping from Soledad. But easier than having you leave me, easier than watching you go out of my life.'

'But Rowley, wait. No. You don't have to go. It doesn't matter about the painting. Let them have it. Horacio will take it and go away. We will stay here with Arthur and Jess. We can pretend we never knew that Arthur was involved.'

'You know that's impossible. We can't pretend. We can't live a lie.'

'Sure we can. We have. We all have. We've all been pretending to be what we aren't. Every one of us.' She began to unbutton her blouse. 'Here, take the painting to Horacio.'

Rowley, seeing she was still wearing the painting felt again the jealousy of the night before. He stayed her hands from the buttons and reminded her, 'You love that painting.'

'So what? I love you more.'

'Beulah, is it true that the painting's insured?'

'I don't know and I don't care.'

'I can't ask you to give up something you love that is also worth all the money you have in the world.'

'Of course you can. I would ask it of you.'

'No, I'm going. I have to. It's the only thing to do. I'm being selfish by going while I can feel you still love me and want me. Because, what I did last night, I'd do again, and again, until you couldn't stand me any more.'

He went to his motorcycle, climbed on the seat. She followed and took his face between her hands. 'Rowley, you're not really going? Just like this! Please don't leave me. The painting doesn't matter to me at all. I swear.' Tears sprang to her eyes. 'I beg you . . .'

'I have to go. I told you why. It isn't just because of the painting.'

'It is. I know it is. You never understood about it. You never let me try to explain. Look, Rowley, there are Horacio and Arthur now, out by the pond.' She pointed. 'I'm going up there now. I'm going to give them the painting. Watch me. Watch me go to them with the painting.' She started walking rapidly towards the two men by the pond.

Rowley stomped on the starter. The bike roared. When she heard the sound, she stopped and turned to him, panic-stricken. 'I'm giving it to them now,' she screamed. 'Don't go!'

He didn't hear her or see her. He was moving away from her towards the gate without a backward glance. He went through the gate.

'Rowley!' She ran after him. She ran through the gate after him but he never looked back, only gave the Duke more gas, gathered speed. She ran after him with all her might, but he drew even farther away from her, disappearing down the long valley, becoming a speck in the distance even as she kept running and running after him and for no reason calling, 'Rowley! Rowley!' – her words falling on a deaf landscape.

When he was lost from sight, she slowed and stopped. She couldn't see him any more. He'll turn and come back, she thought. She watched and, as the time passed, she saw many specks in the distance transform into cars then pass her by. He wasn't returning.

She felt as if her heart were broken, as if her whole body were broken, full of excruciating pain, as if she'd been in an accident, run over by a truck. She stood there, feeling this immense pain that was because of his abandonment of her but, worse, was the pain of her own failure – her failure to return his love enough.

Then she thought of Horacio and Arthur and felt furious. She turned abruptly, began to run again. Full of rage and adrenalin, walking and running, she returned to the estate.

Arthur and Horacio watched Rowley motorcycle away with Jenny running after him, eating his dust. They were silent.

Then Horacio got one of the loungers, brought it over, set it down, and lay on it, turning his face to the sun. He spoke.

'That was a really good plan, Arthur. Subtle. You're right about understanding your people. Percipience seems to be the key all right, that and being subtle.'

'Oh, shut up,' said Arthur.

He got a chair and sat down by Horacio.

Jess came out to them, still looking dazed. 'Did you notice that all the flowers on the whole estate have been picked. I thought an enormous herd of deer had come in the night and grazed them all away then, imagine, I found them all in Beulah's room, just lying there, dying. What on earth does it mean?'

'I think it's all part of Arthur's subtle plan,' said Horacio.

'Arthur, darling, you look horribly depressed. You don't look well.'

Arthur was too down to respond.

Jess and Horacio chatted together, then Jess disrobed and entered the pond for a swim.

Horacio sunned, Arthur stewed. Within the hour they saw Jenny come running through the gate. Walking fast, she was red of face and wet with perspiration.

'Here she comes,' said Horacio. For some reason he jumped from the lounger to his feet, ready for action.

Jenny looked desperate.

Arthur, too, got up from his chair. Jess, oblivious, was still in the pond, paddling easily about among the lilies – probably because they were the only flowers left.

Jenny marched over to them. Her eyes flashed with fury. 'He's gone. Rowley's gone. You've driven him away. Aren't you ashamed? He went away so as not to leave me in a vulnerable position, so that I would not have to give up the painting to you. And I won't give it up. Why should losing Rowley be all for nought? No, I won't give it up – I'll *rip* it up. I'm going to rip it up now, right before your eyes.'

Horacio was astounded to see her take off her shirt. It didn't seem to go with what she was saying, with her terrible anger, flashing eyes, beet-red face, and trembling, devastated voice. Why would she say these things and then take her shirt off? It didn't make sense. He felt as he did when Arthur was trying to explain the plan.

'I hate you,' she said. 'I hate you both for your horrible greediness. Ready to destroy whole lives for money.' She began to remove her bra.

They watched her, confused and abashed.

Jess, seeing her remove her blouse, called to her from amongst the lilies, 'Are you coming for a swim? It's lovely.'

Jenny pinned the two men with her angry eyes, the force of which neutralized them. She removed her bra and her pale round breasts sprang from their confinement, looking tremulous, like two surprised little wild animals.

'My dear . . .' Arthur began pathetically, sounding like an old man.

'It won't be easy to rip this up.' She waved the bra in their faces and they saw that the painting, enclosed in plastic, was attached.

For God's sake, thought Horacio, so that's where it was.

She was wearing the damn thing.

'Because I love it. I love this painting. I believe in its art. It is fine and intuitive, lovely and true. But I am going to destroy it before your eyes, before all your eyes, because it is only a thing, an object, not a human being, and therefore it is intrinsically worthless.' She began to cry. 'Compared to Rowley, it is completely worthless. This is something we will all learn now while I destroy it.'

'My dear,' Arthur tried again. He went to the heart of the matter. 'He'll come back.'

'No he won't. And even if he does, I won't be here. And he doesn't even know who I am or where I live. I just realized. He's the only one who doesn't know who I am and he was the one who should have, who deserved to know. I cheated him. Oh Arthur!'

Oh Arthur, she cried beseechingly, because he was still her friend and counsellor. She couldn't bear him to be her enemy now when she needed him so much, when she had no one.

The painting hung at her side, forgotten now, still absurdly attached to her bra. She looked exhausted, dejected, the tears flowing down and down, even wetting her breasts. 'He won't come back,' she said. 'I've failed him. I didn't love him enough. I was the greedy one – not you.'

'Thank you. I'll take that.' It was Laveen speaking.

It was Laveen. He stood before them as if materialized from the ether. Dressed in white, he seemed to flash in the sun. His black gun did flash.

He walked over to Jenny and took the painting from her hand. Then he stood back so that he could cover them all. His eyes were commanding. The atmosphere was charged. Horacio could almost *hear* everyone's adrenalin rushing around.

'This has worked out well,' Laveen said. 'Despite your hopeless descent into sentimentality, you gentlemen did succeed in flushing out the painting for me. Thank you. You understand, however, that it will not be a third for me, it will be all.'

'That's damned unjust, Laveen,' said Arthur. 'I'd counted on that money. My winter plans!'

'Ah, but you've always said, it's not the winning, it's the game.'

'True, but I was younger then. Be a good fellow, Laveen, and put that gun away. You know my feelings . . .'

'Your feelings are a matter of complete indifference to me. In fact it would give me pleasure to use this gun on one or two of you. You see, with me it's not just the winning, it's the seeing others lose – not just the game, but each other.'

Jess crawled out of the water. Since she was naked, Laveen turned slightly to cast a glance at her. He'd already had a little trouble keeping his eyes off Jenny, who was only half naked.

Horacio, alert, prepared to make his move. But it was not necessary, as it turned out . . .

'Arthur,' Jess was saying, as she crawled from water to land like the first amphibian and, unlike the first ape, rose. gracefully to her feet, 'I do believe I see Laveen again. Now that really is too bad. He'd only just gone. I'm simply not up to his returning so soon. My good nature is exhausted. I am Laveened-out.'

As Jess spoke, and Laveen turned slightly towards her, and Horacio prepared to make his move, a rock flew through the air and hit Laveen on the side of the head with a loud thunk. He fell while his gun fired. The bullet entered his leg with a splash of red on white. he fell, and it seemed to Horacio, from the way he fell, and the way he looked as he gave way, that it was a final fall for Laveen.

Therefore, with the same rush he'd begun towards Laveen, he carried himself instead towards Jenny, who was as ghastly pale as she'd been red a moment ago, and in an ague of trembling. Horacio knocked her out cold.

Arthur, also pale, had a hand over his heart and was gasping for breath.

'Sit down, dear,' said Jess. 'You know how violence distresses you. Everything's all right now. It's all over.' She turned to Horacio. 'Why did you do that to Beulah? Was that necessary?'

'Yes. So she wouldn't know she'd killed Laveen.'

'Did she? Little Jenny? My baby?'

'She must never know,' Horacio said fiercely. 'We must all take the secret of his death with us to the grave. Later on, we'll take a blood-oath on it. Come on, Arthur, we'll have to dump Laveen somewhere. And fast.'

'I can't,' said Arthur, sounding choked. 'I feel poorly.'

'I'll help you, Horacio,' said Jess. 'Let me just put on some clothes.'

'No, you stay with Arthur. I'll do it. I'll do it myself. It's better that way.'

'Are you sure he's dead?'

'He looks it.' Horacio laid a finger on Laveen's neck to try to find his pulse but Jess stopped him, saying anxiously, 'Horacio, first help me get Arthur to his bed. I think he should lie down. He doesn't look well at all.'

Arthur put an arm around each of their shoulders and they were able to help him to the bedroom. Jess got his pills for him and a glass of water.

Horacio went back for Jenny, carried her to the living-room, and laid her down on the couch. He covered her with an afghan. Returning to the bedroom, he told Jess, 'When Jenny comes to, just tell her Laveen got away with the painting.'

'I will.'

'Are you all right, old Uncle?' Horacio asked Arthur, who lay with his eyes closed, his colour grey.

'Look after Jenny,' Arthur said.'

'I have. She's on the couch. She's OK.'

'No. I mean, look after her.'

Jess walked Horacio to the bedroom door and whispered, 'I think you'd better call an ambulance for Arthur. It's his heart. I feel worried.'

Horacio went to the living-room phone, called emergency, then, feeling his own emergency, bundled Laveen's body into the Porsche, after first stripping off his disguise so that when he was eventually found it would be as the much-sought-after Hairless Harry Huntington. He put the painting

205

in his secret compartment. Then he headed for the hills just as he began to hear the first thin sounds of the siren heralding the ambulance for Arthur. He was full of wonder at all that had transpired.

And to think I believed that Jenny would never cause a scene, he said to himself. I've never experienced a worse scene in all my life. She could teach a class.

In the bedroom Jess sat by Arthur, stroking his brow.

'I'm dying, Jess.'

'My darling . . .'

'Tonight we will dine in heaven.'

'Very well, then,' she joked. 'I will wear my Pierre Cardin, the lavender, and you can wear your –'

'Merde alors,' they said together, smiling.

'Heaven will be so boring, Jess. Deadly.'

'No place will ever be boring for us, as long as we're together. Arthur?'

He didn't answer. Nor would he ever answer her again. Jess took a while to absorb this information. She went to the bathroom, combed her hair, freshened her face, got something. When she heard the sirens, she lay down beside her beloved and slit her wrists. Before she died she was able to take his hand in hers.

40

On a blustery autumn morning, ten days later, Jenny and Horacio drove out of the valley in the white lady, back to their homes in Mill Valley.

Damon Carner, (still on this side of the white bone door)

was driving back Jenny's Alfa. He had driven down to the memorial service with Mrs Hunt, Jenny's grandmother, thinking that with Arthur dead, Jenny might need him. Although why Jenny would ever need him again, Mrs Hunt wondered (and said to him), she couldn't imagine.

Jess and Arthur were buried. The house was up for sale. Horacio had inherited Arthur's estate. Laveen's body had not yet been discovered. Soon it would not matter whether he was in disguise or not.

Jenny and Horacio were going home to:

'Resume our lives,' said Jenny. 'That keeps going around in my head, that we're going to resume our lives. As if all this, all that took place with us at Arthur's was just an interruption of some sort, a negligible way-station in my passage through life. And now I have only to take up where I left off before I came here. But I was another person then: so frail, so scared, so – nice. Now I feel completely changed. There's no way I can *resume* my life. Do you feel changed, Horacio?'

'I don't think so. I feel depressed as hell, but I think I felt that way when I arrived at Arthur's, so I'm going home to resume my depression.' He thought of his bed but not with any particular fondness or longing.

They were passing yellow fields dotted over with bales of hay. In some fields, the bales had been stacked high as buildings. Despite the wind, the Speedster hugged the road as if on tracks. Horacio drove too fast. It didn't matter.

They were silent for a few miles, then Jenny spoke.

'Jess really did it. She said she could not live without Arthur. I thought it was just talk. She was always so dramatic.' Jenny choked back a sob. 'She really loved him that much. It awes me.'

Horacio didn't comment. He'd seen examples of love on that last day that were too profound to contemplate – from Rowley, Jess, Arthur, even, he supposed, from himself.

After a while, she said, 'So they're still together. Or at least they're not apart. Their death makes everything else seem unimportant, but some day I'd like to be told, and to understand, the whole story, all about you and Arthur and Laveen.

One thing I know is that I don't want any more deceit in my life. I'm not going to hide myself or my feelings any more.'

Horacio remained quiet. One thing he knew was that he was going to stay deceitful to the end.

'Are you still going to be a thief? Will you resume your life of crime? You don't need to. Arthur's house alone will bring you a million.'

'I never *needed* to be a thief. That wasn't the reason.'

'So you will be – still?'

'Quit asking questions. I don't want to talk.'

She was quiet. Then, after a time she said, 'Well, I don't want to be friends with you if you're still going to be a crook.'

'What do you think Rowley was?' he growled.

'Was is the key word. He wasn't any more and won't be again.'

There was bitterness between Jenny and Horacio because of the questions she could not bring herself to ask him yet. Questions that Horacio, when she did ask, could not bring himself to truly answer ever.

'He paid,' she added maddeningly. 'Rowley served his hard time. You never even paid.'

'I'm paying now, having to listen to you nag at me.'

Jenny laughed a little then felt like crying again.

Twenty minutes later, as they entered their town, Horacio suddenly said, 'Just before Arthur died, his last goddamn words to me were, "Look after Jenny." Laveen had got away with the painting, you'd fainted and hit your head on the lounger. When I asked Arthur how he felt, he said, "Look after Jenny." I thought he meant I should be looking after you right that moment, instead of him, so I said you were on the couch resting. Then he said, "No, I mean look after her." He meant for life! Deathbed words,' Horacio said gloomily.

'Don't worry,' she said tightly. 'I can look after myself.'

'Sure you can,' he said hopelessly.

'I can. Really. I've changed.' She started to weep again because Arthur had thought of her at the last. 'It's so touching that he said that. But I absolve you from those words that grew so portentous only because he died after uttering them.

I believe I'll be OK now. It's as if so much bad has happened, there's nothing more to fear. When, all in a day, you lose your lover, your closest friends' – and your painting, she couldn't help but think – 'and you survive, it steels you. I've been through the crucible now. I do think I lost my mind again too. Briefly, and for the last time. I have a memory of losing it, or of not having it for a while, which is why I can't remember much of what happened at the last. You say that when Laveen came, I fainted and hit my head on the lounger – but I don't even remember Laveen's arrival. I remember Rowley leaving, my chasing him . . . Well, even if some memory is gone, I have my mind. I'm well. I feel so sane. In a way there's something missing now that I'm sane. There's an edge gone . . .'

'To be on the wire is life,' said Horacio.

'Without a net. I never had a net. Maybe I should look after *you*. Maybe if I'd been at his bedside, Arthur would have prevailed upon me to look after you. And, of course, I'd hate it just as much. God, what a burden that would be.'

'Here you are.' Horacio stopped the car.

'You knew exactly where my house was,' she marvelled. 'Oh, I forgot that you came here one day and rifled it. I hope you left it tidy. I hope you left me my jewels.' She got out of the car, took out her bag and box and canvases. 'Goodbye, Horacio. Will you be in touch?'

'Do you want me to be, desperado that I am?'

'I don't know.'

'I don't know either.'

He reached over and closed the door. Already she missed him. She ran around to his window. 'Wait! I do want to be your friend, regardless of your criminal ways. I want to see you. And I don't want you to resume your depression. I care for you – a lot.'

'Why?'

'I can't think of a reason.'

At the last they tried joking and failed. They looked at each other, hopelessly unhappy. Two lost, grieving, bewildered people, shaken by recent events that were still reverberating inside them, shaking them up. But the events themselves were reverberations of thier own actions or omissions, going back how far? Maybe they were both still reverberating from being born.

The motor was idling. He gunned it, an angry sound, and drove away, raising a cloud of dust.

Jenny shouldered her bag, picked up her other things, walked up the steps to her house.

41

Horacio was unable to sleep. The wind had worsened and there was a branch hitting against the roof of his bedroom, driving him nuts. Or more nuts. The rhythm of the knocking of that branch had got into his very pulse, entrained with it.

Finally, finding it unendurable, he threw back the covers, got out of bed, slid open the glass door to the balcony beyond, and looked up at the offending branch of the big pine tree. He retreated indoors to get a small saw then, holding it in his teeth, he climbed the tree to ten feet above the roof, where the branch joined with the trunk. The night was luminously lit by the stars, and by the moon when the clouds weren't skudding across it. The wind didn't seem to be connected with the weather of the night; it was some turbulence conjured from the not-too-distant sea, or from the houses of man, or from their minds – more likely his own mind, he thought.

He sawed away the branch. It fell in a slow, easy, wafting motion to the earth below, slowed by the parachutes of its needle clusters. It hit the earth then slid down the hill until it fetched up at the trunk of another tree.

It was a nice fall, a nice way to go; gentle, easy, wafting, hitting, sliding, stopping, and lying there to become one with the undergrowth, in time to decompose.

Why not let himself go the way of the branch?

Are you all right? He seemed to hear Jenny's voice.

No, Jenny, I'm not. Help me.

A gust of wind, hitting him at this weak, foundering moment, dismantled him. He fell – not in a slow, easy, wafting motion. He fell fast and hard. He tried to break his fall, grabbing at branches, tearing his hands.

This is a stupid way to go, he thought, falling.

And I haven't unpacked. Jenny will find the painting and she'll know. She'll know she killed Laveen. I can't let that happen. Can't die, he thought, hitting the ground.

42

Almost a month went by. Jenny resumed her life. She painted, took up with her friends, made new ones, visited her grandmother, and others. Now, when her car said, 'Where do you want to go, big boy?' the answer wasn't the market. Jenny was always on the go. She thought, pretended, it was because of her new sense of freedom, freedom from the burden of wealth and the burden of her mind, but she knew it was a kind of agitation that was driving her hither and yon, an unaccountable restlessness as if somewhere she might find the gap in her memory and all would become clear and perhaps, by so doing, revive Arthur and Jess.

She did not hear anything from Horacio. When she finally began to try to get in touch with him herself, it transpired that he had no phone. And there came no answer to the letter she wrote, or to the notes she slipped under his door once she found his house. He must have gone away.

Where had Horacio gone? Where was the man who fell from the tree? Had he gone to heaven to dine with Jess and Arthur? To hell, to reconnoitre with Laveen? Or was he, like the sawn branch, becoming one with the undergrowth?

Returning to that windy night, Horacio fell from the tree, hit the ground, lived. When, with alarm, his mind registered, 'the painting!', then did his memory begin to work in that mythic way it does in dreams or at death, going with the speed of light, so that even as he was hitting the ground and breaking all to bits, in that millisecond before the advent of pain, unconsciousness, or death, he realized he had to prevent his termination – or else Jenny, discovering the painting among his souvenirs, would realize that his story of her fainting while Laveen made off with the painting was a hoax. Then she would remember rocking Laveen, killing him, and so beyond a doubt would kill herself. She'd told him that if she ever harmed someone she'd be unable to live. Then would there be a clean sweep of all of them who had been at Arthur's.

In short, if he died from this fall, she would die. And that would not be, as Arthur had enjoined him on his death bed, 'Looking after Jenny'.

He was responsible for her never learning the intolerable. Arthur and Jess had taken the secret with them to the grave – no need for a blood-oath after all – but he could not take it with him. He had to live, not only to see that she never learned the truth, but that she never *remembered* it. He was the only witness who could swear that what had happened, hadn't. That what hadn't happened, had. For as long as he lived, his word would carry more power than any memory of her poor, lost mind. If he died, no one could look after her. Certainly if he died with the painting still in his house, she was doomed.

Thinking all this at the very moment of contact with the ground, Horacio put all his intentionality, all his strength and robust health, all the courage of his newly enlivened spirit, on surviving the fall. And he felt a strange joy – not that he would live, but that he had a reason to live, a reason, after all, to be.

Horacio broke one leg in two places. He broke three ribs and one shoulder. That left him, when he came to, with one arm and one leg with which to drag himself along the ground to the road. His stomach muscles helped, too, to inch his body forward, for inches were the measure of his progression.

He passed out more times than he could count. When he came to he'd have to remember it all again: where he was, what had happened, why he didn't want to die, couldn't die. After a while, he couldn't remember the answer to any of these questions but he still inched forward because, although he no longer knew why he wanted to survive, or even what he was surviving, he realized that inching forward was the work at hand, was the name of the game. Horacio was a man of action and this was his current act: to get his body to the road and never mind the reason, to inch.

Six hours later, he had gone seventy feet but he was still not at the road. The sun was shining. A dog was barking.

A man, observing Horacio's property above, saw, while looking up the hill, Horacio's horribly arranged body. He didn't look up by chance. He looked because they were turkey vultures hovering near the spot, waiting. There were five of the big brown birds, three in flight, hovering, two in a big pine tree. The vultures were what the dog was barking at.

Horacio opened his eyes to see the man bending over him.
'You're alive.'
'What happened?'

Jenny continued the custom, learned at Arthur's, of the cocktail hour, although more and more she was returning to cups of tea or coffee as her reading was once again important to her. Her friends, aware of her practice of opening a fine bottle of wine at around six, sometimes dropped by, so, hearing a knock at her door one evening, she simply called,

213

'Come in,' and hardly looked up from her book.

When she did look up, she jumped to her feet with joy. 'Horacio!' But then she stopped cold with dismay, seeing him on crutches with a full leg-cast.

But his broken body wasn't what stopped her as much as his face, which had the bitter, haunted look of a cripple, not a recent cripple, but a man who had been crippled for years. Heretofore, his face had been blandly good-looking, a poker-face, except when he flashed his heart-breaking smile. Now his face seemed to have taken on the responsibility of expressing who he was – a man who was old, spent, tough to the point of ruthlessness, cynical, bitter, sad, and, to Jenny, much more attractive. It was an heroic face. There was a light to the eyes that hadn't been there before, as if, by being crippled, he had been made whole.

Jenny herself looked different to Horacio. He couldn't put his finger on why. She looked austere, grounded, somehow distinguished. 'You look different,' he said.

'So do you. Sit down. Where will you be most comfortable? I've been trying to reach you but I guess you've been in the hospital the whole time. I'm furious that you didn't tell me. I see you have a new ear. It looks fine. But what happened to your leg? Is there a leg under that thing? I hope so.'

'The night we returned from Sonoma,' he said, stretching out on the couch, 'I was up in a pine tree, sawing off a branch that was bugging me because of the wind and then,' he said ambiguously, 'it seemed like a good idea to fall out of the tree.'

'Thank God you're all right. Oh, I'm so happy to see you. I missed you so much.'

She told him all that she'd been doing during the last month, showed him a new painting she'd done, then she began to reminisce. 'I've been thinking so much about my time at Arthur's. I think I've learned some things.'

Horacio felt his body stiffen with alarm. Had she remembered? He prepared to do all-out battle with the memory if she had.

'The bad thing I did was to misuse Rowley's love. He loved

me so much and I took of his affection, let it nourish me, without making any full return or any commitment in my heart to him. Worse, I put the painting before him. I truly did. I cared more for it than for him. He accused me of this and I defended myself like crazy, but he was right. I was more committed to the painting, a material object, than to him.'

None of this was news to Horacio. She'd said as much, just before Laveen came, when she prepared to rip up the painting. 'You can't say that's a bad thing,' he said, 'to be unable to return a feeling. It would be worse to fake it or to force a feeling that wasn't there. Anyhow, he didn't love you that much. He didn't stay to look after you, just made his big-deal, dramatic exit, leaving you to eat his dust and feel bad about yourself. And he blew the whistle on Arthur, who'd done nothing but be kind to him.'

'But I used him,' she tried to explain. 'I was so starved for affection and he was so ready to give. I took without a thought for the future or of whether I might hurt him.'

'So what else is new? Everybody does that.'

Jenny felt angry. In her happiness to see Horacio, she'd forgotten how easily his cynicism griped her.

She drank the wine and it conjured up visions of Jess and Arthur. This one, a Glen Ellen Chardonnay, was the first wine she'd drunk with them. 'I would like to ask Rowley's forgiveness,' she said, 'but he doesn't know my name and I don't know his. I'm sure it isn't Rowley, since he must have been travelling incognito too. I wonder where he is now.'

Horacio, feeling exasperated by her tender feeling towards Rowley, said meanly, 'How many deaf and dumb escaped cons are there? You'd have to do more than change your name. I'll be surprised if he's not back in the joint right now.'

Horacio would be surprised. Rowley was in Montana, working on a boys' ranch similar to one in which he'd spent a good part of his youth. He no longer looked anything like the face on the Wanted poster – that closed-down, secluded young face. Nor did he pass out cards saying he was dumb. He talked. And if no one understood him, that was all right. That way he'd at least have a chance of finding a person who did.

The boys made fun of him at first, then grew to care for him. He understood them. He'd been through everything they had – with spades. He didn't take any crap from them but he was kind. They were drawn to his happiness. He radiated good spirits, even merriment. He was learning how to laugh.

Rowley had transcribed his love for Beulah into a religious experience. He felt he had sacrificed himself for her and was ennobled thereby. It gave him joy to feel that through her he had become a good person. His good feeling about himself and the world was a testimony to their love. Someday, when he could find the person who understood him, he'd tell all about it. Or, one day, maybe he'd write about their love and Beulah would read the story and learn how happy he was, how useful, learn how ever since knowing her he had walked in her beauty, been touched by her grace.

42

Another month went by. Jenny was at Horacio's. They had kept on seeing each other as friends, even though they didn't get on. He was mean. She thought it was because his body was still healing, that he still hurt a lot, so she tried to be forgiving. He limped badly. She called him 'Cripple', which shows that she was mean too. It had always been their style from the first to tease each other, and they'd enjoyed their ability to be natural together, like brother and sister, to say anything that came to mind. But it wasn't just innocent joking any more, nor light-hearted raillery. It wasn't fun, it was hurting. Especially if she ever mentioned Rowley. Especially if she mentioned Rowley with a quiver in her voice. Then he really lashed out at her.

Sometimes Jenny felt that if she could only clear the air, everything would be better for them. She would try to get him to talk honestly about all that had happened at Arthur's, fill in the blank spots. But he wouldn't. He was evasive and mean.

Then she would tell herself, to hell with it and with him, and she wouldn't see him for a while but, in time she would see him again – soon again – because she truly cared for him, felt bonded to him by the tragedy and the mystery, and she could tell he was glad to see her when she came back. But then, soon, it would all disintegrate as before.

As far as she could tell he wasn't seeing other women – which wasn't his style, but he seemed to want it that way. He had driven off his old hangers-on. But not his kids. He was more affectionate and welcoming than ever to them, and there was often one or two around the house. They had learned about each other and seemed to rejoice in their extended family, even though their mothers didn't rejoice one bit.

He had insisted on paying her for the painting, taking the blame for its loss. He was immensely rich, what with his and Arthur's combined fortunes. The five hundred thousand he offered her was a drop in the bucket to him. She said she'd only accept the original hundred she'd paid for it. Damon, as it turned out, had not insured it. In all the excitement of leaving Jenny and going to put a bullet in his head, he'd forgotten. Poor Damon, with none of Jenny's money left to lose, moped about and tried to advise her about other things, but she wouldn't listen as attentively to him as she used to, or even at all.

On this day, Jenny was lying on Horacio's living-room couch. He'd gone down-town to get some food for dinner. She was thinking about his house. He said he'd been working on it for the last month, but she couldn't see anything dif-

217

ferent about it. The floors of the cavernous living-room were still plywood. The royal bathroom off his bedroom still had the shower but no toilet or sink. Another bathroom had a toilet but no shower. The stairs were without banisters, the other bedrooms semi-plaster-boarded.

And yet, he spoke of his work with real satisfaction and absorption.

She got up and wandered around. She went to his bedroom, to the brick fireplace in the corner, warmed herself by it. She noticed that one of the bricks was a little awry. It extruded a little more than the others. Touching it, she found it was loose. She removed it. Inside the cavity was a button. She pressed it. She waited, heard a noise, turned. The wall between his roll-top desk and big wooden soldier had opened. She walked into a small room with windows and a skylight. The room was newly built with finishing work still to be done by way of baseboards and light fixtures. There was only one thing in this room – the painting.

In a flash, Jenny remembered, and she understood, but it wasn't a remembering or reasoning process. It was a seeing, an intuitive leap of the mind. The gap was filled.

She saw the scene by the pond at Arthur's: Laveen with the gun, Jenny picking up a rock, Jess coming naked from the pond, Horacio starting for Laveen, Jenny throwing the rock, the sound of it hitting his head, Laveen falling, the gun going off, Horacio coming at her, striking her a terrible blow.

'He hit me,' she said aloud. 'I didn't faint in the least.'

She grasped that Horacio hit her so that she wouldn't see Laveen fall by her own hand. Or had he done it to get the painting himself? Without her knowing? Or both? Then what? Where was Laveen now? Who was Laveen?

Who was Laveen?

Horacio had been deeply depressed on the ride home from the valley. Perhaps his fall from the tree was a suicide – she remembered him on the building – but he saved himself because of the responsibility he felt towards her.

Later he must have tried to get rid of the painting but, as

218

she had done before him, he fell under the spell of its magic and could not. She could see now that her behaviour had not been crazy. The painting had real power. It affected the hardbitten Horacio in the same way it affected her. He had actually gone so far as to build this room to house it, knowing it must have light and air. How incredible. Dear Horacio. He was looking after them both.

She saw that Horacio loved her – in his way. Now she must learn the truth of it all from him, and the only way to do that would be to get close to him, to allow for the expression of a mutual love between them wherein they could reveal themselves to each other.

Hearing the white lady arrive, she hastened to the fireplace, pressed the button, replaced the brick.

When he came in and put down the bags of marketing, she came into his arms and gave him a warm kiss. 'What's going on?' he asked suspiciously.

'I've decided we should try to be more loving together.'

He smiled and his smile went right to her heart. It was as if he'd waited all this time for some expression of affection from her.

She thought about the power of the painting – that she would wear it and that he would build an entire room for it! Their love for each other would seem somehow to depend on it. Thinking this, she felt apprehensive. What might it cause to happen next?

The important thing was not to confront him with her discovery but to allow him to tell her the truth in his own good time. Meanwhile, difficult though it might be, she must continue to pretend to believe that Laveen had taken the painting away. But where was Laveen?

Horacio was putting away the shopping.

'I think we should love each other and be happy together, while we may,' she told him.

Again he smiled at her. 'We'd better be quick about it. While-we-may isn't very long.'

'Oh!'

'What's wrong?'

Suddenly, as if in a much-delayed reaction, she thought: What if I killed Laveen?

She convulsed with dread.

With tenderness and concern, Horacio took her in his arms, held her close.

It was nightfall. Horacio and Jenny at last had consummated their caring for each other. They lay together in the darkling firelit bedroom next to the secret room where the presence of the painting throbbed like the tell-tale heart.

'I'm so happy,' Horacio said. 'It's amazing. I can't believe we really got together. I suppose I'm stuck with you now. Hey, what's the matter? Aren't you happy too? Oh Lord,' he groaned, 'Who would have thought that the great lover, the jewel-thief stud, would have to ask a woman if he made her happy. Why, it's a given. Jenny?'

Jenny, feeling post-coitally vulnerable, could not sustain her vow to herself to learn the truth from Horacio in his own good time. 'I'm sorry. I am happy. I mean, I want to be. I should be. But all I can think about now is Laveen.'

Horacio rolled his eyes and swore under his breath.

'I feel – that he is dead and that' – Jenny took a deep breath – 'that I killed him.'

Horacio sat up, throwing his legs over the side of the bed, his back to Jenny. He said nothing.

'I have to know. You see, Horacio. I have remembered throwing the rock at him. It's all come back to me. I'm afraid I can't handle it, can't live with it. I have to know what happened after you hit me.'

Horacio started laughing. It wasn't a nice laugh. It wasn't Horacio's laugh. He stood up, pulled on his pyjama bottoms, went to the fire and slashed at it with the tongs so that it blazed up violently.

Feeling startled and dismayed, Jenny sat up, holding the bedcovers tightly to her breast. 'What is it? Why are you laughing?'

'Because you didn't kill Laveen and I can prove it.'

'You can? But why – why does that make me feel even

more scared?'

It was as if the whole scene of love had done a flip into another realm, into vengeance. 'I don't think I want to hear what you're going to say.'

'Oh yes you do. It will make you glad. You will be enormously relieved.' He turned to face her, spread his arms wide, smiled thinly. 'You see, I am Laveen.'

'What?'

'Yes. I am Laveen. Alive. Aren't you glad? You threw the rock at me. Then Horacio dumped me off in the hills to decompose. But I was not dead. Horacio is a fool. He did not bother to check whether I was alive or dead. He just assumed.'

Jenny got out of bed, feeling weak and ill. She could hardly stand. She clung to the wooden soldier. 'Where is Horacio?' she whispered.

'Dead.' He folded his arms. 'Yes, it is he who is dead, not me. He fell out of a tree, you see, the night he returned here. The next morning, I came to his house. I had a bone or two to pick with him. I found him on the ground, broken to bits. You can imagine how surprised he was to see me. "You're alive!" he exclaimed. As I drove him to the hospital, he died. Such a pity. I decided to switch identities. It was particularly easy as there's a family resemblance. My bad leg, of course, is due to the bullet I inadvertently shot into it. Horacio's death was fortuitous for me, both financially and emotionally. I got two fortunes, his and Arthur's. I got the painting, too. And, oh yes, I got you, didn't I? You'd be surprised to know how that pleases me more than all the rest.'

Bile rose to Jenny's throat. She swallowed it down. 'I bet he didn't die on the way to the hospital. I bet you killed him. Oh poor Horacio! Poor, dear Horacio . . .'

Laveen grinned. He actually rubbed his hands together and cackled like the melodrama villain she'd once imagined him to be.

Seeing his hideous pleasure gave her strength. She grew angry and the anger pulled her together. She stopped clutching the soldier as if it were a lifebuoy. She drew herself up,

221

stood square on her feet. 'You are a horrible monster. I wish I *had* killed you. I wish it with all my heart. You're a crumb. If I could throw that rock again, I would, only harder. Much harder. If I had a rock now, I would happily bust your head open with it. A rock – or anything!' She looked wildly around the room for an object to throw. As her anger grew, she honestly felt she would kill him with her bare hands if she had to. Perhaps she could knock the wooden soldier over on to him. If she could lure him closer. Or – the brick! The loose brick in the fireplace. She ran to it. As she reached for it, he grabbed her hand.

'Hey! How did you know about that?'

His villainous Laveenness was dropping away. He sounded awfully like Horacio. She remembered his smile after she kissed him hello earlier when he arrived with the shopping. Only one man in the world had that smile. It was inimitable even if she hadn't seen much of it until today.

'You are not Laveen,' she said furiously. 'This is all a big act. Laveen would never in a million years have built a whole room to house that painting. He'd have sold it immediately.

'Son of a bitch! How did you find out about that room?'

'You just pretended you were Laveen so I wouldn't think I killed him, didn't you?' She shook him and screamed at him. 'Because I did kill him, didn't I? Didn't I? Damn it, tell me the truth!'

'I don't know!' he shouted back. 'I don't know the truth.' He grew quiet and went to sit on the bed. 'Maybe you killed him. Your rock hit him hard. He fell. But he also shot himself in the leg. There was a lot of blood. He could have hit an artery. The truth is, the real truth is what happened just now.' Jenny was standing before him and he took both her hands in his. 'When you said you'd kill him again if you could.'

'Yes. Yes, I did say that, didn't I.'

'Throwing the rock at Laveen was entirely justified in the circumstances. It was not the work of a looney. He was a vile person. He had a gun on us all and he would have used it without thinking twice about it. You weren't trying to kill

222

him, only trying to stop him. You acted in an emergency, like the full-blooded woman you really are. You took charge.'

She sat down beside him and threw her arms around him gratefully. 'Thank you. Oh, thank you, Horacio. Tell me more. Help me.'

'There are times when one has to do bad things, brutal things, even when it goes against the grain.'

'But I didn't save anybody by my act. Jess and Arthur still died.'

'Yes they did.'

'Maybe Laveen didn't die,' she said hopefully. 'Maybe you didn't check to see, in the confusion of it all. We could go back to where you left his body and see!' She looked searchingly at Horacio. 'He is dead, isn't he? You know that he is.'

'Yes. Laveen is dead. And don't you see, Jenny, that even if he weren't, it still wouldn't bring back Jess and Arthur?'

'Yes,' she said sadly, 'I see.'

'What matters is that you're well. You're as normal as I am.'

Jenny could smile now. 'That's *real* normal,' she said.

'It is. I'm better too. I had to break my body all up in order to find . . .' He looked shy, a strange expression for Horacio.

She finished for him, 'That you loved me.'

They were silent, exhausted from these desperate exchanges that weren't at all their style.

'Would you have gone on pretending to be Laveen for me if you'd had to?' she asked.

'I wouldn't have been able to; you'd have killed me in a couple of minutes. The whole thing was pretty spur-of-the-moment. I think I was pretty damned convincing.'

'You convinced me. It was horrible. I thought I was going to puke.' She pondered. 'I think you went a little overboard with the cackling and hand-rubbing.'

'Not at all. A subtle touch. Percipient.'

They hugged each other, kissed.

'Maybe we have the painting to thank for our wholeness and oneness, Horacio.'

'Promise you won't steal it back from me?'

'I don't know. It's pretty powerful. Let's go look at it now.'

Still with their arms around each other, they went to look at the painting, and it was amazing because it did not move them at all, not in the least, it was just sort of pretty and blurry. It looked very ordinary, very powerless, especially when compared to each other's face.

'*And I am near my desire,*' Jenny remembered. '*Nor has life in it aught better . . .*"

She smiled at Horacio. 'Where shall we eat dinner?' she asked. 'What shall we wear?'